"S-stop!"

Gillian tore her mouth away and moaned as Trace circled the delicate rim of her ear with his tongue.

"Mmm?" He rubbed his face through her fragrant hair. She could not possibly mean that.

"We've got to stop," she insisted, but without conviction.

"Who says?" He kissed the tip of her nose. "You don't want to stop. I don't want to stop. So we're stopping?"

"Yes." She said the word softly, but with no compromise this time.

"Mind telling me why?"

She laughed incredulously. *"Trace!"* He could feel her shake her head. "In a word? Lara, that's why."

He swore silently, viciously, then tipped back his head to consult the invisible rocks above. *Let me explain!* Except that he couldn't. He coul̶d̶n̶'̶t̶ ̶b̶l̶o̶w̶ his cover while there was one chance in a mil̶

And he wouldn't have d̶ her. Being undercover day till you were done rule.

Which meant he could come to Gillian only as Trace Sutton, faithless gigolo, not Trace Sutton, heart-free bodyguard....

ABOUT THE AUTHOR

For ten years Peggy Nicholson lived aboard a boat moored in Newport harbor. Nowadays, during southeast storms, she can hear the rumble of waves breaking against the Cliff Walk from her office window. She often runs the cliffs at dawn.

Books by Peggy Nicholson

HARLEQUIN SUPERROMANCE

Don't miss any of our special offers. Write to us at the following address for information on our newest releases.

Harlequin Reader Service
U.S.: 3010 Walden Ave., P.O. Box 1325, Buffalo, NY 14269
Canadian: P.O. Box 609, Fort Erie, Ont. L2A 5X3

HER BODYGUARD
Peggy
Nicholson

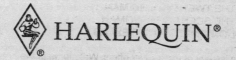

HARLEQUIN®

TORONTO • NEW YORK • LONDON
AMSTERDAM • PARIS • SYDNEY • HAMBURG
STOCKHOLM • ATHENS • TOKYO • MILAN • MADRID
PRAGUE • WARSAW • BUDAPEST • AUCKLAND

ISBN 0-373-70874-2

HER BODYGUARD

Copyright © 1999 by Peggy Nicholson.

HER BODYGUARD

CHAPTER ONE

SHE TRADED YOU FOR A CAR. A shiny red Mustang—
that's all you ever meant to that little lady. Now, why
would you want a mother like that?

"I don't," Gillian said to the door she stood facing.
One of two double doors, twelve feet tall, carved from
some golden wood varnished to gleaming perfection.
They barred an entrance almost wide enough to admit
a Mustang car, shiny red or otherwise. She clenched
her hand to knock, but her arm stayed straight at her
side. *I don't want* her, she'd told the lawyer—a horrible little man—nearly two years ago. *I want the*
facts. My facts.

Like the name of her father. Whether she had any
brothers or sisters or grandparents. Whether she might
be deathly allergic to anything else besides bee stings.
Facts that it seemed, some days, the whole world was
conspiring to hide from her.

The people who'd raised and loved her, the doctor
who'd delivered her, the lawyer who'd arranged her
adoption, the woman who'd borne her almost twenty-
eight years ago—every one of them had lied or
twisted or forgotten or lost or hidden her facts. Or
simply refused to give them.

Her facts lay behind this door and she'd come to
steal them, since asking politely had gotten her nowhere.

Had gotten her much worse than nowhere. Her letter of shy and hopeful inquiry last year had earned her a stinging, contemptuous response: *"If I didn't want you when you were born, why would I want you now, Sarah, if that's who you really are? So go get a life! And stay the hell out of mine!"*

And so I will, Mother. Just as soon as I have my facts. Gillian Sarah Scott Mahler raised her fist, held her breath and knocked, then noticed the doorbell and jabbed that, too.

But of course a woman who owned a mansion in Newport, Rhode Island, a millionaire by marriage and a queen of television soap opera in her own right, didn't open her own front door. How idiotic to have expected it. Gillian blinked at the frowning older woman who swung back the door. "I..." She swallowed and tried again. "I have a ten o'clock appointment with Mrs. Corday. About the job. I'm Gillian Mahler."

"And just how did you get in here? Nobody buzzed the front gates," declared the woman.

Must be a member of the household rather than a maid, Gillian guessed, if she felt free to quiz visitors. She might even be a relative, an aunt or cousin, though Gillian could see nothing of herself in the dour and freckled face, the short square body, of her inquisitor. "I walked in," she said as the woman tapped one foot impatiently. "Someone was driving out as I arrived, and waved me through."

"Those kids!" The woman glared over Gillian's shoulder toward the massive iron gates at the end of the driveway, although the couple, a blond young man and woman in a Range Rover, were long gone.

"I really do have an appointment," Gillian insisted. She didn't care if she'd broken some unwritten rule of the household. No one was turning her back now, not when she was this close.

"Well, come on, then." Leaving her to shut the door herself, the woman marched away.

Gillian hurried after her, dimly aware of high, high ceilings, cool marble that clacked underfoot, a grand staircase that swept up to the floors above. Her mother's house. Assuming Lara Corday—Lara Leigh to her adoring fans—was really her mother. *And she is. Same birth date. Same high-school photo. Of course she is.*

So why wouldn't she acknowledge her own daughter?

Traded you for a car and never looked back, the lawyer assured her for the thousandth time in memory. *That's all I can tell you.*

If that trade had set a girl named Laura Lee Bailey on the road from a ramshackle cabin in the hard-scrabble mountains of West Virginia to this palace, maybe it had been the smartest deal a girl of fifteen had ever made. But why—

"Wait here and I'll tell her you've come." Gillian's guide opened a paneled door, waved her inside and closed it firmly behind her.

"Whew!" Gillian leaned back against the door and pressed one hand to her thundering heart.

"*Damn* it all!" A golf ball rolled across the carpet before her. It bypassed a crystal vase laid on its side and disappeared under a sofa. "So much for my birdie!"

A man stood in front of the fireplace, glaring after his errant putt. He lowered his golf club and leaned on it, then turned his attention to her. "And who the devil are you to mess up a man's game?"

"I'm G-Gillian. Gillian Mahler." *And who are you?* Not Lara Corday's husband, the famous TV writer and producer. Richard Corday had died in his sleep two years ago. And Corday had been in his late sixties, not mid-thirties like this man.

So friend of the family then, or even a relative— Lara's relative and therefore hers? It was conceivable. Gillian was tall for a woman, yet he was taller. Six-one or -two easily. Hair darker than her own light brown. His eyes were too deepset to see the color from where she stood. Still, she felt an odd shock of…something. Recognition on some instinctive level?

Or maybe it was just the mood of him as he glared at her from under his black level eyebrows that made the impact, and her sense of kinship was entirely false. Everyone was a potential relative once you learned you were adopted. You found yourself staring at faces as you walked down the street.

He crossed one running shoe over the other and slouched more comfortably against his putting iron. "You sky-dive, Gillian Mahler? Or maybe you made your approach by sea." He tipped his head toward the six pairs of French doors that formed the entire south wall.

Beyond them stretched the lawn, then the back side of the estate's unbreachable granite wall, and then the cliffs, with Newport's famous Cliff Walk meandering high above the blue waters. Gillian had strolled that path often enough these past four months, staring up at this mansion. And now she stood inside it, about to meet her mother. At last.

"You scuba?" the golfer prodded mildly. "Left your wet suit and fins out on the terrace?"

Why was everyone so intent on learning how she'd gotten in? "Helicopter, actually." She edged away from him toward the windows. *I don't want to talk to you, whoever you are. I came to meet my mother.*

"Funny, I didn't hear it. Didn't even hear the buzzer for the front gates." He straightened and ambled across the room to the sofa, then stooped with ease to peer beneath it. "You climbed over?" he hazarded idly, and swept his well-muscled arm under it for his ball. "Grappling hooks and all that?"

The ball he sought had rolled out in front of the sofa. Gillian picked it up and toyed with the notion of stuffing it into his mouth. *Would you please, please shut up?* Her whole life was about to change. Knowingly and unknowingly, she'd been coming to this encounter for almost twenty-eight years, and now, just when she needed to savor the moment, prepare for it, rehearse the role she meant to play and the first cautious words of her script, this big babbling…jock wouldn't leave her in peace. "I walked in the gates when a couple drove out, all right? They saw me. It isn't as if I snuck in."

They'd barely seen her. They'd been too busy laughing at some private joke to spare her more than a glance, their smiles fading for a moment, their cool eyes passing through her. The boy had flipped her a careless wave, then turned onto the avenue and roared away. Those two hadn't been concerned about any intruders.

"Toby and Joya," the man murmured, his trim rump in the air as he groped beneath the sofa.

"We didn't introduce ourselves." Gillian knelt and

thrust the ball under the sofa, toward his sweeping fingertips. "Here."

"Where?" His hand closed instead on her wrist—and tightened when she tried to withdraw.

She was suddenly angry out of all proportion to the act, whether he was teasing or only hopelessly dim. Their hands connecting in the dark, touch their only link—her skin shivered with the unexpected, unwelcome intimacy. "In my hand. Where do you think?"

He slid warm, surprisingly hard fingers down her wrist to trace the ball she clutched. "Oh." Then he lifted it delicately from her palm. "Thanks."

She sat upright, started to wipe her hand on her skirt, then chose a throw cushion, instead. Its silky chintz fabric didn't wipe his touch away but seemed to drive it into her bones. She bounced to her feet and retreated to the wall of French doors, scowling through the glass at the lawn beyond. Such a velvety expanse of green, a symbol of wealth more potent than a Rolls or diamonds. Why didn't he take his toys and go golf out there?

"I suppose you're here about the job," he said behind her. "We've been up to our chins in would-be companions all week. Short ones, tall ones, nice ones, crabby ones."

If *he'd* been the welcoming committee, she didn't doubt the crabbiness! Gillian swallowed and gripped her elbows. For some reason she hadn't thought there'd be many applicants for the job. Somehow she'd seen it as...fated. Earmarked for her and her alone. But if there'd been that many applicants... And her qualifications—she was really reaching to think they'd do, but somehow she'd thought...

Wished. *If wishes were horses, beggars would ride,*

her aunt Susan—her adoptive aunt, Gillian corrected herself—had always said. She'd been foolishly wishing...

"Funny," the pest said behind her. "You don't *seem* very companionable."

Could he possibly be coming onto her? "Companion to a woman was the job description, I believe," she said coldly, without turning.

"Companion/personal assistant to a business-woman" was the actual wording of the ad in the *Newport Daily News*. Responses to be directed to Mrs. Lara Corday, Woodwind, Bellevue Avenue, Newport. There had been no mention of the celebrity who lived at that address, who presumably required the assistant. That Mrs. Lara Corday was actually Lara Leigh, star of the long-running soap opera *Searching for Sarah*, was one of Newport's best kept secrets. The locals might know it, but they were used to bumping into movie stars at morning coffee, presidents on the harbor launch, princes at the post office. To stare or to show yourself impressed was to mark yourself an out-of-town yokel, a tourist. And the locals didn't tell secrets to tourists.

"Getting a bit stuffy in here, isn't it?" A big hand slipped past Gillian's ribs, reaching for the door's brass handle. His tanned forearm rubbed along her waist. She gasped and shied to her right. And stumbled over her heels.

"Hey, *easy!*" His other arm hooked around her waist to steady her, then draw her upright again. "Sorry. Didn't mean to startle you like that. You could have jumped right through the glass." His arm tightened around her for an unbelievable, outrageous moment, pulling her backward. Her hips bumped his crotch.

"I'm fine!" she snapped, jamming one elbow into his ribs. *"Perfectly—"* He let her go instantly and she whirled around. "F-fine."

Or not. He hadn't withdrawn one inch. Standing toe to toe with him, she was trapped by the door at her back. A pair of broad male shoulders filled her entire horizon. He wore his white golf shirt unbuttoned, showing her a curl of dark hair at the V. She tipped back her head and found him smiling.

"Sorry," he said again, too softly. "I didn't mean to..."

Right. She sidestepped along the wall, careful to give him no excuse to "help" her again. He opened the first pair of doors, then the next, heading her way. She shied off to the center of the room and scowled at his back. *Could* that have been an accident?

"You don't need to be so nervous," he said, swinging open a third pair. The whisper of distant surf filled the room. "It's just a job like any other."

"I'm not—" She stopped and shrugged. Did it show that much? Being on edge, maybe she had misread his actions.

Dark against the brightness silhouetting him, he turned back to study her. "I suppose you're a local girl, a Vod-islander."

That mockery of the upstate accent marked *him* as hailing from other parts, she thought absently. "No." His expectant silence at her one-word response dragged more words from her. "I've been here since the spring." She'd meant to stay only a day or two, a week at most. Still wounded by Lara's letter of rejection, she'd intended only to catch a glimpse of her mother, see her in the flesh once, then go.

Oh, she'd seen Lara Leigh a hundred times or more by then watching reruns of *Searching for Sarah*. But she'd felt no sense of reality, no connection. That beautiful, mobile, weeping or laughing face on the TV screen hardly seemed a real person, much less a person connected to her as no other.

"Living here in Newport?" he prodded.

"Yes." Her first week, she'd stayed at a bed-and-breakfast a quarter mile down the Cliff Walk. Had haunted that stunning path morning and night, sure somehow that if Lara was any relation to her, then this was where they would meet. Her mother would love the cliffs, too. Living so near, she'd be bound to stroll there, drawn by the cry of the gulls, the cool breeze off the glittering ocean, the rumble of the waves grinding the rocks below.

And her certainty had proved right—proof more clinching than any DNA test, to Gillian's mind, that they were of one blood. Walking the cliffs on a misty dawn, her third in Newport, she'd looked eagerly toward Woodwind, its tall chimneys slowly taking shape through the fog. Looked—and had seen a slim figure step out through a wooden door hidden among the wild rugosa rosebushes that hedged the cliff side of the high estate walls.

The figure set off at a long-legged, floating run and vanished around a bend in the path. Gillian caught her breath and jogged after. *Wait, Lara! Wait for me!*

If the runner was her mother. Gillian rounded the bend and glimpsed silvery hair the same shade as Lara Leigh's. Then more rosebushes intervened, black against the pearly mist.

But no hurry, she told herself. She was fifteen years younger and a runner herself. She could overtake Lara whenever she chose. Cliff Walk edged the ragged peninsula jutting out into Rhode Island Sound for another two miles or so. She had plenty of time.

Mist dewed her face, beaded in her lashes, as she ran. A loon called its weird laughing cry from the gray waters below. Gillian came to a set of mossy stone steps and bounded up them, then down another set, her ears straining for footsteps ahead, hearing instead the rip of a wave combing down the black pebbles of the shingle beach fringing the base of the cliffs, some seventy feet below. The path skirted the very rim of the drop-off, and here someone had built a waist-high chain-link fence to keep unwary sightseers from stepping out into echoing space. Wild white daisies softened the craggy soil, trailing downward from rock to rock. Elephant-high clumps of rugosas pressed in from both sides of the Walk now. Blossoms of magenta and white brushed her shoulders as she ran. Through gaps in the bushes Gillian snatched glimpses of the black silhouette of a lobster boat idling in toward a line of pots laid along the cliffs. On a clear day you could see twenty miles out to the islands, but not this morning, when visibility was measured in yards.

And somewhere ahead…Gillian stepped up her pace. She passed a trail that led up between the mansions on her right toward the avenue, but somehow she knew Lara wouldn't stray from this path. A woman who lived most of her life in the public eye would surely treasure this gorgeous solitude.

And what do I do when I catch her? Glance sideways? Say something inanely pleasant, as runners of-

ten do when they pass each other—*Nice day, huh?*
Or should she run a little farther, then wheel and con-
front her? *Mother, it's me,* she could say, *Sarah.* But
she never would dare. Not after that savaging letter.
Gillian pulled up the hood of the orange sweatshirt
she wore till it covered her hair. Tightened the string
at her throat to keep the hood in place. There was no
reason to think that Lara might recognize her, but
still...

Mind focused on the bow she was tying and on the
coming encounter, she rounded another bend and
shied violently sideways, grazing the bushes, thorns
plucking at her sleeve. For all her fascination with
vistas, she had a healthy fear of heights, and this was
a spot she never liked. Just as the path passed a wide
gap in the bushes, it dipped, then tilted subtly toward
the cliff edge. Here, water ran off from the hillside
above, carving a notch in the cliff. Someday the path
would be entirely undermined; the hillside would
cave in and fall. Cliff Walk, Gillian had learned, had
been crumbling for time out of mind, the sea taking
the land inch by inch, the soft slate cliffs eroding year
by year. The path was perfectly safe, but still, you
could feel the abyss calling. Three wincing steps and
she was by the gap, looking ahead again.

Lara? The path sloped downward; the highest cliffs
were behind them now. The surf sounded louder and
the fog was thicker, as if it had chosen this low spot
to crawl onto the land. Gillian looked down, picking
a route around a puddle in the path, looked up—and
Lara burst out of the mist. Retracing her steps, home-
ward bound already.

No time to think at all. As their strides carried them
closer, their eyes met and locked. Hers were a gray

so light as to seem silver, fringed by lashes as dark as Gillian's own. Lara's lips parted, Gillian opened her mouth to speak, but the only word that sprang to mind was *Why? Oh, why?*

Gillian slowed, her steps faltering, her mind stumbling. *That's her!* Near enough to touch! Near enough to question—if only she dared.

She didn't. Not this time, anyway. So instead she ran on, reliving the moment, trying to hold that startled, questioning face in her memory. Seeking from it some likeness to her own.

Finding none—

CHAPTER TWO

A HAND WAVED BEFORE HER face, then dropped as she focused on it. "Do this often, do you?" inquired the man. His lopsided smile was whimsical; his eyes missed nothing.

They were hazel, she noticed for the first time. "Do what?" She'd entirely forgotten he was in the room! For only a minute or so? It might as easily have been an hour.

"Vanish down a rabbit hole. Not a very nice one, by the look of it."

"I...was trying to remember if I'd turned off the stove."

He didn't buy it, but he cocked his head obediently, then one eyebrow. "Don't hear fire engines."

Newport wasn't large. Whenever the trucks turned out, the whole town heard the racket. "I believe I did turn it off after all."

"Ah." He'd jammed his hands into the pockets of his chinos. Eyes fixed on her face, he strolled around her. She suppressed an urge to spin warily with him, and let him instead inspect her profile, then her backside. Clenching her teeth, she tipped back her head to study the chandelier above. She'd thought meeting her mother would be the ordeal of the day. Now she looked to Lara for rescue. *Somebody deliver me from this...this...whatever he was.*

Bad news, that's what he was. Elegantly packaged bad news, from his sexily too-long, razor-cut dark hair, to his runner's shoes, which probably cost more than her monthly rent. With all stops in between just as scenic. Not handsome exactly, but something more potent, topped off with a whiff of...unpredictability. Not a trait she cared for in someone who was shaping up to be an opponent.

"You know she's been ill," he said idly from somewhere behind her right ear.

Ill? That was hardly the word Gillian would have used to describe a fall off the Cliff Walk.

Shattered? her mind supplied, and she shivered suddenly. It had been two days after their encounter before she'd heard. She'd picked up a day-old *Daily News* in the Waves, the town's favorite coffeehouse, and sucked in her breath at the headline: Woman Survives Fall From Cliff Walk! Somehow she'd known what had happened even before she'd read about it. "I heard she had...an accident," she murmured, picturing for the hundredth time the stumble—a shoelace perhaps coming undone, or Lara catching the tip of a toe. Then the horrified nosedive, the frantic snatch at the brush on the rim, a flailing cartwheel into space, the rocks rushing upward, the ice-cold sea...

The article said the woman had been lucky, unlike others over the years. She'd fallen at half tide, when a few feet of water covered the jagged beach. Luckier still, a lobsterman tending his pots had seen her from his boat, and rowed frantically over in time to save her from drowning.

The woman had a fractured skull, the article went on to note, and broken bones. She'd been rushed to Rhode Island Hospital in Providence, where the most critical cases were sent. Her name was being withheld pending notification of relatives.

Like me? Nobody told me!

Checking the date of the paper and counting backward, Gillian deduced the fall had occurred the morning of her encounter with Lara, probably within minutes after they'd passed each other. "Name withheld" was a dead giveaway. It took money and power to keep a person's name out of the papers, especially when that person was a celebrity.

The newspaper had been circumspect, but still the rumors had made the rounds. Gillian had heard them from the women in her aerobics classes at the YMCA, heard them murmured over cups of coffee at the Waves. It was Lara Corday—you know, *that* Lara—who'd fallen—

She glanced up as a humming came from somewhere overhead. The crystal pendants on the chandelier trembled and a shard of rainbow danced across the ceiling.

"The elevator," the man said at her elbow.

At last! Gillian swallowed and glanced desperately around the room. Her mind had gone utterly blank; all her endlessly rehearsed words had flown through the open doors and out to sea. There was a carriage clock on the mantel, she noticed, showing the time as ten-thirty. *Half an hour, she kept me waiting.*

But why should that surprise her? A woman who'd discarded her newborn baby like a worn-out shoe, who'd apparently made her climb to the top her highest priority—why should a woman like that worry that she kept others waiting? Whose time but her own would she value?

The door opened behind her and Gillian turned, dimly aware of the man beside her turning, as well.

"Darling," he said warmly, and went to meet the woman framed in the doorway.

So that was his place in this household, Gillian realized at last with an odd jolt of dismay. The boyfriend. A virile courtier to replace the aging husband Lara had outlived. It explained his supreme confidence, his proprietary air. He put a hand to Lara's elbow and led her into the room.

She barely spared him a glance. Her silvery eyes locked on Gillian, and it was the Cliff Walk encounter all over again. An awareness like a path of silver light, a moonbeam tunnel down which they both drifted, until only a few final feet divided them. "Do I—" Lara Corday smiled and shook her head. "I don't know you, do I? My memory these days..." She gave a tiny, rueful shrug.

"Maybe you do," suggested the man at her side. He'd advanced with her, one hand resting at the small of her back. "Newport's a small town. You bump into everybody once a week or so." His voice was tender, almost coaxing. His eyes flicked to Gillian and she could feel them bore into her.

Let him stare. It was Lara's gaze that held her. "I don't think so," she answered cautiously. *Oh, do you know me?* But how could she? One of the few facts Gillian had pried from the lawyer was that Laura Lee Bailey had signed the relinquishment papers two days after Gillian's birth. *You saw me once or twice, maybe—that was it.*

"Oh, well." Lara smiled, dismissing the notion. "I know your name, of course, from your application,

Gillian. I assume you and Trace have introduced yourselves?''

''More or less,'' he said dryly. ''Trace Sutton.'' He clicked the heels of his running shoes and gave her a mock-formal nod.

A charmer when he wanted to be. Gillian didn't trust charm.

Lara touched her elbow. ''Come sit down and tell me all about yourself.''

I'm taller than she, Gillian realized for the first time, as they moved toward the two couches that formed an L facing the French doors. By five inches or more. It was a measure of Lara's presence that she hadn't noticed till now. *I'm too tall, with different hair. My eyes are light brown and hers are gray. Why, we're nothing alike!* What if she'd gotten it wrong somehow? A birth date and a photo—what did they prove? She'd wanted more than paper proof. She'd wanted resemblance, a physical explanation of who and what she was manifest in an earlobe, the shape of a chin, *something...* Instead all she had was this elusive sense of...connection.

''You said on your résumé that you're working right now at the YMCA, teaching fitness,'' Lara said gently, an actress nudging a forgetful understudy back toward her lines.

''Ah. Yes. I've been there since May.'' She'd applied for the job the same day she learned of Lara's accident. Somehow the accident—or perhaps their encounter on the cliffs—had changed her plans. She'd meant to stay in Newport no more than a week. After the accident she could not leave. Not till she learned that Lara was out of danger, she'd told herself.

But one month had slid into the next, and here it

was September. "I taught aerobics, tai chi, weight-shaping classes while I worked my way through college. It was a good way to earn money and stay fit." She'd thought it best to stick to the truth wherever possible. "So when I saw the opening here..." She let her words trail away. *I grabbed it. A foothold in your town.*

"But I've also worked as a secretary, through a temp agency," she hastened to add, not mentioning she'd been less than a rousing success in the clerical world. What else to say? She should be selling herself, not simply staring. Lara had cut her hair since she saw her last, Gillian realized suddenly—or no, perhaps they'd shaved her head in the hospital. It was boy-short, making her lovely eyes seem enormous. Purple shadows smudged the delicate skin beneath. Her gaze also seemed shadowed, with pain or worry.

"That's *excellent,*" Lara said. "I'm looking for someone to deal with my mail and other paperwork, but if you're athletic, as well—I'm *so* out of shape—we could train together. An exercise buddy would get me off my duff, get me moving. Can you lay on the guilt? I'm *hopelessly* lazy!"

"Oh, I can guilt-trip with the best of them." Gillian laughed. "I learned from an expert—my mom." Her laughter jammed in her throat, turned to a fit of coughing that brought the tears to her eyes. *Mom, how could I?*

But it was true. Her adoptive mother, Eleanor Scott—her Real Mother any way you counted—had wielded that parental weapon with surgical deftness. Gillian couldn't recall a single spanking in all her childhood years. A few well-chosen words of reproach, or one look of loving despair, was all it had taken to make her toe the line. She glanced up to find her own sorrow reflected in Lara's eyes.

"You love your mother," she said softly.

"Yes." Gillian rubbed her lashes. "She died two years ago." *Why am I telling you that?* Perhaps because that had started it all. After the funeral they'd found the key to the safe-deposit box. And the letter waiting there for Gillian, which had turned the first twenty-six years of her life into a lie. She wasn't— never had been—who she thought. So who was she?

Only Lara knew, and in one savage letter she'd closed off all possibility of Gillian's ever asking.

"I'm sorry," Lara said. "I understand what it's like to...miss somebody."

She was nice! Gillian had expected anything but niceness. How could this woman have written that soul-crunching letter?

She's an actress, she reminded herself. And a fine one, if winning an Emmy signified anything. Give her a role and presumably she could make it live. But still—

"You went to college. Where?" Trace Sutton cut in briskly. As if he'd heard enough emotional female meandering and it was time for some facts.

"University of Texas at Austin," she answered in kind. "A double major—art and education."

"So you should be teaching art in a public school," he challenged. "Why earn a poor living doing jumping jacks at the Y?"

She could really dislike this man! "I...don't have the temperament for teaching." Not at the high-school level anyway, where she'd tried for three years, then resigned. She had no taste for the profession's disciplinary side, and the paperwork had been a nightmare. "I hope to illustrate children's books someday." The truth again, though she'd turned the clock back. She already had three children's books to her credit, was contracted to finish a fourth by Christmas. That didn't pay her whole way, but supplemented by the exercise classes, she made do. "For now..." She shrugged. "I'm enjoying traveling around, seeing new parts of the country."

"So you wouldn't plan to keep this job long," Sutton suggested gently. *Drifter,* his eyes jeered.

He really, really didn't want Lara to hire her. Why? "On the contrary." She gave him a look of limpid sincerity. "I've fallen in love with Newport. If I could find an interesting job that allowed me to stay here..."

"Then I doubt this position would suit you. Lara lives in New York whenever she's acting."

"But that won't be for months, probably not this year at all," Lara interjected. "They've written me out of this season's scripts. My doctor doesn't think I'm quite ready to—" Her shrug was apologetic, as if she'd willfully chosen her horrific fall in a fit of selfishness. Then she brightened. "Still, all this fan mail keeps pouring in, piling up in corners, and I *really* need to get back in shape, so when do you think you could start, Gillian?"

Trace Sutton coughed and bumped Lara's shoulder.

She bit her lip. "If I decide to hire you," she added like a good child reciting a lesson. A tinge of pink brightened her pale cheeks.

"I could start right away," Gillian said promptly, refusing to even glance at the overbearing brute. "That is, if you don't mind my juggling this job around my aerobics classes for a few weeks till the

Y can find a replacement. I think I could swap some of my day classes with a woman who teaches nights and—''

''That sounds *perfectly* satisfactory.'' Lara laid a slim hand on Trace's arm as he stirred again. ''Gillian, is there a phone number on your résumé I can reach you at? Good,'' she continued decisively when Gillian nodded. ''Then may I call you later today with my decision? I'm afraid it's time for my physical therapy session at the hospital.''

''Of course.'' But Gillian knew the verdict already. A lover's word carried all the weight in the world. She searched her mind for something to prolong the interview, but short of crying *I'm your daughter! You really ought to give me a chance this time!* she could think of nothing to do.

Except swear to herself she would never *ever* forgive Trace Sutton for wrecking her best, probably her only, chance to learn the truth about her origins. Inwardly raging, she maintained a stony silence as he escorted her not only out of the house but all the way down the long, curving driveway to the front gates of the estate. What did he think—she might hide in the bushes, then pop out at Lara's car when it passed?

''I figured you'd appreciate a boost over,'' he said gravely as they arrived at the gates, an eighteen-foot barricade of ornately curlicued wrought iron topped off with vicious spikes.

He could joke while he snatched a job away from her? Maybe he didn't realize what this meant to her, but still, for all Sutton knew she might desperately need employment. *Terminally selfish, that's what he was!* All she could conclude was that he wanted Lara to himself. No doubt he'd make sure she hired some grim-faced old bag who typed a hundred and fifty words a minute.

"Or if you don't want to climb," Sutton continued when she refused to smile, "you walk between this electric eye and that one." He nodded at two knee-high metal posts implanted at intervals along the driveway. "They decide you must be a car heading out and—voilà." The gates swung majestically open. "Goodbye, Gillian," he added gently. "And...don't get your hopes up."

"I—" She spun and stalked off, tears of rage gathering in her eyes. *So close, so close!* All but for that selfish...brute.

CHAPTER THREE

HANDS JAMMED IN HIS pockets, a reluctant smile quirking his lips, Trace Sutton watched her go.

Most people tightened up with rage. Gillian swung off on those long, long legs like a woman on a mission—a tiger to shoot or a city to sack. As if she'd just heard about a summer sale on silver platters. *She needs one for my head,* he acknowledged ruefully.

He leaned against the bars of the gates to keep her in sight as long as possible and crossed his arms. After a moment he noticed he was rubbing his right forearm. It still tingled where he'd snugged it around her waist. With a grimace, he shoved his hands back into his pockets.

She hadn't been toting; he was reasonably certain of that. A weapon tucked in her waistband had been the logical assumption since she'd worn a loose, gauzy overblouse that hid the top of her skirt. But his lightning frisk had found no gun, no knife—only vibrant, willowy slenderness, a feminine shape that fit his arms as though molded to his personal specifications.

Given her skirt, there was only one other place Gillian might be packing. He'd pictured himself smoothing his hands up the inside of her long, honey-colored thighs—strictly searching for a shiv or a gun taped in place, of course. But try as he might, he hadn't come up with an excuse for doing it that the lady would buy.

Except that I'm an oaf, and she thinks that already.

Far down the street, he noticed, she reached a corner and turned left. Which checked out. That was the most logical route back to the address she'd given on her résumé.

He'd thought it was too damned convenient to Woodwind when he'd first noted her street. But Newport had a layout unlike most cities, where the rich lived on one side of town and the poor on the other. Situated on a long, meandering ridge that encircled a harbor, Newport divided its social classes not by horizontal miles but vertically. The "summer cottages" built at the height of the Gilded Age graced the top of the ridge, while the bungalows and triple deckers that had once housed the Irish maids, the gardeners and cooks and stable hands who had serviced those mansions occupied the lower slopes.

So in itself the proximity of Gillian Mahler's place to Woodwind was no grounds for suspicion. Still... "Something doesn't fit," he murmured aloud. She'd looked like a winner to him, and that didn't jibe with the profile.

But looks and manner aside, there was the fact that she'd drifted here from afar. And she lacked a steady, full-time job.

Which describes just about every kid in the city, he reminded himself. Newport had a well-earned reputation as a good-time town. The young swarmed here from all over the country, even from abroad, to work the summer jobs at the hotels, restaurants and bars. After hours they partied the night away, then spent their mornings drowsily perfecting their tans at the beach, before it was back to work again.

So explain away Gillian's rootlessness and still he had that look she'd given him when he'd stopped Lara from hiring her. If looks could kill. And rage was definitely part of the profile.

Maybe she just needed the job. He squared his shoulders, shrugging off that twinge of guilt. He had one goal here and one goal alone, and nothing would deflect him from it.

So, put her on the shortlist?

His list was damned short. Twenty-seven applicants so far and he had only three candidates, losers all, but not one he'd bet his money on.

So, Gillian? Profiling was hardly an exact science. And those emotions he'd sensed once Lara had joined them… They'd raised the short hairs on the back of his neck.

Powerful, inappropriate emotions were definitely part of the profile—though oddly, he couldn't quite swear which woman had been transmitting.

Or both? *Did I miss something? Or add something that wasn't there?* Usually he trusted his instincts in these matters. This time, something seemed to be jamming the signals.

An image of long graceful legs, of smoldering lioness eyes, drifted across his mind. Trace grimaced. He didn't like to think of sexual attraction crossing his wires, but he'd seen it happen to so many men in his business he'd be a fool to consider himself invulnerable.

And a greater fool to let it interfere with his job.

Well, the solution to that problem was easy. *Keep her at a distance.*

But put her on the shortlist, he decided also, and headed up the driveway. *Maybe even the top of his shortlist.*

LARA HAD GONE UPSTAIRS, Trace found when he returned to the mansion. He took the steps two at a time—she really did have a physiotherapy appointment within the hour. He entered her unlocked bedroom without knocking, then paused. "Lara?"

His pulse jumped a notch when she didn't answer. His eyes swept the big sunny suite, half bedroom, half sitting room, then the balcony beyond, with its magnificent view of the sea. Nothing out of order. Nothing smashed or overturned. Lucy, the downstairs maid, had told him Lara was up here, but maybe she'd—

He sensed a presence and turned to find her standing in the doorway to her dressing room. Silent and unsmiling, she gazed at him for a moment, then withdrew.

So…he had offended her. She'd been so docile and subdued since her fall, he'd grown used to taking the lead. Surprised when she'd gone her own way during the interview this morning, maybe he'd brought her back into line a little too smartly.

"We need to leave in ten minutes," he said, coming to stand in her dressing-room doorway, wondering whether to apologize or let it ride. The little room, lined with mirrors and louvered doors that hid her wardrobe of stunning simplicity, was empty. Lara had retreated all the way into her bathroom, a room that by unspoken agreement was off bounds to him. But the door was open and today wasn't just any day, since they so rarely disagreed.

"Lara?" He stopped in the doorway to her bathroom. She stood brushing her hair before her mirror, a gesture that would have expressed her irritation beautifully four months ago, when those silvery locks had been a foot longer. In her imagination, they probably swirled around her shoulders still.

In reality, short as her hair was now, it stood up in silky tufts, then fell softly as the brush passed. She looked like an outraged downy fledgling. He had to work not to smile. "We'd better go."

"I wanted that one, Trace," she said with fierce determination, staring at herself in the beveled glass.

"You know it's not in the plan." He desperately needed a second person to spell him. Backup hadn't been a problem those first two months after her fall, while she'd stayed in the nursing home. He'd brought in three capable private-duty nurses and alerted them to the danger. Whenever he'd left her bedside, he'd known she was in good hands and he could rest easy.

But these past two months back at Woodwind... There was too much ground here. Too many people for one man to cover. Even for a low-profile assignment, this was ridiculous, as he'd tried to tell her from the start.

A typical shift in his business was twelve hours. He was doing twenty-four, day after day after day. His concern wasn't exhaustion so much as growing stale. No one could live at the pinnacle of alertness without stand-down time.

"So let's *change* the plan," Lara muttered.

Trace breathed in, held for a count of three, breathed out. A centering exercise in karate: achieve serenity first, then take action. "What was wrong with number seven?" he asked finally. "Liz Galloway?"

Galloway wasn't a member of his own security firm, Brickhouse, Inc., but she'd come with the highest recommendations. To maintain her cover, she'd applied for the job in the same way as all the genuine applicants.

The brush paused midstroke. "She...intimidated me."

Trace snorted. "Don't be silly." Lara was one of the bravest people he'd ever met, man or woman. The pain she'd endured without whimpering, those first few weeks after her fall... He remembered looking down at those big haunted eyes set in that swath of bandages and wishing she *would* cry out, complain, weep—anything but lie there bleakly accepting, as if pain were only her due.

"I'm not! I felt as if she was measuring my neck for a collar and leash. As if she'd expect me to heel every time we went out for a walk. Well, *no,* thank you. It's bad enough having you—" Lara stopped, carefully set the brush aside. Reached for a bottle of lotion and fidgeted with the cap.

"Having me...?" he prompted mildly, though he knew what she'd say. It was the perennial problem between bodyguards and their clients, almost always the reason a bodyguard's contract was terminated prematurely. Along with protection came loss of freedom. Spontaneity. Privacy. Once the client's original fear diminished, resentment inevitably followed.

"Having you living on top of me," Lara mumbled without meeting his eyes. "If I was stuck with Liz, as well, I think I'd go..." She shrugged. "Nuts."

"I'm sorry. I try to not cramp your style." Yet the requirements of the detail made it all but impossible.

He was here under cover, and only one role allowed him to plausibly stay by her side day and night.

"Oh, Trace, I didn't mean it that way! You've been—" She turned and smiled up at him. "I'm *very* lucky to have you—I can't believe how lucky. But if I can't have my privacy, at least I want to be…comfortable with the people around me. And besides," she hurried on as he opened his mouth to argue, "we agreed that whoever was hired, she'd have to really function as my personal assistant. Liz Galloway just didn't have the—the warmth or the tact the job requires. Some of those fan letters are so *silly*, the people who write them so—so desperately needy… The job takes somebody with sensitivity. A sense of humor."

"Ouch, poor Liz!" But he could see what Lara meant. The ex-policewoman wouldn't score high on the warm-and-fuzzy scale. "All right, then. I'll see if I can find somebody else." Inwardly he groaned. Female BGs were rare, and therefore in demand, and of the few available not just anyone would do. He'd hire only the best for Lara. And for himself. A partner he couldn't trust was less than useless, endangered everyone.

Laura shook her head. "Don't bother, Trace. I want her. Gillian."

"Out of twenty-seven women you've interviewed, why her?" The one who worried him most.

Laura shrugged. "I don't know. She…" She shrugged again. "I liked her."

"Okay, well, let me tell *you* why not. For starters, Mahler's not a bodyguard." And that was only for starters.

Lara tipped her head in a tiny gesture that meant,

"So what?" She reached for his wrist and turned it, making a comic face at the time on his watch, then nudged him ahead of her out the door—as if he were the one who'd been delaying them. "Does it ever occur to you," she said lightly, following him into the bedroom, "that four months have passed since anyone tried to...hurt me?"

"I haven't exactly given anyone a chance," he reminded her. And if she hadn't snuck out onto Cliff Walk without him that morning in May, no one would have laid a hand on her then. "But aren't you forgetting your pen pal?" She'd received two letters since her fall, five before, for a total of seven.

Those disturbing letters, with their effusive admiration, their seething frustration, ominously mounting expectations, coy allusions to death and violence, had been sent by a fan who signed herself Sarah XXX, and had persuaded Lara to consult him in the first place.

Lara looked stubborn. "I'm not so sure they're connected to...Cliff Walk."

This was an old, old argument between them. "I'm not sure they're not. And even if we do have two separate problems—*two* crazies—that only strengthens my point. You need another bodyguard, not a ditzy aerobics instructor."

"If I'm to stay cooped up indefinitely at Woodwind, I'm more in danger of losing my girlish figure than my life! Gillian would be a big help there."

"Any competent BG can train with you, if that's what you—"

"I don't want a *drill* sergeant, Trace. I want a—" She paused, tears gathering suddenly in her wonderful eyes, then blew out a big gusty breath and gave him a wavering smile. "I want a friend, okay? All my real friends are back on the set in New York, you know. Nowadays I only have you, and you're *useless* for the girl stuff."

"Thanks, I think." He ushered her to the door of the suite, stepped out first and glanced both ways. She made her usual face at him. More and more she was considering him a worrywart, his precautions a nuisance. They walked down the hall to the tiny elevator installed in a dumbwaiter shaft and he waited till the elevator door had closed behind them. "Look, Lara, you hired me to protect you. Well, it's my considered professional advice that you still need protection."

She mulled that over while they walked through the house, out through the kitchen door to the carriage house that served as a garage. She waited obediently at a safe distance while he inspected, then started the car—he didn't expect bombs with this kind of situation but why take the chance?—then she settled onto the front seat beside him. "You know, it...wouldn't have happened if anyone else had been there to witness it or to scream. I mean, that was the act of a coward, wouldn't you say—jumping out from behind me like that and...?" Her voice trailed away.

He nearly took her hand where it lay fisted on the seat between them, then suppressed the impulse. *Brave girl,* he applauded her silently. This was the first time she'd broached the fall of her own accord. Every other time, he'd had to lead her through it, word by halting word.

He didn't agree with her assessment, though. Someone had jumped out of the bushes behind her as she jogged or had overtaken her silently. Had—in broad daylight!—gripped Lara's hair with one hand, close to her nape so she couldn't look back. Had grasped the waist cord of her sweatpants with the other hand, then forced her, step by struggling step, over the cliff edge. To his mind, the act took nerve, determination—and terrible hatred. It wasn't the act of a coward, however it might comfort her to think so. It was the act of a risk taker.

Worse yet, a well-organized, premeditated risk taker, who'd chosen his or her place of ambush with intelligence and care—a gap in the bushes, a spot where the path skirted the drop-off, where twists in the trail blocked the view at both ends.

"Gillian's a big girl," Lara went on when he didn't speak. "If she'd been there with me, no one would ever have dared…"

Yes, Gillian was a big girl—five-nine or -ten. And despite her slenderness, if she taught aerobics, tai chi, she'd be strong for her size… Strong enough to shove a smaller woman off a cliff? Definitely.

"How about a compromise?" he said, instead. "It may take me a week or two to find a female BG you can live with. In the meantime, why don't you hire one of the other applicants—"

"*No.* I want to hire Gillian."

As the gates swung ponderously inward, he studied her exquisite profile. Her chin was tipped in defiance, her arms crossed tightly across her chest. He swore to himself, then pulled out onto the avenue and stepped on the gas. For weeks he'd been silently rooting for her, hoping her spirit would mend along with her bones. But why did she have to regain her spunk today of all days? "Is there something you're not telling me about Mahler?" he asked as they passed the Newport Casino, which had the oldest grass tennis courts in America. "You're sure you've never met her before?"

"I..." Lara shook her head finally. "It's f-funny, because that's what it feels like, but no...I'm sure not."

Under stress, she had a charming hint of a stutter. The question was what was he missing here? "Then why her, Lara? You didn't even ask her how fast she types, whether she's computer savvy, if she can—"

"I think she'd be good for me."

Said with ominous finality. You could give a client advice, but you couldn't make her take it, Trace reminded himself. The cardinal rule of his profession and the most frustrating. He could push no further. He *could* give Lara an ultimatum: insist on Gillian, and you'll have to get yourself a new bodyguard. But he wasn't ready to do that. For one thing, hiring Gillian Mahler might be no more than Lara's harmless whim.

Or it might, just might, prove suicidal.

Either way, he'd stayed too long on this assignment to quit now. He meant to see it through till Lara was freed from danger. Unlike most security firms, the Brickhouse credo was that they solved the client's problem; they didn't just make their money off it.

And if Gillian was the problem?

Well, he'd meant to investigate her anyway. He just hadn't expected his prime suspect to be dropped in his lap. Trace smiled at the image—couldn't help himself—then glanced at Lara.

"All right. You're the boss, boss."

The smile she gave him was a fair trade—more than fair—for all the headaches this whim was bound to cost him in the end. They didn't speak again until he turned into the parking lot across from the Newport Hospital.

"You asked me to tell you if I ever remembered anything else about that morning," Lara murmured. "And something did come back to me a little while ago while I was brushing my hair. The runner I saw that morning out on Cliff Walk?"

The unidentified runner, sex unknown, wearing a hooded orange sweatshirt, who'd passed Lara only minutes before her attack. Trace's best bet for her assailant. It would have been easy to spin around and follow Lara back through the fog, catch her just as she passed the fatal gap... "Yes," he said without inflection. *Come on, Lara. Give me the goods and I'll nail the creep.*

"I told you I thought it was a college sweatshirt, with University of something with an M—Michigan, Minnesota, Montana?—printed on the chest."

"You did."

"It was University of Miami."

"You're sure of that?" he said quietly. Her recall of the last few minutes before the accident was piece-meal and fuzzy, a result of either head trauma or sheer terror.

"Absolutely."

He parked the car and turned to look at her. "So what brought it back to mind?" Sometimes the as-sociation that sparked the memory was more telling than the clue itself.

"D-don't know. It just came to me."

CHAPTER FOUR

Dearest Lara-Mommy,

Something told me that today I'd be SURE to get a letter from you!! I went to my mailbox four times—one, two, three, FOUR—but it never came. At least, the man behind the counter said it didn't come. I'm starting to wonder about that guy. Could he be stealing my mail?!! He stares at me every time I come in now. But maybe that's just because he thinks I look EXACTLY like the famous TV star Lara Leigh? People are always, I mean ALWAYS, staring at me on the street and thinking that. I stopped and gave one woman who was staring my autograph the other day. She thought that was *so* NICE of me to give it to her without her even asking.

But then, I'm not conceited like some people we know. And all *I* want to know is, WHY do I have to keep asking you for a letter? Asking and asking and asking and ASKING for one…CRUMMY…LETTER—what kind of mother makes her daughter beg for just the scraps—any old scrap—of her love? Just a crumb of attention? I guess the same kind of mom who sells her baby to finance her way through med school, huh?

Well, I'm getting very, very tired of asking. Tired of walking to my mailbox, then home again, then back again, then— I know every line in the sidewalk on the way to my mailbox. I play Step on a Crack and You'll Break Your Mother's BACK. Do you remember that game? It's a children's game. If you'd been there for me, Lara-Mommy, instead of devoting all your selfish life to your lousy CAREER, we could have played it together. And maybe then, if you'd been there to guide me I'd have amounted to something. Is that it? Is that why you won't answer my letters anymore? Because you're ashamed of me?

I promise you won't be when we meet. Soon. It's time for a mother and daughter reunion, don't you think?

But till then,

WRITE ME, YOU *BITCH!* (HA-HA—Just kidding!!!) your loving Sarah XXX

WITH A SHUDDER of disgust, Trace dropped the letter on his desk. He stood, switched off the lamp, then moved to the window and leaned out, greedily breathing in the sweet night air, as if the letter's cloying brew of need and hatred had contaminated his lungs as well as his mind.

His office looked out on the front grounds of Woodwind. Even with his thoughts elsewhere, his eyes roved automatically over the darkened lawn below, seeking movement, any shape that departed from the normal outlines of the lush landscaping. Nearly midnight and not even a skunk waddled across the lawn in search of grubs.

He glanced back to his desk. He'd been combing through Sarah XXX's letters for the past hour, searching for any clue he might have overlooked. That letter was number four of the collection—rather, a copy of number four, since the original was filed with the Newport police. The stalking case against Sarah XXX had to be meticulously documented so that if—*when,* he corrected himself—Trace finally tracked her down, they could prosecute.

Like all the other notes, number four was a textbook example of the kind of mash note celebrity stalkers sent the objects of their twisted affections. Whatever the words, the underlying theme was the same: terrible, unappeasable neediness. The echoing emptiness of a person who has no identity in the normal sense of the word. Because for whatever pathetic reason—neglect, abuse, psychological dysfunction?—the typical stalker possesses no self.

Like Dorothy's Tin Man, who realizes he lacks a heart, the stalker is still human enough to know he lacks something. Even if he can't describe the problem, still he senses the void within—the black hole that in a normal person is filled by a sense of selfhood. *By a soul.*

And the stalker knows he needs to fill that void. Yearns most horribly to fill it. Believes with unshakable faith that to ever be happy, to ever be normal, he *must* fill it.

So just as the Tin Man set off to ask the Wizard of Oz for a heart, the stalker goes bumbling through life, searching and searching outside himself for a solution to the problem that lies within.

Until one fine day the answer comes to him. He has a black, sucking hole where his identity should be? He'll fill it with someone *else's* identity! *Someone else's soul.*

And since the void is so big, he'll need a big identity to fill it. Somebody important, however the stalker defines importance.

A generation ago, importance was a politician. Today, importance is most often a celebrity. So one day, the stalker flips the pages of a magazine—and sees a photo. Or turns the TV channel just as a certain actress walks into a room—and wham!—there it is. A person staring into his eyes, seemingly speaking to him and him alone, promising him the solution to his whole rotten, lonely life. Promising recognition, belonging—identity.

All he has to do is win that person's love, the stalker thinks. Except he doesn't know what love is. His underlying urge is darker, deeper. He doesn't want love; he wants possession. Wants to merge with. Become. Seize that soul and swallow it whole. *To eat it.*

Trace switched the lamp back on and sat again. So with zombies like that wandering the world, what does Richard Corday do for his new, beautiful young wife?

Already the creator of five hit TV shows, Corday sets out to create a showcase series for Lara. The perfect wedding gift for an actress, he must have thought. *A role to die for.* Like a master jeweler crafting the perfect setting for a matchless diamond, he creates an evening soap opera called *Searching for Sarah.*

In which, for the past thirteen years, Lara had played the part of beautiful young Dr. Laura Daley, who has a secret sorrow. At the age of seventeen,

Daley sold her illegitimate baby in a black-market adoption and used the payment to finance her way through college, then med school. Lara had assumed the role when she was thirty—at that age, she could still play the part of a teenager—and she'd been playing it ever since. The role had evolved over the years, with Dr. Daley changing from career-driven girl, to brilliant med student, to sexy resident, to glamorous pediatric surgeon in a big city hospital. She needed only one thing to make her life perfect: reunion with her lost, never forgotten, deeply regretted daughter. Because, since episode three of the show, Dr. Laura Daley had realized her dreadful mistake. She'd been frantically searching for Sarah for thirteen years now.

The premise was guaranteed to speak to every wacko in the country—at least every female wacko, and doubtless some of the males. What could be more seductive to the loser nobody needs than a TV diva who needs you and you alone? For somebody lost to know that lovely Dr. Laura Daley is frantically searching for you?

Searching for Sarah was like a Help Wanted ad, broadcast one night a week for thirteen years. The one part waiting for an actor to fill it was the role of the missing, longed-for daughter.

Was it any wonder Sarah XXX wanted the position? The only wonder was that Trace didn't have a dozen—a hundred—wannabe Sarahs to contend with. Lara had been damned lucky to escape a serious stalking as long as she had.

How serious a stalker was Sarah XXX? That was the question.

Six days after Sarah XXX mails this letter from Boston, promising—threatening—a mother-daughter

reunion, somebody pushes Lara over a cliff. The sim-
plest explanation wasn't conclusive, but Trace firmly
believed in starting with it first: one wacko, not two.

So all I have to do is find Sarah XXX.

And maybe he had. He reached for letter number
five, then selected, instead, the top page from a
thicker stack of papers. Gillian's résumé.

He paused as the buzzer tucked in his pocket quiv-
ered soundlessly against his thigh. Lara. He waited,
eyes unfocused, breath deepening, preparing himself
for action if this was a call for help—then let out a
little sigh of satisfaction when the buzzer stopped vi-
brating after three seconds. Good. *And good night to
you, too, Lara.*

Buzzers were a bit of proprietary technology that
Brickhouse used in any case where physical attack
was a possibility. The client was instructed to wear a
special locket on a chain around his or her neck at all
times. Press the button concealed in the locket's design, and a silent buzzer would alert the Brickhouse
bodyguard that he was needed—and needed *now.*

He glanced at his watch. Midnight. Which meant
it was nine in Seattle, not too late for his night-owl
younger sister. He picked up his phone and dialed.

"Mmm, 'lo?" a drowsy voice murmured in his ear.

"Asleep already?" he said easily. "Lazy bum."

"Dozing," Emily insisted. "I'm lying here on the
couch with Duncan on my chest." Duncan was one
of her four tomcats, the surly orange one. "And he's
emitting sleep rays. I was fighting valiantly, but—"

"Well, throw him off and go look at your computer." Trace had scanned Gillian's résumé into his
computer, then e-mailed it to Emily an hour ago.
"Got somebody I want you to check out for me."

His younger sister was not a partner in Brickhouse, God forbid, but an associate. They farmed out much of their research to her, especially anything that could be learned over the Internet.

"Rush job or in my own sweet time?" she inquired around a yawn.

"Like *prontissimo*. I want it yesterday."

"So my—lemme go, you cockleburr!" On the far side of the continent, something heavy hit the floor— twenty-two pounds of cat, Trace assumed. "So my brainstorm worked?" Emily continued. She'd suggested Trace run a want ad seeking a personal assistant for Lara, because if Sarah XXX had come to Newport in May, then maybe she'd stayed.

That wouldn't be untypical—the stalker's life spiraling inward in tighter and tighter circles around her target as her obsession grew. And if she'd stayed, then she'd be frantically seeking some way in past Woodwind's unbreachable walls. "So offer her a way in," Emily had urged. "Run a want ad with the Woodwind address and see who applies."

"I don't know if it worked," he said, "but it turned up a few possibles. And this is the one I want you to start on."

"Gillian S. Mahler," Emily murmured, reading Gillian's résumé on her screen.

"N. Mahler," Trace corrected absently. "The first thing I want you to check out is—"

"S," Emily interrupted, know-it-all kid sister to the end. "That's an *S*. And I'd say your Gillian's a leftie, correct?"

"*S...*" Trace stared at the spiky, backhanded letter. He'd taken it for a *N* in running script, not an *S* practically lying on its back. "By God, I believe you're right!"

"That's significant?"

"That, duckie, might be point, set and game. Okay, in that case here's what I need from you, and I need it as quick as you can. What does the *S* stand for?"

"And if it's Sarah?"

"Then bingo! I've found my pigeon."

THREE DAYS LATER, on a morning as bright as her mood, Gillian leaned out her car window to study the device that apparently controlled Woodwind's gates. Topping a metal post at a height convenient to the driver, it was an intercom of some sort, with a keypad and a speaker. Printed below the keypad was the instruction Press * To Call. She pressed the star sign, then waited.

"Yes?" the speaker said after a moment, in a metallic imitation of Trace Sutton's voice.

It would be him, playing gatekeeper. "It's G-Gillian. I'm here." Lara had called her two days ago to say she was hired, and could she please report for work on Monday. So here she was at last, with all the possessions she'd acquired in Newport packed into boxes and suitcases that filled the trunk and back seat of her car. Because along with the job came an unexpected, quite wonderful bonus: a carriage-house apartment on the Woodwind grounds. Given Gillian's recent problems with roommates, she might have accepted the job on those terms alone. Considering that the job and the housing gave her round-the-clock access to Lara, she couldn't have asked for a better chance to get to know her.

There was no welcoming comment from Sutton,

but slowly the gates swung inward and Gillian steered her ancient Toyota up the winding driveway. At the top of the low hill, the road divided. The right fork curved off grandly to lead front-door callers to the mansion's covered portico. The left fork wound around back, past concealing shrubbery, to the carriage house built to one side of the mansion and a bit behind it.

On the raked gravel before the carriage house, Trace Sutton stood waiting, a sardonic half smile on his face, his hands jammed into the pockets of a pair of impeccable white tennis shorts. The very picture of a gentleman of leisure.

"That's the door to your apartment." He indicated a human-sized entrance to the left of the five garage bays.

She parked before it and stepped out. "Good morning."

"Is it?" he said pleasantly.

Well, it was for me till now. Why did he dislike her so? She glanced past him toward Woodwind. "Where's Mrs. Corday?"

"She's not up and about yet. She had a bad night." As he spoke, he opened the rear door of her car and lifted out a box. "So meantime I'll show you your apartment and help you get settled."

"Oh, that's really not necessary!" She reached for the box, but he didn't relinquish it. "If you'd just give me the key, I'm sure I can…"

But he'd already stepped around her and started off. "Nonsense. It's no trouble at all."

"But—" She didn't *want* him intruding on her new space or on her new-job excitement. Fuming, she grabbed a couple of smaller boxes and followed him up the covered staircase that was built on the outer wall of the carriage house, then through a door at the top of the stairs. "Oh!" The slanted ceiling was set with skylights.

"Nice, isn't it?" Sutton said from the far end of the long room, where he waited in a doorway. "I used to live here myself."

"You did?" Perhaps that accounted for his proprietary air. Still, Gillian didn't like it. He rubbed her wrong; the vibrations he'd left behind would bother her, too. Frowning, she followed him into the bedroom, and stopped short in delight.

The end wall was mostly glass, a gigantic Palladian window that looked out on the side lawn, then over the distant back wall. Beyond that all was blue— robin's egg sky, a slash of aquamarine sea.

"Yes, I rented this place for a month this spring, before I moved in with Lara."

So their relationship was quite new. Must have blossomed almost overnight, given that Lara had spent most of her spring and summer in hospital. One of those sickbed romances—he'd wooed her when her resistance was at its lowest, chocolate and flowers and reading to the invalid? "I see," she said evenly. He'd set her box of clothes down on the bed. The top flaps, which she'd interlocked, had somehow come undone. She dumped her own boxes beside it. "What did you mean by 'a bad night'? Pain?" She straightened to find his eyes locked on her face.

"Nightmares," he said bluntly.

"Oh." Yes, she could imagine that. She shivered, and watched him note it. Why was he staring like that? The memory of his arm sliding around her returned abruptly. She'd put any notion that he might have been making a pass aside after his obvious attempt to block Lara's hiring her. Rationally, one action didn't follow the other. If Trace was attracted, then why would he object to her working at Woodwind? He wouldn't. Since he *had* objected, therefore that fumble at the windows had not been a pass.

Now, with his eyes lingering on her mouth, she wasn't so sure of her logic. "Er, there's lots more in the car." She ducked out the door.

They brought up a second load, Trace in the lead again. He swung her suitcase onto the bed, then opened a sliding door to reveal a closet. "There're plenty of hangers. Why don't you hand me your things and I'll hang them up."

Funny, he didn't look in the least domestic. "Thanks, but I'd rather do it myself." Later, without an unblinking audience.

Her words hung between them in the small room, a little too emphatic, a little too prim. Maybe she was wrong to take offense. Maybe this was no more than the kind of service a slightly younger man grew used to giving an older, richer woman. She found herself wondering for the first time what Sutton did for a living.

His smile deepened at the corners, but he didn't rush to fill the uncomfortable silence. So she did. "It's just that I've been living crunched into a tiny apartment with too many roommates." When she'd taken the place back in May, she'd signed on to share a two-bedroom apartment with its original tenant. Then Debbie had lost her job. To pay the rent, she'd taken in another two girls, college sophomores in Newport to party for the summer. "Dirty dishes in the sink, people coming and going at all hours or, worse, declaring parties at all hours. Laundry hanging all over the bathroom.'' And Michele, who'd decided she preferred Gillian's clothes to her own and who borrowed without asking. ''It's been too much togetherness by half. So it'll be heaven doing for myself for a change.''

Trace cocked his head. ''Let me guess. You're an only child.''

One minute he doesn't like me, the next he wants to know all about me. She was tempted to brush him off, but she didn't need an enemy at Woodwind. Lara's desire to hire her had overruled her lover's opposition. Still, Gillian didn't know by what margin. Better to play it safe. Try to win him over, too.

''Not quite,'' she said lightly, leading him out of the bedroom and back toward the stairs. ''I have a brother.'' By adoption. ''Chris. But he's fourteen years older than I.'' And when her adoptive parents had divorced back when Gillian was eight, Chris had gone with his father. She had stayed with Eleanor Scott—her adoptive mother—and had wondered for years why her father, Victor Scott, had dropped out of her life so completely.

Because I was never his in the first place! Because it was Mom who wanted to adopt a child, not him— he had Chris by a previous marriage and Chris was quite enough. So many mysteries of her childhood had come clear when she opened that safe-deposit box.

''And Chris lives back in Houston along with the rest of your family?'' Trace prodded, coming down the stairs at her heels.

Houston. She hadn't told him she came from there. *He read my résumé,* which listed Houston as her previous residence and the location of her last two jobs. "Oh, he's here, he's there, he's everywhere," she said with a smile over her shoulder. "He's a delivery captain. Moves other people's yachts around."

There wasn't much family beyond that to claim, in Houston or anywhere. Aunt Susan, Victor Scott's sister out in San Diego. And Ed Mahler, the lovely loony man who had married her mother when Gillian was fifteen and had adopted her, never knowing she was adopted already. He had been as thunderstruck as she at Eleanor's deception. Ed was an engineer in the merchant marine, and after her mother's death, he'd signed on for a regular run on a tanker between Kuwait and New Jersey.

Reaching the car, Gillian found herself still smarting at Trace's invasion of her privacy. It was silly to be so irritated. Perhaps he'd helped Lara cull all the applicants, deciding which were worth an interview. Still, his big hands on a paper that described her life...she didn't like it. "So what about you?" she said recklessly as she opened the trunk. "Any siblings?" Two could play the prying game.

She looked up to find a distinct frown on his face. *You'd rather question than be questioned?* Good. She cocked her head at him inquiringly. *I bet you're the youngest brother, with two older sisters. You're comfortable hanging around with older women. Pleasing them.*

Trace accepted her challenge with a wry smile and said, "Three. A younger brother and two even younger sisters."

So much for her betting instincts. "Then that makes you the responsible, conscientious one," she observed. And it would account for his air of command. The eldest was always the kid left in charge. "And what is Trace, a nickname your family gave you?" Might as well keep him on the run once she had him there.

He pulled her portfolio and the big wooden box she used for a paint kit out of the trunk. "It's short for Tracy," he said amiably, and turned to face her. "And what does the *S* stand for—your middle name?"

Touché! she thought wryly. He wasn't one to run far. *S* stood for two names in one. Sarah and Scott. But Sarah was the name Lara had given her at birth— Gillian knew that from the papers her adoptive mother had bequeathed her—and then apparently her adoptive parents had retained it. Simply because they liked the name Sarah? Or as some sort of salute to Lara's wishes?

Scott was the surname of her adoptive parents at the time of Gillian's adoption. The name she'd refused to give up in a fit of teenage defiance when her mother married Ed Mahler.

So Sarah Scott was how she'd signed her letter last year, when she first wrote to Lara asking if they might be related. And Gillian had no intention of risking exposure by giving it now. Probably she should have changed the S to something else on her job application, but all her ID showed her as Gillian S. Mahler.

She met Trace's eyes and realized that her hesitation had stretched for a minute or more. That he stood motionless, his face as intent as a cat's at a mouse hole.

"My middle name?" She smiled. "*S* stands for Seymour."

CHAPTER FIVE

"Now, TAKE A DEEP BREATH," Lara laughingly advised, as she paused, hand on a doorknob. Despite the nightmares Trace had mentioned, she seemed in fine spirits this morning. Trace and Gillian had collected her from her bedroom suite, where she had taken a late breakfast. She'd led them on a leisurely tour of the public areas of the house, the high point of which, to Gillian, had been an exercise room, complete with lap pool, in the basement that she might use whenever she pleased. The conclusion of the orientation was Gillian's new office, located upstairs in the same wing as Lara's suite, all the way at its western end. "And remember," Lara continued as she opened the door, "it isn't as bad as it looks."

"It's worse," Trace lazily assured her. Apparently having nothing better to do, he'd tagged along on the tour and Gillian wasn't sure if she was grateful or annoyed. On the one hand, his presence diluted the intensity of her first extended interaction with her mother, so that she wasn't constantly "onstage," having to pick and choose her words every minute. But on the other hand, his presence prevented her from connecting with Lara on a more intimate level.

"Hush," Lara commanded as she opened the door.

"If this is *bad*," Gillian murmured, following her into the office, "I don't know if I could stand good.

It just might kill me!'' The large room ended in a gigantic, three-sided bay window, with tiny stained-glass diamond panes trimming its upper reaches; at eye level, half-moon expanses of plate glass framed the outrageously splendid view. A long cushioned seat was built in below each facet of the window; a coffee table was placed in the alcove thus created. Gillian could see the tops of the rosebushes that edged Cliff Walk peeking above the estate walls, then 180 degrees of ocean glittering in the noonday sun.

"It is gorgeous, isn't it?" Lara agreed. "This used to be Richard's—my husband's—office. I never did understand how he could write here. But then, he used to sit with his back to the view." Her smile wavered for a moment. She swallowed, tipped her head in a movement that seemed to say, *Oh, well,* and continued. "It was Joya—my stepdaughter—who turned the desk to face the windows last year when she took over."

Her stepdaughter! Somehow Gillian had thought, if she hadn't been told by now, that Lara had no children.

"Up until last year, I'd had the same assistant for nine years. But when Beckie left to be married, Joya asked for the job..." Lara went on, glancing around the room with a faint frown.

"And you can see what a good job she's been doing," said Trace, nodding at the boxes lined along one wall.

A dozen boxes at least, Gillian estimated, filled with— "Yikes! Is that all—"

"Fan mail," Lara said with a look of comic guilt. "Still want the job?"

"Well, yes." More than ever. Lara wasn't like anything she'd expected. There was some mystery here that needed unraveling. "Who's afraid of a little fan mail?" And now was probably not the time to admit that she had suffered all her life from mild—okay, moderate—dyslexia. Reading required intense concentration and exacted fierce headaches. "Am I looking at a week's worth of mail or—"

"Oh, just today's," Trace assured her blandly.

Lara elbowed him in the ribs. "Sit down and hush *up* before you scare Gillian off the job, you brute!"

"Your wish, oh heart, is my…" Trace retired obediently to a window seat. He selected a catalog from a pile arranged on the coffee table, opened it, and seemed instantly absorbed.

Lara turned back to Gillian with a smile. "It's six months' or more accumulation. Joya fell behind some time before last Christmas and the poor darling never caught up again."

"Though she tried valiantly," Trace murmured without looking up. He turned a page.

"She was only working part-time," Lara defended her stepdaughter. "She and Toby—her brother—were attending college here in town, at Salve Regina…"

A brother, as well! Gillian's stepbrother, also, or was Toby Lara and Richard Corday's son? Which would mean that he was Gillian's half brother. She found herself hoping keenly for the second alternative. Her own adoptive brother had been plucked from her daily life with her parents' divorce. She would have liked a full-time sibling or two.

"What with her midterms and a paper she had to write…" murmured Lara, still defending the absent Joya. Trace rustled his catalog too loudly. Lara shrugged. "Anyway, all these letters need answering. So here's how you go about it."

She selected a letter from the last box in line along the wall, opened it and pulled out a printed get-well card featuring a doleful rabbit on crutches, his ears bent, his head bandaged. She laughed to herself and held it out to Gillian. "They're filming the fall season's episodes of *Searching for Sarah* already. Since I won't be returning for another six months or so, the scriptwriters have written me out of the story. They've decided that I had a dreadful accident while skiing in Switzerland, and no one knows if I'll ever walk again—art imitating life, but not too closely, thank God."

She lifted the card from Gillian's fingers. "Anyway, somehow *Soap Opera Digest* got wind of that plot twist and ran it as their lead story last month. Ever since it came out, half my mail is get-well cards and the other half is outraged complaints."

Either way, Gillian's job was to respond. Lara switched on the computer on the desk and showed her the various form letters. As time and inspiration permitted, she should add a sentence or two to customize the form letter, thus making the fan feel she was receiving a personal response. "I wish there were time to send each of them an answer from scratch, but there just isn't. Still I'm really grateful for their concern. For their…loyalty. Some of them have been writing me for years. Which reminds me—"

Lara showed Gillian how to check to see if the fan was new—in which case the name was to be added to a database Lara maintained, along with a code that showed which form letter she'd received—or if the fan was an old one, then Gillian should review the file to make sure a repeat response didn't get sent.

Autographed photos of Lara were stored in this drawer, prestamped envelopes in that. "And that's about it for the fan mail," Lara said at last. "Except for the...special cases."

"The reality impaired," Trace murmured.

Lara rounded on him fiercely. "They're *not* all—"

"There?" he supplied gently. "Any woman who thinks she might be Sarah? A fictional long-lost daughter of a fictional Dr. Daley, star of a prime-time soap opera? Anyone who believes that isn't playing with a full deck, Lara."

Gillian had wondered herself, of course. Dr. Laura *Daley* was fiction. Lara's maiden name was Laura *Bailey*. Both women, the fictional one and the factual, had sold their babies—one for the money to go to med school, the other for a red sports car. And it was Lara's own husband who'd created the Dr. Daley character. *Why?* The story was just too juicy to pass up? But how could Lara have allowed Corday to use her own life as fodder for a soap opera?

On the other hand, people did it all the time, selling their real-life tragedies or scandals to TV, to be dramatized as a movie of the week. *So why couldn't Lara sell her own story—sell me—all over again?*

"They're a little confused," Lara admitted, regaining her good temper. "So we try to straighten them out gently, pointing out that *Searching for Sarah* isn't based on reality."

Except that it is. Almost. Gillian found herself nodding to hide her confusion.

"I have a form letter for the special cases," Lara went on, "but those I handle personally. If you run

across any letter where the fan thinks she might be
Sarah, you bring that *right* to me and I'll deal with
it, okay?''

Straightening them out gently, she'd said. Except
that when Gillian had written Lara a year ago to say
that maybe, just maybe, she might be Lara's birth
daughter, Sarah Scott, Lara's response had been fe-
rocious, not gentle: *If I didn't want you when you
were born, why would I want you now?*

''*Laaaara.* Lara-darling?'' The owner of that car-
oling soprano paused in the office doorway. Gillian
recognized the blonde in the Range Rover, who had
coolly nodded her through the gates on the day of her
interview. This morning she radiated warmth. ''Oh,
there you are, darling!'' Her blue eyes switched to
Gillian and widened. ''And you must be my poor,
poor replacement!''

''Gillian, this is my daughter Joya,'' Lara said, and
completed the introductions while the girl glided
across the hardwood floors to offer her hand. Her
palm was marshmallow soft, her grip fashionably
limp; her inch-long mauve fingernails made shaking
hands a bit of a hazard. Gillian could see why she'd
gotten behind in her paperwork.

''Did you need something, sweetie?'' Lara asked.

The girl turned a dazzling smile upon her. ''Just
your car for a little bitty while? Stupid Toby took the
Range Rover back to the dealer. He says it's lost its
new-car smell and the dealer should have some sort
of spray to make it smell new again. I mean, I ask
you, so it smells like it's three months old instead of
three days? Who cares? Anyway, I told Duffy and
Pooh I'd meet them for lunch out at Bailey's Beach,
so could I pretty, pretty please take your—''

"No," said Trace from the window seat. "I may need it."

Sunshine gave way to storm clouds in the blink of an eye, as Joya whirled to face him. "Well, too bad! I asked first!" She glanced over her shoulder at Lara. "Didn't I, darling?"

Lara bit her lip, glancing from one to the other. Trace shook his head slowly and Joya caught the movement from the corner of her eye. Her head snapped around.

"You stay out of this, Trace! It's none of your business."

"We could drive you, I suppose," Lara said. She put a soothing hand on the girl's arm.

Joya shook it off and backed away. "I don't *want* to be driven to lunch like a snot-nosed child. I—"

"Then stop acting like one," suggested Trace.

Joya stamped her foot. "You shut up!"

Gillian drifted back a step...another, then turned. If there had been some way to creep out of the room she'd have taken it gladly. Next best option was to act as though this ugly little scene wasn't happening, go about her business. She stooped by the last box in line and examined its contents.

Behind her, Trace's voice overrode Lara's placating murmur. "If these so-called friends of yours can't be bothered to drive a mile out of their way to pick you up, then call a taxi. You can afford it."

"Trace—" Lara interposed on a note of pleading.

"At least *I* pay my own way here," Joya declared in a vicious singsong, advancing on him. She snatched up the catalog he'd set aside, flipped its pages at random. "Unlike *some* of us who just lounge around, preening and *flexing*—"

Trace laughed aloud. Gillian chose a letter from the box at random. This one was a manila envelope and seemed to contain something thicker than a letter. A gift from an admiring fan? She could ask Lara to show her what to do in cases like that. Lara looked as if she'd welcome a distraction, but Gillian hadn't the nerve. Joya was standing over Trace, her hands clenched as though she wanted to smash his upturned, gently smiling face but didn't dare. Frustrated as the girl appeared, she might lash out at the next person who spoke or moved.

"Flexing and preening and sucking up to older women. Getting Lara to buy you goodies. What are you shopping for this time, Trace, another set of custom golf clubs? Or were you a *very* good boy last night? You deserve a gold Rolex this morning?"

"Joya, that's enough!" Lara said sharply.

Gillian stood, opened the envelope. Any distraction was better than this.

"Enough? It's not half enough," Joya snarled. "It's time somebody said something! If Daddy could see this—this big lapdog who's taken his place. I bet he's spinning in his grave! Spinning and puking!"

The package held something wrapped in several folds of a plastic bag. Pulling it out and unwrapping it, Gillian drifted to Lara's side. From the bag she removed a mottled white-and-brown card, folded loosely around some oblong object. "Mrs. Corday, excuse me, but this letter contained some—"

"If you don't mind, honey," Joya snapped, "you can wait your turn! I'm—"

"Stop!" called Trace, lunging to his feet and swinging Joya out of his way—just as Gillian shook the item free of the card and into her hand.

Her gasp feathered out, loud in the sudden silence.

White fur…the hardness of bone beneath…the stench of rotten meat. Trace caught her wrist and turned it, flipping the object off her palm and onto the desktop.

"Oh, gross!" cried Joya.

"Oh," said Lara, as she sank onto the office chair.

LARA'S "GIFT" WAS THE FOOT of some small animal. *Rabbit's foot,* Gillian thought with revulsion. But not a commercial, sanitized rabbit's foot you could buy on a key chain. Horrible as she thought those were, this was much worse. A homemade job, it looked like, with dark stains on the soft fur.

She became aware that Trace still held her wrist. Warm and oddly comforting, his fingers curled around her. She could feel her own pulse, slamming against the base of his thumb. And his slower, heavier beat, like an answer you could depend on.

"You're not going to faint on me, are you?" he asked absently, looking up from the rabbit's foot into her eyes.

"Of course not," she said, though she did feel— detached. Floating a few inches off the floor. As if she could tip forward and fall into his deep hazel eyes—pools of slate green spangled with gold and gray. Aware, also, that even if her knees did buckle, he was strong enough to hold her upright.

"Of course you're not," he murmured on an odd note, something almost with an edge to it. "And what have you got there?" He reached and caught her other wrist and lifted it, scowled at the bloodstained card she still clutched. "Drop it."

The wrapper fell to the desk and he released her at

last. She stood, rubbing her wrists. Trace used the eraser ends of two pencils off the desk to push open the curled card and pin it flat to the blotter. Lara wheeled her chair up beside her to watch. Joya also crowded closer.

On the inner surface of the bloody card were printed the words:

Lara-mommy! I saw this and thought of YOU. You could use some luck—maybe more than you know? See you SOOOOOOON. Your loving SARAH XXX.

"Gross!" Joya repeated. She sounded more excited than repelled.

"I'm sorry," Gillian said, glancing at Lara's troubled face.

"Why?" Trace snapped.

"What?" Swinging to face him, she found his eyes had gone darker, the pupils expanding like those of a cat when it sees a bird.

"*Why* are you sorry?" he demanded softly.

Bewildered by his intensity, she shrugged. "Of all the letters I had to choose..."

A two-heartbeat pause, then Trace looked down again. "Most unfortunate," he agreed smoothly.

"I'll say!" Joya sniggered. "First day on the job and the girl hits a home run! Way to go, Gillie."

"It's hardly Gillian's fault," Lara protested. "Not her fault at all! If anyone ought to apologize, Gillian, it's me. I should have warned you. Once in a blue moon you'll get a fan who's a little..."

"Or a lot," Trace observed wryly. He was using

his two pencils now to maneuver the manila envelope across the desk to his side.

"Oh, pick it up, for Pete's sake!" Joya reached for it. "Ow!" she yelped as he rapped her knuckles with the eraser end of a pencil. "Did you see that?" she demanded of Lara. "I'm supposed to put up with this crap?"

"Fingerprints, darling," Trace murmured, bending to study the envelope. When he straightened again, there was a stillness about him that hadn't been there before. "This envelope came from which box, Gillian?"

"Th-the one on the end." Whatever Joya might think, this man was nobody's lapdog. Gillian had met rottweilers with kinder eyes. "Why?"

"This is today's mail. Postmarked Saturday in Boston. So today, Monday, is the first day it could have been delivered. So who brought it up to the house?" His eyes swung to Joya.

She squirmed, shrugged, looked up at him with an odd defiance. "Okay, so I did, so what? When Toby and I came in from breakfast, it was there in the mailbox, so I brought it up—brought it here to the office. So what?"

"I believe we had an understanding, Joya. *I* bring up the mail."

"You think that's all it takes to earn your keep around here?" she jeered, backing away from him toward the door.

"Joya!" Lara protested.

"Oh, spare me. I don't want to hear it, okay? I'm late for lunch. Gillie, call me a cab and tell it to meet me at the front gates." Joya stalked out of the room without a backward glance.

CHAPTER SIX

AT SEVEN-THIRTY IN THE evening, a rosy light still lingered in the western sky. Standing at his office window, Trace could see, beyond a hedge of lilacs, a shadowed stretch of the service driveway. "Come on, Gillian." She'd told Lara that she taught an eight o'clock class at the Y Monday nights. Women's weights, she'd said. "Get a move on." She'd have to leave the carriage house any minute now to make it on time. And he couldn't move till she did.

Just one more roadblock in a day filled with frustrations.

After that ugliness in the office, Lara had gone straight to bed. She'd claimed a raging headache and Trace didn't doubt it. Since her fall she was subject to those, and stress looked to be a trigger. But it wasn't just pain troubling her, he'd thought, when he brought her her lunch on a tray.

The lady was blue, it struck him, in spite of her brave front. Not frightened, which seemed the more reasonable response to such a blatant threat, but deeply depressed. And not willing to talk about it—at least not with him. Not till he'd apologized for thwarting Joya.

But Trace had no intention of apologizing to the silly brat. He'd explained to Lara that he didn't want her car out on the street unsupervised, where it might be sabotaged. But he couldn't say that to Joya, since she and Toby lived in a state of blissful ignorance, unaware that Lara was being stalked. Or that their stepmother's "accident" on Cliff Walk was no accident. Only the chief of Newport police and his top detective, Jeremy Benton, were privy to that secret. Lara had wanted to avoid publicity. And Trace felt he had a better chance of nailing her assailant if no hue and cry was raised.

Since the last few minutes, even hours, before a traumatic head injury were often wiped from the victim's memory, whoever had pushed Lara off the cliff had good reason to hope she'd forgotten the assault. Let him or her think so, Trace had urged. *The better to catch you, you freak!*

For the same reason, he lived at Woodwind under cover, with no one but Lara and his police contacts knowing his true role in the household. Because he didn't want to deter a threat—postpone Lara's troubles till he'd gone. He wanted to lull the stalker, lure him or her into his reach. *Look, here's poor little Lara, protected by no one but her bumbling gigolo. Come and get her!*

Or be gotten.

TRACE STRAIGHTENED as headlights blossomed beyond the lilac leaves, then wheeled downhill toward the gates. Gillian's little Toyota. He breathed a sigh of relief. Action at last.

He left the mansion by the kitchen door, checking that it locked behind him. Barbara Heath, Lara's longtime cook and housekeeper, and Maureen, the upstairs maid, had both retired to their third-floor apartments. As had Harriet, Woodwind's perpetual houseguest.

The resident layabouts, Toby and Joya, were out for
the evening. If they followed their usual pattern, they
wouldn't return till the bars closed at one o'clock. Or
later, if they found an after-hours party.

And his client was locked in her impregnable suite
with his locket buzzer around her neck. He didn't like
to leave her, but it was Lara's choice to hire only one
bodyguard. There was only so much he could do.

Nail Sarah XXX and he could stop worrying.

Trace circled the noisy gravel of the courtyard, then
approached the carriage house through a flower bed
on the downhill side. The copy of the key he'd made
two days before—without telling Lara—fit sweetly
into the lock and turned. At the top of the stairs, he
glanced at his watch—7:55 p.m. He'd give himself
till 9:00 to toss the place. It took longer when you
meant to leave no signs of a search.

Inside, he paused, listening to the silence. Smelling
it. Already the air carried a suggestion of Gillian.
Lemons? New-mown hay? The same sunny, subtle
perfume that clung to her tawny hair. He'd noticed it
that first time he held her. Must be imagining it now,
surely.

He padded into the room. After he'd disposed of
Sarah XXX's latest offering, Gillian had spent the rest
of the morning working on the fan mail. In the afternoon she'd retreated to her apartment. To unpack and
settle in, she'd said. Noting a vase of wild roses on
the table in the window nook, Trace smiled in spite of
himself. Whatever else she might be, she was all
girl.

His smile faded. *Whatever else she might be.* He
didn't want Gillian to be his psycho. Found it almost
impossible to imagine she could be. But if she was?

Then the odds are very good that the lady owns an orange University of Miami sweatshirt, he reminded himself. Find that, and his search was over. Trace headed for the closet in the bedroom.

"GOT A NOTE TO YOU FROM your class," said the front-desk attendant at the Y. "One of them called it in."

Gillian unfolded it on her way up to the locker room:

Gillian, we forgot to tell you that it's Jennifer's BIG FORTY tonight. She opted for champagne instead of tummy crunches, so we're carousing at Yesterday's. Join us, why don't you, and bring the rest of the class. The Rat Pack.

Gillian laughed and shoved on into the dressing room. The Rat Pack were five women friends who'd signed up together for her weight class. A good time was always their first priority; shaping their figures with small free weights ran a distinct second. With those five truant, she'd have only two students tonight.

She'd changed to her exercise togs before leaving the carriage house, but she stopped by her locker to drop off her thigh-length cotton sweater. "Well, blast!"

"Blast?" inquired Bobbie, the sixth member of Gillian's class, sitting down on the bench behind her.

"I'm missing a sweatshirt and I was sure I'd left it here." Her favorite orange sweatshirt, which her brother, Chris, had sent her years ago, when he was attending the University of Miami. She'd looked for it this evening to wear to class and not found it. But if it wasn't back at the carriage house, wasn't in her car and wasn't here in her locker, then— *Michele!* "One of my roommates has struck again. She puts meaning on the word 'borrow' that would make a burglar blush. I'm down three pairs of earrings, a baseball cap, two T-shirts and a pair of 501 Levi's, at last count. And now my favorite sweatshirt." Gillian slammed the locker, then checked the clock on the wall. "Well, ready to hoist some metal?"

Bobbie glanced around the room. "Where are the others?" Two swimmers chatted quietly as they toweled off, but otherwise the place was empty.

"Birthday party for Jennifer at Yesterday's, to which we're invited after class. And looks like Nancy is a no-show tonight. So you get my full attention, kiddo."

Bobbie responded with a wan smile and a shake of her head. "You know what, Gillian? I almost didn't come tonight. I'm having cramps... Would you be hurt if I weaseled out on you and sat in the sauna, instead?"

"Not at all!" She'd be delighted to call it a day herself.

LEANING OUT THE WINDOW of her car to reach the keypad, Gillian punched in the code to open Woodwind's gates. Lara had given her the number that morning, and a good thing, since the mansion was dark. Eight-thirty and everyone had gone to bed? Lights in Lara's suite, situated on the oceanside of the house, wouldn't show, though, come to think of it.

Bed sounded inviting. The day had been a long one, crammed with too many impressions, too much emotion. That horrible letter. *If that's life as a celebrity, Lara can have it!* She shuddered and put the letter from mind while she parked the car.

After entering her apartment, she turned to lock the door, turned back—*"Oh!"* She flinched against the door, one hand to her stuttering heart.

Standing at the counter in her kitchen, Trace Sutton glanced over his shoulder. "I'll have to buy you a decent corkscrew." He held up the simple bartender's device he must have found in her utensil drawer, then jabbed it into the cork of a wine bottle.

Her wine, she realized, recognizing the label. Her heart was still stampeding, but fright was giving way rapidly to rage. How *dared* he simply walk in like this? "Wh-what d'you think you're doing here?"

The cork popped softly. He poured the bardolino into two glasses.

"Well?" she demanded, throwing her sweater on the couch and stalking toward him. The creep had kept a key to her apartment—that much was obvious!

He lifted the glasses, began to walk toward her— and stopped, his eyes dropping to her legs.

Which were bare below her nylon gym shorts. As were her arms, since she wore a sleeveless T-shirt. She swerved toward the sweater she'd abandoned too hastily, then stopped herself. *Show no fear.* With the thought, a twinge of alarm skated along her nerve endings. He was very large and already he'd proven he didn't respect normal boundaries.

"I thought your first day at Woodwind was a little...rough and you deserved a drink." Trace handed her a glass.

"Of my own wine?" If she dashed her drink in his eyes, would that slow him down enough? The distance to her door was twelve steps at least, and then she'd have to throw the dead bolt. Remembering the speed with which he'd crossed the office that morning, she abandoned the notion as soon as it formed.

"I'll do better next time," he assured her.

There won't be a next time, buddy! Was he that vain that he thought he could simply barge into a woman's apartment and be welcome? That with one smoldering look she'd fall into bed with him? Granted, no woman could deny his appeal, but still...

And what about Lara? God, she'd forgotten Lara! Trace wasn't just a sexy lout; he was *Lara's* lout. Too angry to speak, she took a gulp of the wine. And rattled as she was, she tipped the glass too far.

A drop dribbled past her bottom lip and fell. "Damn!" On the slope of her breast, a blood-red spot stained the white cotton.

She looked up to find his eyes aimed at her heart, his pupils gone wide and black as gun bores. His eyes lifted to hers, then slowly one of his dark eyebrows rose in a question. *Well?*

As she imagined his lips on her breast, his hands clamped on her waist, the pressure of his mouth bending her backward, a wave of raw heat washed through her. A tingling awareness spread from the back of her shaky knees and climbed. It didn't matter that he was a vain and faithless brute—in his mind he was kissing her breast and in *her* mind she was responding helplessly. She turned away—felt his eyes caressing her hips and spun back again. "Get out!"

She stalked past him to the sink. Found a dishcloth and dabbed furiously at the spot. A useless effort, of course.

He came to lean on the counter beside her, so close

she could feel the heat of his big body. Stood sipping wine and watching. "Seltzer?" he suggested huskily at last. "That's what my sisters always use."

Sisters, seltzer and spot removal. The sheer domesticity of the images banished fear. And there were rules at play here, even if she didn't understand them. Trace wanted her, that was clear enough, but he wouldn't use his size to take what he wanted—he'd have done so by now.

He expects me to give of my own free will? Oh, he was unspeakably vain! She threw down the dishcloth and wheeled. "I said, get *out.*"

He tipped his dark head in mocking acquiescence, then said, "May I finish my wine first?"

May I. Her sense of control grew with the question, and after a moment of icy silence, she nodded. She wanted him out—meant to have him out—but she didn't need to make an enemy. Because faithless or not, Trace was Lara's lover. She'd seen who won the battle over Lara's car this afternoon. Trace had the clout at Woodwind. He could persuade Lara to fire her, if he really wanted to; of that she was certain now. *So I walk a tightrope here.*

He took another savoring sip. She watched his strong brown throat move as he swallowed. Another sip. He had a beautiful mouth, though very masculine. She could see why a woman might want him hanging around. Why he'd expect a woman to want him. Did Lara know he was unfaithful? Or was that simply an accepted part of the celebrity life-style? Maybe Lara didn't care. Not everyone valued fidelity as Gillian did.

"You know, you've been worrying me," he said softly, rousing her from her trance.

"Oh?" Her ever-ready sense of guilt came alive. She didn't want to worry anyone at Woodwind. She'd come here to be the fly on the wall. To silently see all, then fly away. Bluff it out, she told herself. She lifted his empty glass from his fingers and set it emphatically on the counter, then tipped her head at the door and moved purposefully toward it.

He pushed off the counter and padded alongside her with the loose-limbed grace of a sleepy tiger. "I've decided that someone who..." He paused and let the silence stretch.

"Who...?" she prompted evenly. He'd noticed some discrepancy on her résumé? Or maybe— Reaching the door, she flipped the dead bolt and opened the door wide. Stood waiting for him to take the hint and go.

He moved one step into the doorway, then swung back, much too close to her. His hand rose slowly.

So this was another pass after all, nothing more. She narrowed her eyes in warning and raised her chin. Watched his beautifully carved lips quirk at the corners with amusement.

Trace lifted a lock of her hair off her shoulder. "Who looks like you..." He gazed at the curl, rubbing it thoughtfully between thumb and forefinger. "Can't possibly be what she seems...."

God, he did know something! What?

He stared deeply into her eyes. "You can't be a Seymour."

Oh...a stupid joke. She breathed again, then tossed her head. Her lock of hair slipped through his fingers.

"So what's the S really stand for, Gillian?"

Or was it a joke? He wasn't smiling now, not with

his mouth, not with those hunting-cat eyes. Could he know?

He could not. Bluff it out, she told herself again. She sniffed. "Did I say Seymour? How silly of me. It's Sylvester, an old family name." End of discussion! She swung the door around till it bumped his track shoes, and smiled meaningfully at him through the remaining gap. *Beat it, buddy.*

"So…I guess this is good night?" he said on a note of quiet laughter.

"I guess it is." He had charm; she'd give him that. "Oh!" she cried as he retreated a step. "I forgot. You know what's worrying *me?*"

Solemnly he shook his head.

"Apparently you have a key to my apartment. So—" she held out her hand "—give."

He surrendered the key without a protest. Dropped it into her waiting palm—and touched the soft skin of her wrist with one lingering fingertip. "G'night, Gillian."

She stood staring into the shadows where he'd been, counting two of her heartbeats for each of his footfalls down the stairs, then she closed the door. And locked it.

"GOT CAUGHT WITH MY HAND in the cookie jar," Trace admitted a short while later. Lemon cookies hot from the oven. He could imagine what her skin would taste like.

"Oh?" Emily said encouragingly out in Seattle.

He'd called to ask how her research was going. And to talk. He'd been under cover too long. You had to touch base with family—and through them yourself—occasionally or you risked confusion. A blurring of your undercover role and your real identity.

Leaning back in his office chair, he told her about the snafu: Gillian's unexpected return, his frantic scramble out of the bedroom, his covering story of an impromptu housewarming.

"And she bought it?"

She bought that I was a jerk, yes. "Seemed to."

"How far had you gotten in your search?"

Far enough to determine she didn't own an orange sweatshirt.

"Not anymore, anyway," Emily murmured. "She might have dumped it after the Cliff Walk attack."

"Might have." But he couldn't see Gillian shoving Lara over the cliff. Couldn't see Gillian as his stalker at all. Yet she'd found the rabbit's foot letter—chose it unerringly out of a box of thirty or more. Go figure those odds. And her middle name started with *S*, plus she'd given two patently ridiculous versions of what the *S* stood for...

"You didn't see anything else that would tie her to Sarah XXX?"

"No." He'd just sat down to the papers in her desk when her car pulled into the courtyard. A pity. Papers always left a trail. "Speaking of Sarah XXX, her eighth letter arrived this morning." He told Emily about the rabbit's foot.

"The heartless bitch!" Emily's voice rose half an octave. She loved animals, had filled their family home in New Hampshire with hamsters, stray cats, half-fledged nestlings, throughout her childhood. She was the protector of anything that crawled or flew. "She chopped up a *bunny?*"

"Maybe it was roadkill," he lied. Stupid of him to

tell her the details. He had some notion from time to time that if Emily was to work for Brickhouse, she'd have to toughen up, but he always regretted any effort to harden her.

"Not if it was white," she said grimly. "Did you phone the local pet shops?"

"Spent all day on the phone." Calling every pet shop within twenty miles, urging sullen or harried employees to try to remember if they had sold a white rabbit last Friday or Saturday—at least, a rabbit with white paws.

Not an easy task when he couldn't see their faces, judge if they were making an effort to remember or simply brushing him off. "Nobody recalls selling a bun." Of course, the luckless rabbit might have been purchased at one of the farms out toward Second and Third Beach.

Or purchased in Boston. Trace grimaced. No, he wasn't going to find Sarah XXX that easily. "So that brings me back to you. What does the *S* in Gillian's middle name stand for?" *And don't you tell me Sylvester.*

Emily sighed. "You know Harry S. Truman?"

"As in President Truman?"

"The very same. Do you know what *S* stood for in his case?"

"What's that got to do with—"

"It stood for *S*, Trace. He didn't *have* a middle name, just an initial to puff himself up. There's absolutely no law that says you must have a middle name. Or that you can't have five."

Here lay the disadvantage in hiring your sister: you couldn't swear at her. "You're telling me Gillian doesn't have one?"

If she had, Emily had yet to find it. It didn't appear in the credit-card databases, the magazine mailing lists. The registrar at the University of Texas, Austin, knew her only as Gillian S. Mahler. So did the phone company in Houston, Texas, the electrical and gas companies. "Maybe it would show on her driver's license, but Texas has instituted antistalking laws like California, you'll be pleased to learn." Emily understood how he hated stalkers. "So I can't tap into those records. You wouldn't happen to know where she was born, would you?"

"No, and I doubt she'd tell me." She was hiding something; he was sure.

"Too bad. If I could find out that, I might be able to get a copy of her birth certificate, now that I've got her social security number off her credit data. That would show it."

"So what now?" His years as an agent with the FBI had spoiled him. The agency had computer jocks who did nothing but track down data upon request. And the government had sources that private investigators couldn't easily access. Still...

"If you'd like to finance a little road trip to Houston—all expenses including cat sitter—that might be the most efficient way. I got her family's address from the UT registrar. They've moved away—I've checked that already. But if I could run down her high-school girlfriends...or a preacher if her family were churchgoers. Or the district where she registered to vote. With some scratching I'm sure I can uncover something."

"Do it. Can you fly tomorrow?" SOOOON, Sarah XXX had promised. "I've got to know her name soon."

HOURS LATER, SOMETHING woke him. Staring into the darkness overhead, Trace lay listening, orienting himself. Lara's bedroom. Slowly he turned his head to the left. He could see moonlight shining through the tall French doors that led out to her balcony. He'd checked them before retiring, and they stood now as then—securely latched.

And no one could have entered through the corridor. He'd hardened the entire suite his first day on the job. Had chosen the locks for her door and the locksmith to install them.

The soft, incoherent sound came again, and he lifted himself on his elbows to look over the back of the sofa.

Lara, talking in her sleep. "Cloudy..."

He scowled and sat up. *Weather reports at 3:00 a.m., Lara?*

"Cloudy?" More sob than word this time. "Cloudy, I t-tried."

He scrubbed a hand through his hair. Whatever was haunting her dreams, she needed hugging. If she'd been his woman, he'd have taken her in his arms and held her. Kissed her awake.

But she wasn't. He'd drawn the line clearly the first day, and he'd never once stepped over it. You don't boff the clients was rule number one at Brickhouse. They'd all seen too many bodyguards come to grief over that one, and had voted a man out of their partnership last year for breaking that rule.

"Cloudy, she—" Not so much sobbing as keening—a heartbreaking, tiny wail, torn ragged by each indrawn breath, then resumed.

He kicked off the covers and stood. Padded to her

night table and poured a glass of water. Sat on the edge of the bed. "Lara?"

"Sh-sh-she... I think she h-*hates* me."

"Who, Lara?" Sarah XXX? Or something she sensed in Gillian? Or, since dreams didn't confine themselves to the here and now, any one of a thousand women Lara had met at any point in her lifetime, from her hairdresser to a first-grade teacher?

"She..."

He put a hand lightly on her shoulder and shook. "Lara."

She jerked awake with a cry, stared at him blankly for a moment, then hitched herself up against the headboard.

He switched on the bedside lamp. "You were dreaming."

"Oh." Her cheeks were wet with tears. She swiped the back of a hand across her lashes, gave him a wavering smile and accepted the glass of water.

He let her drink, then asked. "About that letter today?"

She shuddered violently, but she shook her head. "My...husband."

Corday had been dead two years, but she wasn't a woman who'd forget a love overnight. Yet Lara had said "she." Still, it wasn't his place to interrogate the client. Trace took the glass from her hands and set it aside. "All right now?"

She nodded, looking like a drowsy, tousled little girl, lost in a bed too big for a child. He gave her a last reassuring smile and stood, flicked off the lights. "Sweet dreams, then, Lara."

"G'night, Trace. And...thanks." A deep, sorrowful sigh feathered through the dark, then he heard her snuggle into the bedclothes.

He walked slowly back to his couch and rearranged his comforter. Lay down. Stared into the blackness again. Knowing by the sound of her breathing that she stared, too. How many people all over the darkened country right now stared at ceilings, their arms as empty as their hearts?

You've been too long without a woman, he told himself wryly, and rolled over. Five months or more.

But to be with just any attractive, available woman... The thought didn't cheer him as it once would have. As soon as Brickhouse was fully viable, had made its rep and could afford to hire some more manpower...say two years, three at the outside...he'd look into that. He thought about his brother Jon and Jon's beautiful Demi...the way she looked at him, when he didn't know she was looking. *Whatever Demi sees, I want a woman seeing that in me.* But not just any attractive, available woman.

Trace curled one arm around his pillow and hauled it close. A pair of golden lioness eyes stalked him into the thickets of sleep.

CHAPTER SEVEN

SINCE LARA SLEPT LATE most mornings, Trace liked to start his day with a workout in Woodwind's basement gym. For once, personal preference dovetailed with professional duty. He could stay fit—the perpetual requisite for a bodyguard—while at the same time he polished his image as the body-conscious gigolo, a self-preoccupied lightweight, no real protection for Lara, no threat to anyone. If anybody was looking...

Gillian, for instance?

After completing his warm-up, he moved to the leg-press machine. Set the weights—he was going for a brisk workout, but not a killer, this morning—then lay back on the inclined seat, his legs straight, his feet braced against the weight board.

Releasing the safety catches, he lowered the board till his knees neared his chest, then he exhaled and pressed up smoothly. *One rep...two reps...three.* The rhythmic thrust and release of the weight freed his mind to drift...make new and unexpected connections. He could choose a problem, then let his mind wander around it at will. Consider Sarah XXX's letters, for instance. They were almost textbook samples of a stalker's mind. *Four reps.* He inhaled, brought the weight board down smoothly. Were the letters perhaps too smooth? *Five reps.* Sarah's transitions from one thought to the next. *Six.* One sentence building on the last, laying the ground for the next—hateful thoughts flowing smoothly...*Seven reps*. An educated, intelligent organization of the contents of each message...*Eight. But who says stalkers can't be intelligent?* Yeah, some of them were off-the-charts intelligent, but smooth? *Nine.* Wounded minds lunged from one concept to another without the normal, sane transitions. *Ten reps.*

Eleven. But the emotions in those letters. The progressive obssession was textbook perfect, building from the puppy-dog anxiety to please in letter number one...*twelve reps*...to the edgy requests of letter three... To the sense of frustrated entitlement of number four...*thirteen*...to the barely veiled hostility of number five, that threat of reunion. *Fourteen*...then after number five, came the assault out on Cliff Walk... *Fifteen and set the safety catches and stand.*

He rolled off the machine, breathing deeply and easily, added five pounds to the weights. Bent over straight legged, till his fingers touched the mat and held it for a count of sixty, then straightened and climbed into the machine again for his second set.

Released the safety catches and brought the weight down smoothly. *Where was I?* Smooth, the emotions reading right, the transitions possibly reading wrong—too smooth? *Make that one rep*... Smooth as Gillian's legs had looked last night...his blood warming, breath coming faster now...*two reps*...and the image of his open hand, sliding up the slim, muscled curve of her thigh... *Smooth Gillian, what are you doing here? She stares at Lara whenever she can, seems fascinated.*

But people stared at stars; he'd guarded enough to know. People stared, wondering, *how are you differ-*

*ent, what do you have that I don't? How could I get
some? Be like you?* Envy and fascination intertwined.

But Gillian had no need to envy any woman…the
way she moved…those eyes… *Six reps.* Last night,
he'd scared her, coming on to her like that. Hadn't
meant to, but on some dark, instinctive level he'd
liked that she tacitly acknowledged his superior size
and strength, the inevitable outcome if… *Down boy!
No ifs, buts or maybes here.*

He punished himself by picking up the pace, breath
hissing in and out, and kept on pushing, no words in
the mind now, not words, but images—soft lips, soft
skin, an all-over softness of spirit that reminded him
oddly of Lara. Sheer femininity, but with an entranc-
ing edge. He'd liked her toughness last night, throwing him out… *Twelve reps.* She liked nothing about
him, demanding her key, which was just as well. If
he couldn't keep her at a distance, then thank God,
she was minding her fences.

Minding them too well? *What are you hiding, Lion
Eyes? Fifteen—* Oh, crap, so much for peace and
quiet, because here came little Joya.

He locked the weights in place and rolled out of
the machine. "'Morning,'' he said, panting, and
turned his back on her while he added ten pounds to
the weights. She was dressed in nothing but a beach
towel, a sullen look and a few scraps of nylon—a red
bikini he hadn't seen before. She'd come to do laps,
apparently, though this wasn't her usual time. Like
her brother, Joya generally slept till eleven, then
swam, then went out to the beach club or a restaurant
for lunch, and was rarely seen again until the following day at eleven.

He glanced her way as he climbed into the machine

again for his last set and saw that she was down on a mat by the pool, stretching in a square of sunlight like a cat. Ignoring him completely, which suited him very well indeed. He had no use for selfish brats, male or female, and she and her brother were quite the pair. Both were offspring of Corday and his first wife...a film actress, he remembered, and a third-rate talent—he'd seen her in a thriller or two. She was the one the serial killer always finished off in the first reel.

Third-rate talent, first-rate face and body, which she'd passed on to Toby and Joya. But something hard went along with the beauty—a silent message that said, *Look at me. See what you can't have, sucker, and weep!* Smart guy, Corday, to trade her in for Lara, an unknown soap-opera starlet without his first wife's icy beauty-queen looks, but with something much better—heart.

Trace rolled out of the leg-press machine and stood. Now for the bench press. He added two twenty-pound weight disks to the barbell, then lay back on the bench. He grasped the bar, positioning his hands slightly wider than shoulder width, then he lifted the bar off its rack and inhaled as he lowered it slowly to his chest. Exhaled as he pushed it up. Counted *one* as his elbows locked.

"A hundred and twenty?" Joya said beside him. "Toby lifts more than that."

And two and so what? Trace could easily lift his own body weight, 180, but only a fool did so without a spotter. Pull a tendon and they'd find you with your show-off weight compressing your chest, while you squeaked softly for help.

She drifted closer and looked down at him as he

lifted, one long, beautifully tanned calf nearly touching his thigh. What the hell did she want?

"But I guess if you're, like, past your prime and that's the best you can do..." She shrugged contemptuously.

He smiled as he raised the barbell and blew out a breath. Still pouting about yesterday, he supposed. *No* wasn't in Joya's vocabulary, or her brother's, as far as Trace could tell. Their mother out in Hollywood had had custody throughout their formative years, and in Trace's estimation, she'd botched the job. Lara and Corday had taken them on at age nineteen and twenty, after they'd flunked out of school out West.

Corday had persuaded Salve Regina, Newport's one college, to admit them—with the help of a generous endowment, no doubt. But they'd dropped out again in their junior year, last spring, without even completing the semester—"to find themselves," according to Joya. Maybe in five months they'd found all of themselves there was to find? And since their inheritance from their father had just come through probate and they now owned half of Woodwind and three million apiece...*I don't see a Bachelor of Arts in little Joya's future.*

Her calf nudged his thigh. "*Are* you?"

Am I irritated? Most assuredly—he'd lost count. Call it thirteen. "Am I what?" he gasped out on his exhale. *Fourteen.*

"Are you past your prime, Trace?"

Fifteen. He racked the bar, smiled and sat up. Swung his leg away from hers and over the bench, stood and walked slowly around the room, breathing hard, shaking his arms out, rolling his shoulders, his neck. She was spoiling his workout. This was his time

to center himself, the time when he did his best thinking. He couldn't let her drive him out, or she'd do it
every morning for the sheer fun of it.

Returning to the bench, he found her seated—no,
posed on it, her thighs spread wide, her lids lowered
in almost a parody of seduction. He swallowed his
startled laugh and said simply, "Move."

She flounced off the bench and started away. He
breathed a sigh of relief, lay back into his position
and lifted the bar off the rack. *One.*

Then she was back beside him, knee nudging his
thigh. "But I s'pose you don't have to exactly be in
your prime to please an old lady, do you?"

Two. It took him a moment to realize she meant
Lara. He snorted. *Three.*

"After forty, I guess you take what you can get,
even if you have to pay for it, huh? Does she pay you
by the…piece or by the hour?"

Four and enough! Trace paused on the upthrust,
elbows locked, and met her eyes. "Sweetheart, don't
you worry about Lara. When she's seventy, she'll still
have something you never knew you were missing."

His biceps shivered in complaint and he brought
the bar down to his chest. Joya swung a leg over him
and sat. *"Uhh!"*

Grasping the barbell with both hands, she leaned
all her weight on it and smiled down into his face.
"What did you say, studmuffin?"

A hundred and thirty pounds at least, added to the
bar's one-twenty. And her hips were compressing his
abdomen, making it hard to breathe. Face hovering
only a foot above his own, her long hair a silken
curtain shutting out his light, she smiled a slow, taunt-

ing smile. "Hmm? What's the *matter,* studly, cat got your tongue?"

He pulled a difficult breath and looked up at her. Enjoying this immensely, she was. Not just a brat but a bully. Why hadn't he noticed that before?

He could let go the bar with one hand, grab her wrist and flip her off him, but there were exercise machines to either side. If she hit her head. Hurt Joya and Lara would fire him; he had no doubt. And Lara needed him.

Joya was pressing the bar forward, as well as down. If it rolled onto his throat while they struggled… He took another labored breath, considering. *Gotta move soon.* The muscles in his arms, already taxed by his first set, were quivering with the effort to hold the bar off his chest. Spasms weren't far behind.

"*Sooo,* you want to take that back?" she invited.

Apologize? Something in her face told him she wouldn't settle for that. The kid wanted groveling, and he didn't know how. Didn't feel like learning. "Move!" he panted.

"*Ohhh,* take your time, Traciekins. *I'm* in no hurry."

But he was. Trace drew a breath—and released the bar with his left hand. As he grasped a hank of her hair, he braced his left forearm against the bar, keeping it off his throat.

Her eyes narrowed to slits. "Hey!"

"This…is what's called…a standoff," he said between his teeth. She shoved the bar toward his throat and he stiffened his arm. "Don't *do* that!" *Unless you want to be scalped.*

The sound of breaking glass caused Joya to jump

against him. They both turned their heads toward the sound.

Across the room at the edge of the pool, Gillian stood staring. "Um, I...I... S-sorry!" she muttered, and looked down at the shattered bottle at her feet. Her shampoo. She'd intended to swim, then wash her hair in the gym shower. Had walked halfway across the room before she'd seen the couple entwined on the weight bench. Joya and Trace! "Sorry," she murmured again without looking their way. And what now? Flee and leave them to it? Or clean up the glass before somebody got cut?

She detected movement from the corner of her eye and looked around to see Joya approaching. The girl's face was brick-red, her blue eyes glittering. "Sorry," Gillian said again.

"Sure you are," Joya snarled under her breath, "Miss Underfoot!" Yanking her towel off a chaise longue, she stalked out of the gym.

And Trace preferred her to Lara? Trace... She stooped hastily and snatched up the shards of glass. *Get 'em and go.* She had no desire to face the man. *Me last night, Joya this morning. What a busy guy!* She glanced sideways at him and paused.

He lay as before, and now she realized he clutched a barbell to his chest. What the—? His elbows wavered. Was he trying to lift it?

Hesitantly she moved toward him. It was really none of my business. She'd barged in enough already. His arms tensed—the muscles jumping under his taut, sweaty skin. He *was* in trouble. "Trace?" She looked down at his face, as red as Joya's had been. "D-do you need some...help?"

"Yes." One word, compressed by fury or exhaustion or both.

"Hang on!" She moved behind him, and grasped the bar outside his hands. "Ready?"

She lifted and it came up an inch—then dropped back to his chest. He couldn't help her at all. She glanced at the weights, one twenty. She couldn't lift the barbell over without his help. "Okay, let's try this."

She moved around to his side, straddled him and the bench, then grasped the bar just inside his hands. "I can lift it a few inches if you could slide beneath."

They measured each other for a moment. He'd have to slip under the bar, then between her thighs and down the bench; couldn't roll off to either side because of her bracketing legs. If she dropped the bar on his face or his throat...

"I won't drop it, I promise."

"Then go," he gasped.

She nodded, bent her knees and lifted, puffing with the effort.

Trace caught the bench on either side and squirmed down it, his rib cage brushing her thighs. Goose bumps everywhere, muscles quivering, she stood motionless. His throat passed under the deadly bar to safety and now there was only his head to go. His eyes were locked on hers. She smiled reassuringly. He squirmed an inch or two more—and stuck, his broad shoulders wedged between her knees.

She bit her lip. *This'll teach me to exercise in the mornings!* Tipping forward on the balls of her feet, she brought the bar down. It hit the bench three inches beyond his head. *"Whew!"*

"Yeah." He patted her thigh as she backed over

him down the bench, then swung one leg across—back to proprietyville. "Thanks," he muttered, sitting up.

"Sure." *And next time, find someplace safer to fool around than a gym!* She backed off a step. Clean up the glass and scram—that was her program. She'd swim another day.

"Can you bend your arms?" she asked, as she realized he hadn't yet.

"No. Cramps, I guess. They should go in a minute."

He deserved no consideration at all, but still. "Let's see if I can help." She half knelt on the bench beside him and took hold of one arm. Dug her thumbs in gently at the biceps, then slid them along the knotted muscle, walking her fingertips up the back side of his arm.

"Ahhh..." He grunted half in pain, half relief. Then he closed his eyes and let her work on him.

She couldn't span his arm with both her hands. He was so graceful in movement that she hadn't realized he was quite so large. Not overbuilt, but wonderfully hard, with gorgeous definition. She massaged her way up his arm to his shoulder, then switched to the other arm before it, too, seized up. He let out a long groan of pleasure and she glanced at him warily. "You shouldn't work without a spotter, you know," she murmured. *Let's pretend that whatever I saw, I didn't see it.* Not that she'd forget.

He nodded assent, and it turned to silent laughter. "Are you volunteering for the position?" He opened his eyes and somehow they'd darkened.

"Nope," she said primly. So much for charity. Give this guy an inch and he'd make a pass. She briskly slapped his shoulder once to say he was done, and backed off.

"Too bad," he said lightly.

Oversexed, that's what he was. God's gift to women, spreading the goodies around. Not her type at all. Yet her hands still tingled with the feel of him—warm velvet stretched over steel. "You might want to take a hot shower," she advised, heading back for her broken bottle.

"Or a cold one," he said softly behind her.

She hunched her shoulders and didn't look back. Next time maybe she'd leave him under his barbell.

CHAPTER EIGHT

Two HOURS OF FAN MAIL, some writers expressing shy admiration for Lara, others demanding her photo or autograph as their rightful due, still others suggesting ways to resolve Dr. Daley's crippling dilemma—perhaps a sexy African witch doctor flown in to effect a cure? Two hours of squinting over crabbed, handwritten notes or lengthy typed epistles, and Gillian already had a blinding headache. She winced as the phone on her desk rang, then grabbed for it. "Hello?"

"Gillian." Lara's warm voice. "Trace said you might be at work already. How's it going?"

Gillian laughed and told her about the witch doctor. "Otherwise it's going fine. I haven't sealed any of my responses in case you'd like to check them."

"I'm sure you're doing beautifully, but I'll look at a few this afternoon if you like. Which reminds me. Trace is driving me to a rehab appointment this morning, but we'll be back in time for lunch. Meet us out on the terrace at one, shall we say?"

"Of course." Gillian hung up the phone and glanced toward the door. Lara's suite wasn't a hundred feet down the corridor. Surely it would have been as easy to deliver that message in person. Was Lara avoiding her? Or just bone lazy?

Either way, if she had no more contact with Lara

than she'd had these past two days, the job was going to be a bitter disappointment. She shrugged and opened another letter, maybe the worst sample of penmanship yet. Frowning, she propped her elbows on the desk and bent over the letter, stayed that way for ten minutes or so, and still the meaning wouldn't come clear. She could make out a word or two on each line, but the rest might have been hieroglyphics twisted from black wire, wires stabbing at her eyes...

"Are you all right?"

Fingers massaging her temples, she opened her eyes. Trace, standing beside her. "Oh. Sure." She sat upright. "Just a bit of a headache." The top of her head coming off, that was all.

He showed her a double handful of mail. "Today's catch. Where would you like it?"

"The end box, right-hand side." He deposited the envelopes and returned to prop a lean hip on one corner of her desk. She glanced up at him warily, then down again at her letter.

"That's a bad one," he said after a moment.

"I'm beginning to wonder if it's English," she admitted, not looking up.

"I mean that's a bad headache." Trace pressed the tip of his forefinger between her eyebrows. "You've got a little vertical line there I haven't seen before." He rotated his fingertip in a gentle massage.

The touch feathered outward across her scalp in slow, delicious waves. She wanted to lean into that soothing pressure. Instead she sat back in her chair. "It's nothing, really."

"Hmm." A sound of polite skepticism. He glanced toward the bay window. "It's too bright in here for a computer screen. If you want drapes, I'm sure Lara would be delighted to—''

"No, really, thanks. I'd rather have any headache than shut out that view."

He cocked his head and considered her, the corners of his mouth deepening. She had a vague sense she'd passed some test, but all he said was, ''I know what you mean. My idea of Hell is a desk job in a windowless room. Give me your hand.''

She shouldn't let him touch her. Each time he did, she felt it for hours afterward. But his hand hung relentlessly before her nose and finally she surrendered. Trace turned her hand over, then ran his thumb in slow exploration across the palm. Her skin came alive, sensations sliding warmly up her wrist to her elbow, a hot heaviness rising from there. ''What are you doing?''

''Acupressure—ah, there's the spot.'' His thumb tip centered on the muscle at the base of her thumb, then pressed with a pressure just short of pain.

Now hot awareness climbed her arm to her shoulder, the back of her neck, down to her breasts. She liked the size of his hand, dwarfing hers, its strength... Liked it too much. ''Look, I've got a lot of work to do and...''

''Hush,'' he said peaceably. ''Just relax.''

Relax? She felt as if she'd stuck her hand in an electric socket. Alternating current, resistance and desire. The tingling had spread to her stomach and lower.

He stopped pressing on her palm. His thumb slid lazily down to stroke her wrist once, then he released her. ''Other one now.''

''Really, you don't have to—''

"Give," he insisted, hand outstretched.

With a little growl of exasperation she laid her hand in his. The same drill again, with the sensation rippling all the way down to her toes this time, then rebounding.

"I wanted to thank you," Trace said huskily as he pressed, "for this morning. I would have been in a jam if you hadn't come along."

"It was nothing." The less said about the whole sleazy incident the better, as far as Gillian was concerned.

His slow smile gave her the lie, but he simply completed the thumb pressure with that same tiny caress across her wrist and let her go. "How's the headache?"

"Flown out the window," she marveled.

"Good." He touched the spot between her eyebrows again. "Then don't work too hard, and call me whenever your head hurts." He sauntered across the room without looking back, closed the door softly behind him.

She sat back in her chair, her body throbbing like a beaten gong. Blast the man! If Lara was really keeping Trace as Joya had hinted, well, he just might be worth every penny.

"SO YOU'RE GILLIAN," said the beautiful young man out on the terrace. Seated beside Joya at a glass-topped table under a candy-striped awning, he made no attempt to rise. "Joya didn't do you justice." Wide and blue as his sister's, his eyes moved over Gillian in an appraisal just this side of insolence. The smile he finally bestowed upon her was all the more arrogant for its approval. "Welcome to Woodwind."

"And you're Toby, I take it?" Gillian said, choosing a seat to his right. And no half brother to herself, she was as certain as she was grateful. He could have been Joya's fraternal twin.

"The one and only." He lifted a pitcher and filled a glass with a yellow liquid. "Have a mimosa, my very own recipe."

"Thanks, but not while I'm working." She tipped a hand up to fend off the drink, but he set it before her with a smack that rang the glass.

"Oh, don't take yourself too seriously," he said easily. "For personal assistant read court jester and you'll hit the right note around here."

"Yeah, Gillie's been a load of laughs so far," Joya said with heavy irony.

And what's eating you? Gillian wondered. *Are you blaming me for walking in on your romp with Trace this morning?* "It's Gillian, actually," she said mildly. Then the thought suddenly occurred. *Are you afraid I might tell Lara? No fear there, honey.* The incident was distasteful, but it was none of her business.

Joya sniffed as Toby drawled, "So tell us a-a-all about yourself, Gillian."

She was saved by Lara's sleighbell laugh, as she stepped out onto the terrace accompanied by Trace. "Sorry to be late. You wouldn't believe the traffic in town!" Passing behind Gillian and Toby, she patted his arm. "Hi, stranger!"

"Darling." He picked up her hand and kissed it theatrically. "Were they too brutal today?"

"Not at all. I had a wonderful session." Lara launched into a comical description of herself wired up to a machine that delivered electrical stimulation to damaged muscles—the dial turned too high, the machine's attendant happily jabbering on the phone to her boyfriend across the room. "My muscles just sort of striding along with no help from me...I felt like Frankenstein's bride—would somebody please, please unplug me?"

Lucy, the maid, relayed trays of sandwiches, bowls of roasted, marinated vegetables and a hot quiche from the kitchen. While they laughed and filled their plates, the dour-faced woman who had opened the door to Gillian the day of her interview appeared and took the last empty seat, beside Trace.

"You've met my friend Harriet Bristow, haven't you, Gillian?" asked Lara, passing the latecomer the sandwich platter.

"The first day," Gillian agreed, "and I've been thinking you look familiar, but I can't..."

"See?" Lara crowed to her friend. "You say no one ever notices you! She's my surgical nurse," she explained to Gillian.

"On *Searching for Sarah*," clarified Harriet without a smile. She hadn't smiled once since she'd joined the table. "Currently unemployed, since Dr. Daley skied off a mountain in Switzerland."

Gillian watched Lara's smile waver, then renew itself. "I am a klutz," she admitted softly, and looked down at her plate.

As if it's your fault you fell off Cliff Walk? Gillian felt like demanding. Harriet's face wore an expression of sour agreement as she helped herself to the vegetables. So Harriet had been written out of the storyline with Lara—what good was a supporting actress, without her star? It had to be rough if that particular role was her sole source of income, but still, to blame Lara?

"Speaking of familiar," Lara said, rallying with a smile, "I keep thinking I've seen you somewhere before, Gillian."

She sat transfixed, glass halfway to her mouth. *Where? In your mirror?* She couldn't see a resemblance herself, though she'd hoped for one from the very start. To find some tangible connection... It was why she stared at Lara whenever she could. There had to be *something*—an earlobe, the shape of a hand—but she'd yet to find it.

"It's extraordinary how often people's paths will cross," Trace mused. "You go on vacation and bump into your mailman in the Caribbean. So what do you think, Gillian. Have you two ever met?"

She could hear the faintest taunting in his voice, though when she met his eyes, his look was one of innocent interest. "Well, certainly I've seen Lara on *Searching for Sarah.* Who hasn't?"

"America's *favorite* pediatrician," Harriet murmured.

"But never in person?" Trace challenged.

Why did he ask? What could he know? She met his eyes squarely and held them. "I don't think so."

But she couldn't rout that level, slate-green gaze. Found herself trapped by it for one heartbeat, two, three. Then he smiled and looked down at his plate. *Oh, really?* was the unspoken message behind that smile.

"Coffee anybody?" asked Lucy, returning with a silver carafe.

"Hit me," said Toby, "and give Joya a double. I don't think she's with us yet this afternoon."

Coffee sounded like a splendid idea. Gillian lifted her empty cup and swiveled toward Toby, bringing it within reach of Lucy's pitcher.

As the maid filled the cup, a bee landed on its rim. *"Oh!"* Coffee splashed as Gillian jumped—and Toby shoved back from the table, cursing. "Oh, I'm sorry!" The bee had toppled off the rim and into the hot brew. "Oh, damn!"

"Take it easy." Trace had risen and now stood beside her. "I've got him." He dipped a fork in the steaming liquid, and the bee crawled up on it. He walked away from the table and deposited the insect on the terrace's balustrade, then returned.

"Silly bitch!" Toby said in a voice so low only Gillian could hear him. He wiped frantically at a stain on his white trousers, then looked up at her, red-faced. "It was only a wasp."

"Way to go, Gillie!" applauded Joya.

"I'm sure the cleaners can fix that," Lara said quietly. "And if they can't, then I can—"

"You can't," snapped Toby. "Not unless you want to fly to Rodeo Drive to replace them. You won't find trousers like these in this dreary town."

"I'm very sorry," Gillian said. "I'm a wimp about bees. You see, I'm allergic..."

"Really allergic?" Trace demanded across the table. "As in anaphylactic shock?"

She nodded. "One tangled in my hair and stung me while I was in a parking lot in a strip mall. I started having trouble breathing..." She swallowed, remembering that horrible sensation of her throat swelling and closing, her skin prickling and itching. "There was a doctor's office within fifty feet of my car. The friends I was with rushed me in there and the doctor gave me a shot of epinephrine..." She shrugged. "And then I was fine."

"Well, you're going to love it around here," Joya observed with relish. "September in Newport it's nothing but bees, bees, bees swarming around. Anything sweet you eat, they want their share of it."

"They're wasps, actually," growled Toby, looking up from his pants. "Are you allergic to wasps, too?"

Gillian shrugged. "I don't know. Last year was the first time I was ever stung and that was by a honeybee."

"Most probably you are," said Lara. "If you're like me. The venom has the same effect."

"You're allergic to bees, too?" demanded Trace on a note of outrage. "You never told me."

Lara shrugged. "You never asked."

And here it was at last. Gillian sat with her eyes fixed on her coffee cup, not daring to look up. *I'm allergic to bees—and so is Lara. This came from her to me.*

She remembered that after the epinephrine took hold and she could breathe without effort, she'd been blazingly mad. A simple side effect of the medicine, the doctor had explained, but she'd known otherwise. How many other booby traps lurked out there, just waiting for her to stumble into them? she recalled thinking.

Because that was one of the things Lara had deprived her of when she'd rejected her all over again. A medical history. Just the simple facts that most people got without having to beg for them. For all Gillian knew she came from a family at high risk of breast cancer or manic depression.

There was no way to guard against risks if she

didn't know about them. And no one had a right to keep her in the dark, she'd told herself. Maybe Lara didn't want her. Well, that was fine. Still, she owed her daughter the facts.

Funny how things worked out. Now here she was, having just learned Lara was allergic to bees, too. There was a certain...sweetness to the knowledge of what they shared.

She looked up to find Trace studying her from across the table, his eyes narrowed in speculation.

CHAPTER NINE

"WHERE'S YOUR BEE STING KIT?" Trace queried Lara when they were alone at last. Gillian had headed upstairs to her office and the brats had wandered off God knows where. Sunny Harriet had mumbled something about her afternoon soaps and departed for her room, which was where she spent most of her time brooding.

Staring out to sea, Lara shrugged. "New York, I suppose. In my apartment, in the medicine cabinet."

"You're supposed to have that with you always." Death by bee sting took about three to five minutes. If you were lucky your heart stopped before you slowly strangled to death.

She gave him a rueful smile and turned back to the view. "I did for a while, but I hate carrying a purse."

He counted to ten. Then twenty. She could be so childlike. "Fine, then I'll carry it. Let's call your doctor. I want one today."

"Trace, really, calm down." She patted his arm. "I'm sorry I ever mentioned it. You're overreacting."

"You pay me to guard your life, Lara. Well, whether you like it or not, this is part of it. No bee is stinging you on my watch."

Her smile was gamine in profile, beautiful when she turned to face him. "Dear Trace..." She patted his cheek, the first time she'd ever done so. "Nobody ever told you that if it's meant to happen, it happens? If a bee stings me..." She shrugged and made a comic face.

There it was, that dark fatalism he noticed sometimes beneath her seeming cheerfulness. *What is it with you, Lara? You miss Corday so much that life isn't worth clinging to?* Or was this some depression born of her present stress, the inescapable knowledge that somewhere out there somebody hated her?

But he was here to guard her body, not heal her spirit. Wouldn't have known how to begin if he'd accepted that mission. "If a bee stings you, lady, then the next thing you'll see is me brandishing a hypodermic."

She laughed softly. "You'd really know how to use one?"

He was as well versed in emergency medicine as any professional bodyguard. Dress a bullet wound. Set a leg. Heimlich a dinner guest. Deliver the odd baby. An injection was nothing. "Piece of cake," he assured her. "Now, let's go call your doc."

"Hello-ello!" someone called cheerfully behind him.

Trace spun and stopped, his body blocking Lara, one hand reaching behind him for her shoulder, ready to shove her to the ground. "Who the hell are *you?*" Before him stood a kid about Toby's age, his wide smile just starting to fade at this welcome. "And how did you get in here?"

"By the front gate. It was unlatched." The boy stuck out his chinless chin. "I'm looking for Joya. She skipped our tennis date."

Lara removed Trace's hand from her shoulder and

leaned around his legs. "Hello, Duffy. I believe she's upstairs."

"Uh, thanks, Lara." The kid vanished into the sunroom through the French doors.

Trace sat, his heart rate gradually decelerating. "The gates were unlatched," he said grimly. If you caught the gate manually just before it closed, you could prop the latch against the lockplate. It would look closed until someone pushed on it. He'd found Joya leaving it propped open for some friend several weeks back, and had persuaded Lara to tell her to stop that. But the Corday kids took plain orders as optional.

"You'll have to speak to her and Toby again. I can't keep you safe if any clown can cruise in here whenever he pleases." It was why he insisted that Lara lock the door to her suite whenever she was within. Because he couldn't guarantee the perimeter with her brats running in and out at all hours. *Crap, if somebody really wants you, lady, I'll be hard put to stop him.* He needed at least two more guards to do the job right.

She sighed and nodded. "I'll speak to them. But it would be so much easier if you'd let me explain the problem."

Trace had covered this ground before with Lara. "I'm sorry, but I don't trust them to keep a secret." They'd find Lara's stalker an amusing morsel of gossip to chew over in the bars with their boozy lightweight friends. *We'd be reading all about Sarah XXX in the* Daily News *tomorrow.* And when all was said and done, they'd still leave the gate unlatched. Because the only thing in the world those two honored was their own convenience.

"You're awfully hard on them," she said.

And you are woefully soft, lady. But that was another thing he couldn't say to a client. He smiled. "Am I?"

She shook her head. "Sometimes I feel like I'm talking to the wall!"

A stone wall between you and whatever comes, God willing. But a wall was no help against the enemies within. Someday those brats would break her heart.

BY THREE O'CLOCK LARA still had not stopped at the office as she'd promised earlier. Forgot, Gillian supposed, or perhaps she and Trace were... She shied away from that thought and went back to work. But a slow, painful throbbing had settled in behind her eyes again and she was in the mood for a break. She completed another letter, then picked up the phone and dialed Lara's suite.

"Hello?" Lara said eagerly. She didn't sound as if she'd been disturbed middalliance.

"It's Gillian, Mrs. Corday. I have a question about a letter and—"

"And it's Lara to you, kiddo! Why don't you bring it down here? I'm bored silly."

Tapping on Lara's door a minute later, Gillian was surprised to hear the sound of a heavy dead bolt turning. *She locks herself in, in her own house?*

"Come in," said Lara, and led her to a long couch that looked out on a balcony, and had another spectacular view of cliffs and ocean. "What's the problem?"

They dealt with the matter quickly. Letters concerning any business deal, be it product endorsements, acting roles, proposals for magazine features, etcetera, should be filtered through Lara's manager in New York. "My mail goes to her first and she's supposed to pull out that sort of business plus all my bills. Then she mails the rest to me. This one she missed because with a handwritten return address it looks like a personal letter. So all you need to do is send it back to Margaret. You'll find a file on the hard drive named Manager, which will give you her address. Excuse me," Lara added as the phone on her bedside table rang.

While she spoke at length with Barbara, Woodwind's housekeeper, about meals for the next few days, Gillian glanced casually around the suite. It was a lovely, light and sunny room, with a spectacular Chinese rug in shimmering pastels, and no sign anywhere of Trace Sutton. Good. She found it hard to concentrate on Lara when he was around. She turned to study her now.

Standing in profile, the actress was totally absorbed in Harriet's wishes for steamed artichokes, Joya's demands for low fat and Toby's insistence on smoked salmon at every meal. "Yes, yes, whatever you think, that's fine," she agreed on a note of laughing exasperation as she ran a hand through her silvery hair.

Silver-blond hair, pale gray eyes. She looks nothing like me. Or vice versa. *But if I don't look like my birth mother, whose child am I? My father's? I skipped a generation and look like a grandmother I never met?* It would be so much simpler if only she could ask.

And she must stop staring. Gillian dragged her gaze away, across the big bed, with its piles of puffy pillows and a big feather comforter. Hard to picture

Trace in such a cream-puff bed. Some emotion twisted uncomfortably in her stomach and she rubbed it absently. Maybe thinking about a parent's sexuality was taboo at any age, even when the parent was a total stranger. Her eyes refocused on something orange indenting the comforter's lush center and she felt her mouth drop. Couldn't be!

She rose and walked across to the bed and picked up the stuffed tiger just as Lara cradled the phone. "Tigger!"

"That's his name," Lara agreed, smiling.

It was eerie! "I have this—this s-same tiger." Packed with the rest of her possessions in storage back in Texas. "My parents gave him to me when I was four." Or to be more correct, she'd seen Tig in a toy store and recognized her soul mate. Had fussed and whined and nagged till they gave in and went back to the shop and bought him.

"You're kidding! I've had Tigger for twenty-seven years and—" Lara's face clouded over as she figured silently "—eleven months."

Which meant, Gillian calculated, that Lara had acquired the stuffed toy roughly one month after her birth. "Someone gave him to you?" A boyfriend or a best friend? It seemed important to know that.

"Oh, no. I...bought him...myself." The words trailed away like stones falling down a deep, dark well. Lara swallowed and stared off toward the ocean.

And so we both like tigers. I guess I got that from you? Gillian stroked the stuffed toy, not quite as ratty as her own, but a fifteen-year-old wouldn't have chewed her toy the way her four-year-old daughter had. "Well..." She smiled at Lara and put Tigger back on his puffy domain. Funny that he still held pride of place now that Lara shared a bed with Trace. She'd have thought Trace would have banished him at least as far as the bedside table.

But then, if Lara paid the piper, perhaps she called the tunes in their relationship, in bed as well as out. Suddenly the walls of the spacious room seemed to subtly draw in. "You know," she said determinedly, "during my interview, you said you'd like me to help you get back in shape. And that I was supposed to nag you. So when do I start?"

Lara laughed. "Whenever you please."

"Now, then. I'm dying to go outside. How about a walk?" She'd need to learn about Lara's present condition before she proposed much more than that.

Lara bit her lip. "I'd love to, but..." She glanced toward the open windows. "It's a beautiful day, isn't it?" she murmured wistfully.

"A short walk around the grounds?" Gillian coaxed. "There's this rosebush with blossoms like I've never seen before. Maybe you could tell me what it is."

"Of course I could. I planted all the roses..." She heaved a slow sigh, then said absently, "Trace will have a cow..."

Gillian frowned. Why should Trace object, or even have a say in how Lara spent her time when he wasn't around? "Nothing too strenuous. We'll take it very slow. Oh, come out and play, Lara!"

Lara laughed. "Yes, you're right. This..." Her eyes moved around her suite. "This is ridiculous. I'll meet you on the terrace in ten, okay?"

FOR HALF AN HOUR OR MORE, they explored Woodwind's grounds. Lara was as lighthearted as a child playing hooky from school. Gillian discovered that another trait they shared was a love of gardening. The antique roses that climbed and rambled along the granite walls had been planted at Lara's behest when she and Corday first moved into Woodwind ten years ago. She glanced back at the mansion. "It was much too big for us then, and now...it seems even larger. But Richard loved to entertain. When he was alive we always had houseguests, and the kids would visit summers. And he bribed me with the grounds—said I could plant as many roses as Napoleon's empress, Josephine, if I liked. I'm still about nine hundred varieties behind, but I've more than a hundred at last count." She stopped and pulled a high branch down to nose level. "Smell this one."

"Heavenly!"

"Tuscany, actually, a variety that goes back to the early 1800s." She plucked the rose and handed it to Gillian. "You realize you're welcome to pick all the flowers you want, I hope. The whole point is to enjoy them."

"Thanks, I will." *She's so darned nice,* Gillian found herself thinking as they wandered on. *So warm. Is she entirely two-faced and I just haven't seen the other side yet?* Apart from her glimpse in the letter.

"And this—" Lara stopped before a wooden door let into an archway in the stone. "This gate leads out onto Cliff Walk."

Yes. It was through this gate that Lara had stepped the day Gillian had first seen her and chased after her. The day she'd fallen from the cliffs.

Lara touched the door's weathered wood. "I used to love to run out there. Every morning at dawn. You start the day in such perfect beauty and how can it go wrong after that?'' She grimaced. "Or so I thought.'' Her shoulders hunched in something that was more shudder than shrug. "Anyway, if you ever want to go out on the cliffs, it's locked, but I always keep a couple of spare keys here.'' She toed a stone aside to reveal a plastic margarine tub, opened it and showed Gillian two keys. "Just be sure to lock the gate behind you.''

Beyond the wall, Gillian could hear the rumble of waves hitting the cliffs. "Feel like going out today? Or have you had enough exercise?" she added as Lara frowned. She'd been watching her for signs of pain or limping and had seen none. Lara was quick to confess her faults, then make fun of them, but Gillian wasn't so sure she'd admit to hurting.

"I...d-don't think I'd better. But please, Gillian, you go ahead if you feel like it. It's such a gorgeous day.''

She looked so wistful that suddenly the thought occurred: could Lara be afraid of the cliffs? After her horrific accident, it wouldn't be surprising if she avoided the path forever. What a shame, though! To be shut out of one of the most beautiful spots in the world, when it existed on your own doorstep? She *hated* for Lara to lose that.

"I should go back to work—only ten boxes of letters to go, you know. But first, why don't we just take a peek. It sounds as if the surf is breaking today.''

Confronting the fear little by little—wasn't this how you cured people of their terror? She bent for the margarine tub, removed a key and rose. "Just a peek?''

Lara stood very still, staring through the wooden door, it seemed. She nodded finally. "Why not?''

Before she could change her mind, Gillian unlocked the gate. The cool southwest breeze off the ocean rushed through the gap, lifting their hair, bringing the scents of wild roses and kelp, the louder rumble and thud of the waves below.

Lara laughed like a child and stepped through the gateway, glanced back, her eyes sparkling with her own daring. "What are we waiting for?"

"Beats me." Gillian locked the door and followed her down the short trail through the bushes to Cliff Walk itself.

"Well," said Lara, staring off over the water. *"Well!"* She looked both ways down the path, carefully, like an intelligent five-year-old preparing to cross a street.

There was no one in sight, in either direction, though by afternoon tourists typically strolled the path. "Well," said Lara, again on a note of triumph. "I usually run this way."

I know, Gillian thought, falling into step beside her. She wasn't sure what obstacle in Lara's mind she'd just overcome, but the outcome seemed to be renewed confidence and joy. *Hurrah for us!*

NOT IN HER SUITE, not in Gillian's office. Damn him for a fool, he never should have left her! Should have insisted she come along when he went to the doctor's for her kit. *Who lured you out, Lara, and how?*

He could make a good guess at that, since Gillian was nowhere in sight, either. *First time I turn my back, she whisks Lara away.* What if she wasn't the innocent he'd begun to think her?

He went down to the first floor to quiz the household staff, but no one had seen Lara. At Gillian's carriage-house apartment he hammered on her door, cursing himself for giving up her key so easily. She could have Lara trapped inside, for all he knew. The door was metal; he'd need a crowbar to break it down. Maybe he should check with Harriet first. He hadn't bothered, because as loyal as Lara was to the actress, she rarely seemed to seek Harriet out. And who could blame her?

Still, he should have a look. But Harriet claimed not to have seen Lara, and Trace nudged her door far enough open while they talked to be reasonably certain Harriet spoke the truth. So what the hell?

Back at her suite he checked for notes—no notes— then used her balcony to survey the grounds. Leaning far out over the stone balustrade, looking south, he could see a stretch of Cliff Walk—and two figures just vanishing beyond the bushes. One of them wearing lemon-yellow, as Gillian had this morning. Damn her! *This is all her fault.*

Was this an innocent escapade, or was she luring Lara off to the cliffs again? One quick shove and—

Not on my watch! He spun and headed for the door. Glanced toward his dressing room, where he kept his gun hidden nowadays. Told himself, *No, not necessary.* With Gillian Mahler? Should the need arise, he could snap her like a potato chip.

CHAPTER TEN

THEY ROUNDED A BEND in the path and there it was, the place where the pavement tilted seaward, the gap in the bushes showing blue beyond. Lara stopped short, took a deep breath and crossed her arms tightly. "This is where...I...f-fell."

"*God,* Lara." Yes, this was the place Gillian had always pictured her falling. It must be low tide—she could hear the shingle beach below, the waves thundering up the rocky slope, then dragging the gravel seaward with an odd rippling growl. "Shall we go back?" She wouldn't blame Lara in the least if she couldn't walk past this spot.

"N-no...not yet." Her face was greeny pale, beads of sweat gleaming at her hairline. She wiped her brow with a forearm, then stood staring absently out to sea. "If..." The breeze whipped her soft words away. She swallowed convulsively.

Gillian moved nearer; the only comfort she could offer was closeness. "If?"

"If someone had...wrecked your life...utterly. Without hope of mending... How mad would you be?"

"Mad as in crazy?" she asked, bewildered.

A little painful laugh escaped Lara. "Maybe that, too, but mad as in angry, I meant."

Whose life had been wrecked? Lara's own, with

this fall or by the loss of her husband? Or could she be referring to Harriet, who acted as if Lara had fallen for the express purpose of derailing Harriet's career? Or...

From the corner of her eye, she saw movement and glanced over her shoulder—to see Trace Sutton approaching at a run, with a look on his face that spelled trouble for somebody. "Um, I think we're about to—" She let out a yelp as his hand clamped on her forearm and he spun her away from Lara. The edge of the cliff whirled past—for a horrifying second she thought he was slinging her out into space! Instead she found that she'd been forcibly do-si-doed. Now Trace stood between her and Lara. His hand steadied her for a moment as she staggered, then he withdrew it.

"Trace!" Lara cried.

"What the hell do you think you're doing?" he demanded in a savage undertone.

"That's *my* line, I believe!" Lara peered around his bulk at Gillian. "Gillian, are you all right?"

She nodded, feeling her face blushing crimson. Could he be so jealous, so possessive, that he couldn't permit Lara out on her own? Or out with anyone besides himself?

"In that case, would you please excuse us?" Trace said, but it wasn't a question.

"Of course." She brushed past him, aware that he loomed over her as she came even with Lara. Setting her nose away from Woodwind and toward the sea, she stalked off. What a boor! What an unspeakable, rude and possessive boor! How could Lara put up with that?

There must be compensations, a voice that sounded eerily like Joya's observed from within.

No skill in bed would make up for that kind of boorishness, in Gillian's book. Poor Lara, if she thought so! Gillian glanced back once as she reached the next bend of the path.

Lara stood toe to toe with Trace, glaring up. She looked as if she'd happily shove *him* off the cliff. Gillian blew a shaky breath of relief and marched on. *Good, don't let him bully you.*

"I SHOULD F-FIRE YOU for that," Lara exclaimed. "You big bully!"

"I may quit for that, Mrs. Corday. You hired me to do a job, and either you make it possible for me to do it or I walk. We had an agreement that you don't stir from Woodwind without me."

"We did, but—"

"No buts, Lara. Somebody wants to kill you, got that? Somebody who's close enough to scout your routine, to learn you run on the cliffs at dawn. Who's got the time and the patience to lie in wait for his opportunity, and then—*wham!* So what do you do? Soon as your bones mend, you go strolling on the cliffs with a woman you know *nada* about."

"You can't think Gillian—"

"I can't rule her out. What's her middle name?"

"What?" Her expression plainly said, *You're nuts!* Then she glanced aside.

A family of Japanese tourists, chatting happily, strolled around the bend. The mother let out a sharp cry as she spotted the gap in the bushes, and her young son, trotting in the lead, stopped and looked back. Catching his hand, she hurried him past the drop-off. Trace and Lara stepped aside, half-bowing nods were exchanged, then the tourists vanished around the next bend.

Trace drew a deep breath. "She claims her middle name is Sylvester, which is plainly absurd."

Lara laughed aloud. "That's what's worrying you? She's teasing you, Trace. Probably thought it was none of your business, and I don't blame her."

"Maybe, or maybe it's something more. What if her middle name is Sarah?"

The color seeped out of Lara's face. He caught her forearm before she fainted. "Lara?"

Her pupils were dilated, black holes rimmed in silver, staring blankly through his chest. "Lara?"

"I should be so lucky," she murmured, and shook herself. Her color flooded back. "And one thing we know for certain is, I'm not."

He turned her gently around to face the sea and the cliff edge. "Walk over there, look down at those rocks, and tell me you're not lucky." He didn't like talk like that. He needed his client's spirit working with him, not against him. Fatalism was not allowed. "You've got a first-rate guardian angel, Lara. But I'd like to give him a hand."

She made a little grimace of resignation, then smiled. "Okay, Trace. I suppose I'm being unfair. It wouldn't do your business any good if you lost a client, would it?"

"It wouldn't recommend me to my next client, no." Yet he didn't want her to play it safe for his sake, but for her own. *Show me some will to live, will you?*

"Okay," she said, turning toward Woodwind, "I'll behave. On one condition, though. No, two. First...

you don't terrorize my household. And that includes
Gillian.''

"But—"

"I mean that, Trace! How you could imagine that
girl sending me that rabbit letter…''

"All right, all right, kid gloves for Gillian." *Which
doesn't mean I don't watch her like a hawk.* First
chance she got, she'd led Lara right here, to the very
same drop-off. And if he'd come five minutes later?

"Second…I'm sick of this circle-the-wagons men-
tality. There's no use guarding my body if I go out
of my mind. We *have* to get out more. I'm out of
touch with my friends, I need a new pair of running
shoes, a manicure…''

"Lara, it would be wiser if—"

"That's *not* negotiable," she snapped. They
walked on in tense silence, then she touched his arm
in apology. "I'm forty-three, Trace, and I don't *do*
wise. Never did. It's a bit late to learn it now.''

*Then take my advice, dammit. I'm wise enough for
both of us.* But he was tired of arguing—and losing.
"You're the boss.''

"I am," she agreed briskly. "So one more condition, Trace.''

"Which makes three.''

"Why, so it does. Condition three," she pronounced as they reached the turnoff that led to Woodwind's back gate. "You scared Gillian back there.
So…apologize.''

GILLIAN WALKED NEARLY TO the end of Cliff Walk,
walking hard to blow off her anger. The path dropped
lower and lower till it meandered along only twenty
feet above the ocean. It grew more and more ragged,

becoming dikes of boulders here and there, riprap laid
to withstand the waves that would break right over
the path in a southwest storm. She came to the first
tunnel in the rock, surmounted improbably by a Japanese teahouse, the upcurved eaves of its copper
green roof decorated with slinky bronze dragons. The
building was a wonderful folly, over a hundred years
old, belonging to one of the summer cottages lying
inward from the cliffs. You couldn't enter the teahouse, but you passed under it in a long tunnel carved
from the rock.

As always she stopped at the tunnel mouth, eyeing
the blackness beyond. Halfway along, the passage
bent in a sharp right turn. No sunlight carried from
either end into its depths. She drew a breath and
walked in. The temperature dropped ten degrees immediately. Cool pounded earth underfoot, rock above
and around, the sound of the waves dying to an echoing whisper. She dragged her fingertips along the
stones till, fifty feet in, she reached the turn and saw
light ahead. Up some mossy stone stairs, then out into
the sunshine, on higher cliffs again, the blue waters
sparkling forty feet below. *I wonder if Lara would
have made it this far.*

Lara… She wasn't at all what Gillian had expected.
And Trace, what the hell was he? Lara's faithless toy
boy? Or something much more offensive, a jealous
lover who abused his power? It was hard to say from
moment to moment who had the upper hand between
those two. *Forget it. It's none of your business, really.
Just feel this gorgeous day, the sunshine, the wind,
the water. Just walk.*

WHEN GILLIAN RETURNED to Woodwind an hour before sunset, it was time to leave for the Y. Aerobics

tonight, a class she'd traded with a fellow instructor, who'd taken her morning assignment. She was committed to teach it till the term ended in three weeks. She drove off without seeing either Lara or Trace. Which was just as well. In spite of her walk she was still upset and offended.

The class—advanced aerobics—calmed her at last. Afterward she showered long and luxuriously, dressed, then paused, looking into her locker. It was here that she kept the manila envelope with all the papers from her adoptive mother's safe-deposit box. It had seemed safer to leave them under padlock at the Y than take them into Woodwind. On sudden impulse she picked up the envelope and retreated to the aerobics room. It was deserted now, and, settling on an exercise mat, she dumped out the contents of her envelope. Would the papers look the same, now that she'd met Lara?

She lifted the single-page typed document from the lawyer who'd arranged her private placement. It described a one-week-old female child, named Sarah Cloud ''Doe'' by her natural mother. The baby had been born in Virginia, legally relinquished by her mother two days after birth, was in foster care and available for adoption.

Cloud. Why Cloud, Lara? On first reading, Gillian had assumed that must be a family name, either Lara's or on the paternal side. The first way she'd tried to research her past was to go to that small town in Virginia and check in old phone books for the name Cloud.

No such family had lived there, twenty-eight years

ago—or ever—as far as she could learn. *A dead end.*
The first of many.

She looked down at the document again. Next her
birth parents were described. The mother was a fifteen-year-old white Anglo-Saxon named Laura
"Doe." In excellent health; religion, Methodist. A
graduate of the tenth grade. IQ, well above average.
Her ambition, to be an actress.

*So you knew what you were meant to be even back
then, Lara.* And perhaps that explained everything.
*You would never have achieved your goal with a baby
on your back, any more than your fictional double,
Dr. Laura Daley, would have made it through med
school with a baby to look after. So you ditched the
load and went on?*

The document didn't say—said no more at all in
fact about her birth mother.

It devoted one paragraph to her father, describing
him as an eighteen-year-old white Anglo-Saxon,
name, William "Smith"; last grade completed,
eleven; IQ, well above average; ambitions for his life,
unknown.

Gillian sighed and slipped the paper back into the
envelope. She'd also had her birth certificate to work
with, which listed her as Gillian Sarah Scott. But
she'd soon learned, once she entered the Alice in
Wonderland world of the searching adoptee, that this
certificate was an officially sanctioned lie. It had been
issued to her adoptive parents at the time of her adoption, with their names substituted for the birth parents.
The real facts were buried by the state of Virginia and
most definitely were not the adoptee's for the asking.

Angrily she blew out a *whuff* of air, remembering
the bureaucrats who'd smugly explained they couldn't

release the facts of who she was or where she came from—as if she were a half-wit, dangerous child who couldn't be trusted with the truth that everyone else had by right. *Right of birth.*

After that dead end, she'd gone to the Virginia lawyer the Scotts had used to arrange her adoption. Her lip curled at the memory: the old man with his oily, stern-uncle smile, his eyes as cunning and detached beneath their weathered folds of skin as a crocodile's. He'd told her next to nothing, pointing out that his only duty lay with his clients, her adoptive parents. He owed *her*—the child whose life he had derailed— not a word, not a fact. Not legally speaking.

"And why would you want to meet her at all? That little lady didn't give a damn about you. Traded you for a car and never looked back."

"A car?" she'd coaxed, sickened by her desperate need to ingratiate herself, when she'd have preferred to shake the facts out of him. "What do you mean?"

The Scotts had paid all her birth mother's prenatal and delivery expenses, the lawyer had explained. "And as I recall, she padded the bill something shameless." He coughed. "But the straw that about broke the camel's back was that the girl demanded a car at the last minute. Said your adoption was off without it.

"So your adoptive momma brought a brand-new red Mustang to me a few days before you were born, and after that the girl was happy to sign your relinquishment papers. So why would you want to find a mother like that? Now, if you'll excuse me, I've got a court appointment in half an hour."

Gillian had pried the rest of that story out of her adoptive brother, Chris, a month later when he called her from Hawaii, where he'd stopped off while delivering a yacht from Seattle to Japan.

"You heard about the car?" he'd asked, the worry in his husky voice coming clear across four thousand miles. She'd written him an outraged letter telling him she'd learned of her adoption, demanding to know why he'd never told her, but this was the first time they'd talked about it. "That damned car, Gillian. I didn't forgive you for that for a long time. It was Mom's car, but it was the car Dad used to teach me how to drive that year. And the understanding was, when I got my full license they'd give me the Mustang and buy Mom a new one.

"But then that sleazeball lawyer called and said he had to have a car to persuade your real mother to sign the papers—and by that time, Dad and Mom had already forked over some twenty thousand in expenses to get you.

"Anyway, there was a real dustup. Dad decided we'd been had, and maybe this wasn't even legal. You can't *buy* a baby, you know, though you can pay the mother's expenses. He said we were way over that line, and it would end in trouble, not a baby.

"But Mom didn't agree. She'd come so far she wasn't quitting when she was this close to you. She stormed out of the house, drove off in her red Mustang and arrived home a few days later by cab. And two weeks later they drove to Virginia and came home with you." He laughed softly. "A damn poor trade for a Mustang, I thought at the time. Took me a while to realize what a good deal Mom had made."

She smiled, tears beading in her lashes. Dear Chris. She glanced up as the door to the exercise room opened. Mr. Sousa, the Y's janitor. He glared at her, announced, "Lights out in ten minutes, girlie!" and slammed the door again.

Gillian sighed and started to put her papers away, then paused as a photo slipped between two sheets and fell facedown onto the mat.

She turned over the picture of Lara. Clearly a high-school photo—you couldn't mistake the format. Chin lowered like a young Lauren Bacall, Lara smiled warily into the camera. But already you could see her elfin beauty. The camera loved her.

Without this photo, Gillian would be still living back in Houston, teaching aerobics and tai chi by night, painting her watercolor illustrations by day, wondering with mounting frustration who she was and where she'd come from. It was this photo that had led her at last to Lara.

On his way back from Tokyo, Chris had stopped off in San Diego to visit their aunt—Chris's real aunt, Gillian's adoptive aunt. Aunt Susan, Victor Scott's sister. During his visit, Chris had mentioned that Gillian had learned she was adopted and was searching for her birth mother.

Gillian turned over the page torn from a soap-opera digest some nineteen years ago. Aunt Susan had found the article in a magazine in a dentist's office and recognized Lara's photo. It was the same school photo that Susan's sister-in-law—Gillian's adoptive mother, Eleanor Scott—had once shown her. But this time it accompanied an article about the promising new soap-opera actress, Lara Leigh, aka Laura Bailey, who'd grown up in a series of foster homes in West Virginia, then run away to New York City and hit the big time.

Nineteen years ago Aunt Susan had triumphantly

mailed the article to Gillian's mother—and she'd had a fit. Had made Aunt Susan promise that she'd never, *ever,* in her life tell Gillian anything about this article.

But now that I think of it, Aunt Susan had written in her letter, I'm not sure if poor Eleanor meant never in my life, your life or hers. And since, bless her, she's gone, if you're hunting for your real mother, well, I guess this is her.

"Lights out!" growled Mr. Sousa at the door.

"Coming, coming, I'm sorry." He dogged her footsteps downstairs to the front door, then locked it behind her.

Gillian stood on the Y's porch, staring out over Newport's vast reservoir, its swans pale, drifting shapes in the moonlight. Downhill to her left stretched First Beach, then the dark cliffs of Cliff Walk, rising beyond. Those lights about a third of the way out the headland must be Woodwind.

Traded me for a car, and ended up with a mansion by moonlight. What kind of deal would Chris call that?

CHAPTER ELEVEN

GILLIAN PAUSED OUTSIDE an open bay to the carriage house. Trace Sutton lay on a rolling cart, his head half under a car. "Uh-oh, trouble?" They were due to leave for a luncheon date with a friend of Lara's in minutes.

"You can come along and pretend to be a real lady's companion," Lara had informed her cheerfully that morning. "I'm tired of moping around the house. Meet us at the car at one?"

"Us" apparently meaning Lara and Trace, since here was Trace, half under the car. "What's up?" She dragged her eyes away from his long legs. His lightweight chinos couldn't conceal the hard planes of calf and thigh.

"Nothing," he growled. "I thought I saw an oil leak. Now, would you mind giving me some room to work?"

"Fine." *Be that way.* She stalked out of the bay and into the sunlight.

"There you are!" Lara stepped out of the flower beds and came to join her. "I was picking roses for Meagan," she said, showing Gillian a half-dozen long-stemmed buds. "She has a passion for the whites."

Trace backed the car out, then rounded its front to

open the door for Lara. Gillian reached for the rear door, but he beat her to it. "Allow me."

He was playing the perfect chauffeur this morning, except for the oddly measuring look he gave her as he closed her door. *Who are you, Trace Sutton?*

Studying the back of his dark, well-trimmed head, she pondered that all the way down the hill to the waterfront, while Lara chatted happily about the woman they were meeting, a watercolorist of some note and one of her few local friends. Trace parked the car in a parking lot before a waterfront restaurant, the Moorings, then, to Gillian's disappointment, accompanied them inside. She'd half hoped he might leave the three women to dine alone, that he'd rather wander along the docks and wharves, admiring the yachts lying alongside. But no such luck.

"SHE'S DELIGHTFUL," pronounced Lara's friend, Meagan Riley, watching Gillian make her way through the crowded restaurant toward the rest rooms. "Have you seen any of her paintings?" The older woman had spoken of her own work for much of the meal, until Lara had proudly volunteered—much to Gillian's obvious consternation—that Gillian was an illustrator. After that Trace had listened with amusement while the older woman ruthlessly pried more information out of Gillian over the course of a meal than he had managed in four days of trying.

The information was interesting—he found everything about Gillian Mahler interesting nowadays—but was it useful? Meagan clearly accepted her as genuinely knowledgeable and accomplished in the art world.

The typical stalker wasn't accomplished in much

of anything, except sometimes guns and paramilitary techniques. But if Gillian wasn't a stalker, why hide her light under a basket the way she had at Woodwind? So she could someday return to the life she'd divided so neatly from the current one? *In Houston she's a budding artist, making ends meet by teaching exercise classes on the side. In Newport she drops the art, becomes a full-time fitness trainer—till she secures a job with Lara. Why? A woman who has worked all her life in the creative and physical realms suddenly develops clerical ambitions? Which give her excruciating headaches?* He smelled a rat somewhere.

And what the hell is her middle name? He'd called his sister, Emily, last night and learned that so far she'd uncovered nothing of use in Houston. The family who might know the most about the Mahlers were off on vacation and due back this weekend.

"Oh, look!" cried Lara, pointing over his shoulder at the harbor. Two awesome, moving pyramids of white cut the blue sky—a schooner sailing past the docks.

He sighed. Here he was in the sailing capital of America and he hadn't set foot aboard a boat all summer. He returned his gaze to the room. A bodyguard always put his back to the wall, kept his eyes on the directions from which danger might come.

Speaking of which, here came Gillian, swaying between the tables. His hands remembered the pliant shape of her waist that first time he'd touched her. She'd had a faint bruise on her left arm, he'd noticed, when he put her into the car. From when he'd grabbed her yesterday. *Still haven't apologized.* He didn't need Lara's prompting for that. He could if she was innocent. If she had lured Lara out of Woodwind's walls without bad intent.

And if not?

No apologies now or ever.

Her smile met Lara's, Meagan's, then faded as she met his gaze. She sat and looked away.

"Is there a line in the bathroom?" asked Meagan.

"Not really," Gillian said. "Just smokers camped out in both stalls, that's all."

Which accounted for the faint smell of cigarettes overlaying her usual sunny fragrance.

"In that case…" Meagan stood. "Lara?"

Trace put his fingertips on the table and half rose. The rest rooms stood down a hall next to the exit. Too easy for someone to slip in to the ladies' after Lara, then make a smooth getaway. He'd have to wait outside.

"I don't think so," said Lara, frowning at him till he subsided.

Gillian hadn't missed much of their interplay. And did not like it, even if she didn't understand it. She swung accusing golden eyes his way as, from over his shoulder, a ray of sunshine bounced off some bit of chrome on the docks to gild her face, turn her tawny hair to fiery bronze. Lion eyes glaring at him out of a burning field.

Something tightened inside him. *I want to bed you! See those eyes looking up at me from a pillow by candlelight.* He turned away, stared blindly out across the restaurant. Damn her, anyway! She was the last woman in the world he should want. What if she was his freak?

Then he'd see her behind bars.

He turned back to find Meagan was making her

farewells. She'd spotted a patron in the bar, a man who'd acquired five of her works so far, and she was going to go over and make nice. Talk up her latest project, a series on the local twelve-meter yachts.

Lara signed for their meal. This earned Trace another skimming glance from Gillian, which he answered with a complacent smile. *Think I'm a useless gigolo, do you? Good.*

He played his part all the way to the car, opening the restaurant door with a flourish as they left, shepherding Lara with a hand on her waist to her usual seat. He unlocked the front passenger door—and Lara said, "Gillian, you sit there."

He scowled at his client. What was she up to this time? God, he'd rather guard a man any day. Simple and straightforward. You knew what he was thinking, what he wanted or needed, before he did—or if you didn't, he told you. None of these curves that a woman threw.

"No, really, I'd rather sit in back!" protested Gillian, looking as alarmed as if Lara had proposed she sit on his lap.

"Nonsense. I'd like to return by Ocean Drive, and you'll have a better view from up there." Lara opened the rear door and sat decisively.

Trace shrugged, opened the front door wider and motioned Gillian inside. Found himself mesmerized as she sank gracefully onto the seat and swiveled into place, her slender calves kissing from knee to ankle throughout the procedure. He'd half closed her door when it hit him.

He hadn't touched the button that unlocked all four doors at once. *Yet Lara had opened the back door.* A bolt of adrenaline shot through him, raising the hairs on his nape and forearms. He spun to face her.

Gillian glanced at him in mild surprise.

He drew a shaking breath. If there was a bomb, it should have gone off by now, under one woman or the other. Probably under Gillian, since it would have been intended for Lara, who always rode in front. No bomb, thank God.

So...false alarm? With relief he felt the first hot surge of anger, the aftereffects of adrenaline. He snapped at Gillian, "Did you unlock the back door when you got out?" He'd hit the locking control as he exited the car, he was sure of that, but if she'd then unlocked it *again* while he walked around to help Lara out...

Her eyes wide with confusion, she swallowed and shook her head. "I don't think so. Or...I'm not sure. Possibly. I thought I locked it, but maybe I—"

"So what?" said Lara from the back seat. "If you did, there was nothing to steal, apart from our bridge tokens. No harm done. Come on, Trace."

No harm done this time, but, oh, lady, it's the little slips that get you in the end. Scowling at Gillian, seeing in his mind's eye a moment's lapse that ended with the dull roar of dynamite, three lives shattered, he started to close the door.

As she reached reflexively for its inner handle.

And at some subliminal level he heard it—smashed her hand up and aside before he knew why.

"Ow!" She caught her fingers with her other hand and stared at him.

"Trace!" Lara cried from the back seat as he yanked the door wide and bent down.

The buzzing rose, then fell like a tiny bomber diving out of the sky—a blur of golden brown stripes and furious motion. A bee, struggling frantically to free itself from the hollowed-out door handle.

"What is it?" asked Gillian, bending beside him, her cheek nearly brushing his.

One second more and she'd have slipped her fingers into the handle and pulled to shut the door. Her fingers would have closed over the bee.

"Oh!" she breathed as she saw it.

He turned his head and his lips nearly brushed hers. "Just a bee. It caught its leg somehow." With the help of a dab of Super Glue.

Another second and her fingers would have pressed down on the outraged insect. A second after that, its venom would have been coursing through her body. Three to five minutes till death by suffocation.

But that death was intended for *Lara,* who now leaned impatiently over the front seat. "Don't touch it—don't move. I'll be back," he said to Gillian, as he opened the back door. "Let's go, Lara!" He almost dragged her from the car and marched her across the parking lot toward the restaurant, his eyes roving all points of the compass, his nape icy, as if he could feel a crosshair lining up on it. Whoever had done this might still be out there, crouching among the parked cars. Might make a more direct attempt, now that his nasty little trick had failed.

His? Hers. This had a woman's indirectness and subtlety, to his mind.

"Trace!" Lara protested, trotting at his side. "Dammit, have you gone mad? What are you doing?"

"I'm sending you home in a cab, Lara. Let me call it, then I'll explain."

"I DON'T SEE WHY GILLIAN can't come with me," Lara fretted. They stood waiting for the cab in the Moorings foyer, looking out through the glass doors. Gillian no longer sat in the car, though Trace couldn't see her.

She was down on the docks, he told himself. Or perhaps she'd lost her nerve finally and split?

"I'd be safer with her along than alone," Lara insisted.

Would you? That all depended on who had glued the bee to Lara's door. Trace's best guess was Gillian. "The police may want her statement, since she's the essential witness," he said, instead. The minute Lara was safely away, he meant to take the car to the police. Have the bee photographed. It was the star exhibit in the case he was building. All he needed was a perpetrator.

He straightened as a yellow cab pulled into the parking lot. "Now remember, don't stop anywhere on the way home. Have him drive you all the way to the front door, then make some excuse and let the maid escort you to your suite. I'll be back as quick as I can."

She nodded unhappily. "You really think this was an attempt...on m-me? It's not some mistake—the silly bee snagged its foot or something?"

"I wish I could say so." He walked her to the cab, gave her an encouraging smile and her address to the cabbie. "Fast as you can," he added, handing him a ten. He didn't like leaving her on her own, but he couldn't be two places at once. He waved her off. When he looked around, Gillian was hurrying up the ramp from the dock.

"Where's Lara going?"

"Home. She isn't feeling well. But she asked you and me to do some errands," he added immediately. *No sneaking off to Woodwind while my back is turned.* "Get in." He nodded at the car.

"Um..." She bit her bottom lip and studied the ground, then looked up under her lashes at him—a move of such incredible unrehearsed femininity it stole his breath away. "W-would you...do something about the bee? It's still trapped. That's why I didn't..." Her voice trailed away. "But don't hurt him," she added.

"Of course not." Okay, now what? If she was innocent, she was only being reasonable to request that he deal with the bee. If she was guilty, she was as cunning as a snake—she was asking that he destroy the evidence.

"All clear," he called a few minutes later. He held the passenger door for her, but she paused, frowning down at the duct tape that now lidded the door handle and muffled the indignant buzzing that sounded from within.

"It's in there?"

"We'll need a pair of tweezers to free its leg without yanking it off. Since you told me not to hurt it..." He shrugged.

She edged away from the door. "Maybe I'll sit in back."

"Coward!" he taunted softly. Suddenly, would-be killer or no, he wanted her sitting beside him. A clear case of testosterone poisoning, but there it was.

She tipped up her chin, gave him a stormy glance and swung into the car.

All the same, he noticed when he sat behind the driver's wheel, she'd slid over to the left side of her seat. He smiled at her and she edged outward three inches, then stopped. Trapped between a rock and a hard place.

But he was in no mood to enjoy her dilemma. In the confines of the car, he could smell cigarette smoke in her hair. *If I wanted to keep a bee still while I glued its legs, say, to a door handle, I'd stun it with cigarette smoke.* The way beekeepers stunned hives of bees when they wanted to take the honey.

From the waterfront to the police station was a mere five minutes. He passed it by, drove down Broadway, then parked in front of Kelly's, a bookstore where he'd picked up several interesting histories. "Lara asked that you buy her a half-dozen books or so. She likes mysteries, the cozy sort with a vicar, an eccentric English lady, poison in the tea."

Her face lit up. "I like those, too."

Swell. Make my day. "Pick her out several of those, plus any biographies of movie stars you can find," he said gravely. "I have to run to the hardware store. I'll be back in twenty minutes."

"SHE COULD HAVE CAUGHT IT in a jar anywhere in the gardens this morning," said Trace, while Jeremy Benton adjusted his lights on the bee. Trace had parked in the cops' lot, behind the station, where Gillian wouldn't see him even if she strolled down the street.

"She could have carried it in her purse—the one she had today was large enough." Then while Jeremy shot a roll of film, Trace described how Gillian left the table at the Moorings for a good ten minutes. "It wouldn't take ten minutes to nip outside, stun the bee by blowing smoke into the jar, then glue it in place. She left her back door unlocked to gain entrance.''

The detective straightened, set the camera aside and removed his lights. "Nasty and neat. I haven't seen better in a long, long time. If it had worked, how could you have taken it for anything but an accident? The bee would have been crushed when the target grabbed it. The glued leg would have torn free as she dragged her hand away. She'd have flipped the bee off or maybe even stomped him.

"And you'd have had no time to consider—either you'd have been racing for the hospital or you'd have been busy injecting her. Later on, who'd have thought to go back and count the bug's legs? Hell, I don't know how many it *should* have. And who'd have noticed a drop of glue no bigger than a pinhead, with one bee leg embedded in it, on the inside of your handle? Neat. You've got a sharp one here.''

"Too damn sharp." Studiously ignoring Benton's raised eyebrows, Trace removed his knife from its ankle sheath. "Done with the bee?''

"You're gonna do the poor bastard?''

"Nope. I promised Gillian I wouldn't hurt it." He bent over the door handle, then paused, hearing his own words.

Benton laughed. "And that's who you make for this—a woman who's deathly allergic to bees but who doesn't want the little creep crunched to kingdom come? Does that add up?''

"Nothing adds up." Slowly he slid the blade along the handle. Minus a toe or two, the bee shot up and away. Would probably be home, warning the other bees, before they'd finished dusting the car. "On the other hand, with stalkers it rarely does.''

"Yeah, that kid that shot the TV actress point-blank a few years back. What was she—twenty-one? I love you to death—*bang!* Stupid freaks.'' He motioned the print technician, who'd been lounging in the shade by the station's back door, over to the car. "Outside and inside of this door, 'specially the inner handle.'' Trace and Benton wandered away, hands in their pockets. "Who else knows Lara Corday is allergic to bees?"

Trace told him about the lunch on the terrace yesterday, and Benton whistled. "Fast response! And nice improvising. But not much patience, if somebody learned about Corday's allergy yesterday, then used it against her today. Who at that table isn't softhearted and *is* impatient?"

Two blond, sulky faces came instantly to mind. "Her stepbrats, Joya and Toby. And possibly Harriet Bristow.'' He told Benton about the sour supporting actress. "The maid, Lucy, I don't know, but she seems a nice kid. She'd be the last on my list of all of them.

"And of course, there's always the possibility of an outsider—that Gillian isn't Sarah XXX but that Sarah XXX *is* in town, shadowing Lara. That she noticed the car door was unlocked . . .''

"And she just happened to have this bee in her pocket?'' jeered Benton.

"Unless she already knew that Lara was allergic to bees,'' Trace insisted, playing out the scenario. "She might have come equipped with a jimmying tool, may have used it—it doesn't leave a mark. Maybe Gillian hadn't locked the car in the first place. She couldn't say.''

"Okay, it's not likely, but it's possible. But how

would Sarah Kiss-kiss-kiss know Corday is allergic to bees?"

Trace shrugged. "Beats me, but believe me, I'll ask." They'd made a circuit of the fenced lot and were now back at the car, where the technician was wiping his powder away.

"Here's one more thing that maybe you haven't considered," said Benton. "What if someone wanted to kill *Gillian?*"

He didn't like even the thought of it, those golden eyes swelling shut, that long slender throat closing, still... After a moment he shook his head. "Lara always rides in front."

Benton laughed under his breath. "Except this time she doesn't. She insists Gillian sit in front. So maybe your boss wants to kill Gillian?"

"Hey, thanks for clarifying matters!" They shook hands. "And let me know if anything turns up on the fingerprints."

"Will do." The detective spun on his heel and sauntered toward the station, then swung around. "And Trace? Whoever it is, the freak's got a hate on, and you're the guy standing in the way. Watch your back."

CHAPTER TWELVE

GILLIAN WAS STILL HIS first choice, Trace reflected as
he drove to the bookshop. Two incidents since Lara
hired her—the rabbit's foot, now the bee. Make it
three if you counted girls' day out on the cliffs, which
might have been an aborted attempt.

That story at lunch yesterday about an allergy to
bees. Possibly Gillian wasn't allergic at all but had
some reason to think Lara might be. Wanting to check
out her facts, she'd spun a tale that elicited an admission from Lara that she was allergic?

Another thing to consider: whoever had glued that
bee in place had assumed Lara didn't carry a bee sting
kit. That a sting would be fatal. But in fact, as of
yesterday afternoon one kit now lived in the glove
compartment. And he carried a second kit in his
pocket and would do so for the rest of this assignment.

So the question was: had Lara told anyone he'd
shot off to the doctor's yesterday to get her a bee sting
kit? If so, strike that person off his list of suspects.
Nobody would have risked sneaking into Lara's car
in broad daylight and gluing the bee if he couldn't
reasonably hope for the big payoff.

Gillian…he wished he could rule her in or rule her
out. He could search her purse. It should contain a
pair of tweezers to handle the bee, a tube of Super

Glue, an empty jar, matches or a lighter and maybe a pack of cigarettes. *Yeah, try to get your hands on her purse without a search warrant.* And if she was really smart—and one look at those lion eyes told you she was—she'd have dumped her tools before returning to the restaurant. *Call Benton,* he decided. *Ask him to assign a suit to do some Dumpster diving this afternoon in the parking lot, the ladies' and down on the nearby docks.*

He parked two spaces up from the bookstore, then saw her, seated on a bench outside the shop, beside a foot-high stack of books. She slung her purse over one shoulder, gathered the books into her arms and came to meet him.

His day brightened, as if the sun had stridden out from behind the clouds and for a moment he was simply a man walking toward a woman he wanted. "Here, let me carry those!" He reached for her load.

She shook her head. "I can manage."

With the gesture, her hair brushed her shoulders and he smelled cigarettes. The day darkened again as he pictured her lighting a fag, inhaling, blowing into the jar containing the bee... "I'm sure you can," he agreed huskily, stopping directly before her.

"Then wha—"

He held her shoulders and lowered his mouth to hers—caught her in midword, her lips parted. She froze, then gasped, and for a moment he forgot his reason for doing this. Then found a better one—her warm, startled softness...a silky dampness enticing him deeper...the barest flutter of a response? His hands tightened on her shoulders, drawing her closer—

Ten pounds of books cascaded over his feet. "Ouch, dammit!" He let her go.

"Y-y-you're—" She tossed her head, at a loss for words, and swept past him toward the car. "Unspeakable!"

He looked down at the books covering his shoes and found he was smiling. That his heart was bounding along, the blood zinging through his veins; that the sun had swaggered out from the clouds again. Because Gillian tasted of the chardonnay she'd had with lunch, melded with an undefinable taste that was the woman herself—honey and sunshine and musk. But no taste of cigarettes, at all, at all.

Doesn't prove a thing, his mind protested. Maybe she'd lighted the cigarette and simply stuck its burning end in the jar. His "test" didn't mean a damn thing.

Tell that to the rest of him.

If SHE HADN'T BEEN WEARING heels, she would have walked back to Woodwind. Gillian sat stiffly, with arms crossed, scowling straight ahead as Trace turned the car uphill toward Bellevue Avenue. She couldn't just let this pass, pretend it hadn't happened. Not with her lips still buzzing, waves of heat rolling through her. "If you ever do that again," she said finally, "I'll…" *What?* she asked herself.

"Do what?" he inquired politely, turning to glance at her. "Tell Lara?"

Oh, he had her there and he knew it! *If Lara has no idea what you are, I'm not going to be the one to tell her.* "I'm not a snitch." Besides, apart from the hurt she might inflict if she told Lara, there was always the chance that Lara would let *her* go. When it

came to choosing between a personal assistant and a
lover, the choice was obvious. Especially a lover who
could kiss like Trace Sutton.

"Good for you," he said quietly. "So what *will*
you do?"

"Slap you cross-eyed to Sunday if you ever try that
again."

"Ah." He stopped for a red light. "Might just be
worth it."

"HAVE YOU HAD ENOUGH OF MY fans yet?" Lara's
laughing voice inquired over the phone. It was the
following day, nearly noon, and Gillian sat at her
desk, letters stacked on all sides.

She had her usual splitting headache. "Well…"

"Say yes, you're sick of them," Lara pleaded,
"and come down to my suite, would you? I need
moral support."

"I'm doing a photo album," she explained, when
Gillian reported for duty. "The perfect rainy day project, I told myself, but it's turning into a bear. I've
never done one before." She gestured at two large
cardboard boxes. "I've always just kept everything in
heaps, but now…" Her smile flickered, then renewed
itself. "Lying there in that hospital the first half of
this summer, I got to thinking of all the things I hadn't
done. That I shouldn't leave undone, if something
ever…" Her voice trailed away and she shrugged.
"Anyway, I've already made a good start." She gestured across the room to an arrangement of photographs laid out in front of the French doors. It strag-
gled a good ten feet or more along the rug.

"Yikes!" *Gold mine*, Gillian thought. Here was

what she'd come for at last. If that was Lara's family history laid out on the floor, then it was also her own.

"Of course, if you'd rather not…" Lara said anxiously. "Lots of people think albums are bores, I know. Especially other people's."

"Oh, no! No. No, I love albums. "Mom was a fanatic album keeper—scrapbooks, too." *But with the real facts tucked away out of my sight.* "So where do we start?"

"How's it go—" Trace paused in a doorway to what must be his dressing room. He was clothed, but his hair was still wet from a shower. "Gillian." He nodded, not trying to hide his irritation. Eyebrows raised, he turned to Lara.

"I decided I needed some help." A note of defiance underlay Lara's cheeriness.

"In that case, maybe I'll—" He swerved toward the couch, but Lara scurried to block his way.

"*No,* Trace, go on to your office. We don't need you moping around here. I'm fine."

"Lara…" His eyes flicked to Gillian, then back to the actress.

What? Gillian wondered. *Are you afraid I'll rat on you about that kiss yesterday?*

"I'm fine," Lara repeated.

"Okay." He didn't look at all convinced. His hand strayed to her collar and he plucked at a chain hanging around her neck, pulling a silver locket into view. "You know where I'll be if you need me."

ONCE HE'D GONE, they settled to work. The first order of business, Lara declared, was a rough sort. "We need to lay out everything in somewhat chronological order. Then we'll see if I can figure out the exact year each picture was taken.''

''I'm afraid I won't be much of a help, not knowing your family.''

''Of course you will. You already know Joya and Toby. Here they are the first year I met their father. Weren't they adorable? They were eight and nine. So if you'd put this one over there...'' She pointed all the way to the left. ''About a foot from the end. Right there, perfect.''

Not perfect at all, Gillian realized, staring down at the start of the time line. ''You look about twenty here.'' She held up a photo.

''Twenty-five,'' Lara said, digging into her box.

''So...where're the early years?'' In her teens, Lara had been raised by foster parents, Gillian had learned from by reading that first article her aunt had torn from *Soap Opera Digest*. Her later research had turned up only variations on that fact, as if it were the only thing known. But before that? *What did you do with my grandparents? Did you have sisters and brothers? Where's the picture of you behind the wheel of your shiny new red Mustang?*

''The...early years?'' Lara murmured, then shrugged. ''They were nothing to speak of. Life begins in your twenties, I always say.''

Recorded life, anyway.

For the next hour, they sorted and arranged every photo in the first box. There were pictures of actors and actresses and backstage people from Lara's early years in soap opera, then later came the *Searching for Sarah* crowd. ''And this is...was...my Richard.'' Misty-eyed, Lara sat smiling down at a photo. ''I don't have many pictures of him. For some reason he was terribly camera shy.'' She passed over a shot of a thin-faced, thin-haired man in his late forties, intelligence shining out from behind a pair of wire-rimmed spectacles, a shy and kindly smile. ''This was the year I met him. He saved my life.''

''Careerwise, you mean?''

''Every which way and wise. I was running with a bad crowd. Had been since I dropped out of high school. I'd forgotten there was any other kind till Richard came along and reminded me.'' She rubbed a hand through her silvery hair. ''And yes, I never would have made it in show biz without him. I was working for the caterer who served lunches on the set, when he noticed me. Got me my first bit part.

''After that he coached me till I could halfway act. He taught me how to talk, how to walk, how to dress. How to think. Made me remember how to feel...'' She sat, head averted, throat convulsing, her hands cradling the photo. ''Sorry...''

''Oh, don't be silly!'' Gillian protested warmly.

''That's me. Silly's my middle name...'' She rose and walked over to the coffee table before the sofa and set the photo of Richard aside. ''Think I'll have a blowup made of that one.'' She pulled a tissue from the box on the table, blew her nose and wandered back, sat on the rug and delved into the photo box again. ''Speaking of middle names,'' she said casually, shuffling photos, ''what's *yours*? Gillian's so pretty. I wondered what your parents paired with it.''

Were they speaking of middle names? Gillian carefully squared one picture with its neighbors. *Trace put you up to this, didn't he?* Lara had stopped shuffling, had fixed her silvery eyes upon her with an almost fearful intensity. ''It's...'' God, she didn't like lying to this woman! "S-Susan. They named me after my aunt Susan." The kernel of truth in the lie, that she really had an aunt by that name, was the barest of comforts.

Lara blew out a long, sighing breath. "I like that. Gillian Susan…"

But you named me Sarah Cloud. Why Cloud, Lara? Why give me such a lovely, poetic name, then give me away?

There was no way to ask, with Lara's rejection engraved on her memory: *If I didn't want you when you were born, why would I want you now?*

Why indeed?

They worked for another hour, till there was less than an inch of pictures left in the second box and their photo train stretched for nearly twenty feet around the room. They broke for lunch—Lucy brought up a tray of soup and sandwiches—then on they slogged. "You don't have half enough space in your photo album," Gillian pointed out. "Joya and Toby alone would fill one."

There were pictures of Lara's stepchildren swimming at Bailey's Beach, sailing their dinghy in junior regattas at Ida Lewis Yacht Club. Of Joya competing in a horse show. Toby behind the wheel of his first car, a Porsche. Pictures of them in evening dress with Richard, at the Emmy Awards ceremony. Gillian plucked an early photo out of the box that was almost an eerie foreshadowing of that one—Toby in a child's tuxedo, Joya in a floor-length gown much too sophisticated for a girl of eight or nine. The two of them flanked Richard Corday, his buoyant smile contrasting oddly with his children's stony stares.

"That was at our wedding," Lara said, peering

over Gillian's shoulder. "They were supposed to take part in the ceremony, ring bearer and flower girl, but at the last minute Joya wouldn't and—" Her laughter was soft and rueful. "Somehow Toby lost the ring. We never did find it."

She shook her head slowly, remembering. "Richard was living in New York and their mother in Hollywood when I met him. The marriage was over in all but name, but the kids didn't know it. Wouldn't have it. They blamed me, of course." She set the photo in its place among those of the early years, then straightened, and stood staring down at it. "Took me forever to win them over…"

Jealousy plucked at Gillian's sleeve. *You wanted them but not me. Wasn't I good enough?* She stirred the remaining photos. "Another inch to go, plus this envelope." It lay at the very bottom of the box, a big tattered manila one, closed with a brass hasp. She turned it over—and Lara almost snatched it from her fingers.

"Oh, don't bother with those!"

"W-why not?" The envelope was dingy from years of handling. It was all she could do not to grab it back. *That! That's what I came for!*

"It's just some old junk…doesn't belong with the rest of this."

"Your childhood?" Gillian asked bluntly.

Lara grimaced, looking down at the envelope. "Such as it was."

"Show me," she coaxed in almost a whisper. *Please, please, please show me.*

"It's nothing much…" Lara's fingertips traced the bent clasp, drifted away from it, while Gillian clenched her teeth and held her breath. "Haven't looked at it in years..."

Oh, Lara, show me!

Her mother's slender fingers lifted the clasp, the tattered flap, reached in and drew out a photo. A young man and woman stood next to a worn old Chevy from the fifties. Whoever held the camera had backed far away, so that the entire car was visible in the photo—which meant the faces of the couple were tiny. The man wore a hat that shaded his upper face, but you could see his wide grin. His long bony arm was draped in casual possession over the shoulders of the tiny, white-blond, beaming woman in the flowered sundress.

"My parents," Lara said as softly as if she and Gillian sat together in church. "The day Daddy bought his new car. He was *so* proud of it."

The car might have been new to him, but this photo must have been taken in the mid-sixties, since Lara had been there to see their pride. Gillian's eyes stung. Such pride, such young hopes. "Where..." She swallowed; she could guess the thrust of the inevitable answer, if not its details. "Where are they now?"

Silently Lara pulled a yellowed newspaper clipping from the envelope. Flood Claims 7, proclaimed a mid-size headline. Bridge Washes Out In Storm Of Decade, it continued in smaller caps. She set it to the far side of her.

Gillian swallowed and nodded. *And so you ended up in a foster home. Or series of homes,* as the magazine article had put it. "How old were you?"

"Twelve." Lara pulled out a high-school photo— a copy of the same photo the lawyer had sent Gillian's adoptive parents so many years ago. "Here's me at fourteen, ninth grade."

And within a year this child was pregnant with me. Would buy herself a stuffed tiger after she'd given me away. A more suitable toy than a baby for this big-eyed, delicate child with the wary smile.

"The photographer was having the darnedest time getting me to smile," Lara remembered. "Finally he told me he'd bet I'd grow up to be a model someday, and that was so ridiculous I had to laugh—and he snapped this one."

"He wasn't far wrong," Gillian observed huskily.

"You could say it's all his fault," Lara agreed. "When I finally ran off, I needed *some*where to run to. And I guess becoming a model had stuck in my mind. Everybody knew you went to New York to be discovered." She smiled and set the photo aside. "But nobody in West Virginia knew you had to be five foot ten before they'd even let you in the agency door. I pounded mile upon mile of pavement before anybody bothered to set me straight."

"You grew up in West Virginia?" It was one of the many mysteries Gillian had yet to solve. She'd first learned that fact from the *Soap Opera Digest* article. She'd assumed Virginia, since her own birth certificate was issued by that state and her adoption decree was granted by a court of Virginia. So that was where she'd looked for her parents when she first started searching. *No wonder I didn't find any trace of you!* Could that muddling of facts have been intentional—perhaps by the lawyer who'd arranged her adoption? Change a state here or a date there and the link between parent and child was effectively broken.

Lara nodded. "I was born and raised in the mountains, yes. Coal country."

"Do you...still have family there?"

Staring into the mouth of the envelope, Lara shook her head. "Nobody."

So... Gillian sat, folding and tucking away her hopes of aunts, uncles, cousins, grandparents, like outgrown but still treasured clothes. *Well, I still have Chris. Sort of. He was such a traveling man that theirs was a phone-and-letter relationship more than a tangible, hugging one. A birthday present arrived every September without fail—one should be arriving any day, come to think of it—and he'd phoned her every Christmas since their parents divorced. That's more than lots of people have,* she reminded herself.

Lara pulled a card from the envelope, a homemade affair with a graceful sketch of a tree in black ink. On its trunk was drawn a heart, with the inscription *W. M. loves L. B.*

L.B. was Laura Bailey, of course, Lara's maiden name. But *W.? As in William?* That was her birth father's name, according to the document the lawyer had sent her adoptive parents. Gillian sat, her hands painfully clasped. "Beautiful sketch," she said finally. Her throat had almost closed on her and the words came out in a croak.

"It is," Lara agreed, setting the valentine on her far side. "He could draw anything."

And so can I! Could this be where that talent came from? A valentine proved nothing, of course, nothing at all; still, the blood hammered in her temples. *So close...so close...*

Lara lifted another photo from the envelope. Her eyes glistened as she stared at it, then she laughed in soft bewilderment. "He's so young and I...I got old."

"Who is he?" Gillian leaned in to stare at the young soldier. He looked...familiar. Something in the slant of his eyebrows or the shape of his face. *Could it be?*

"My first true love," Lara murmured. "He flunked out of high school—he was so smart, but he couldn't read to save his life. I used to do his homework for him." She smiled, lost in some long-ago sweet memory.

"What happened to him after that?" *Tell me. Oh, tell me!*

"He found some recruiter who helped him lie about his age, joined the marines. They shipped him off to Vietnam a few months later." Her smile faded. "He came home after training to say goodbye. I never saw..." Lara gulped, shook her head at the words that wouldn't come, then spun in relief as the telephone rang. She set the photo gently on the carpet and went to answer the phone.

Gillian stared down at the picture. *Never saw him again? Why, Lara? He died in the war, or he never came home again, or he found another girl?* She could imagine a dozen reasons. Eyebrows that seemed familiar... She longed to take the photo to the nearest mirror and compare it feature by feature with her own. *Is this my father? Flunked out of school because he couldn't read. And now here am I, a woman who scrambles her alphabet, who confuses numbers with letters, when she reads.* She'd never thought of dyslexia as a gift before.

CHAPTER THIRTEEN

"WHAT NEWS?" TRACE demanded when Jeremy Benton came on the line. "Any word back on the prints?"

"Yeah, I got word," Benton said, " for all the good it did me. Had to call in some favors to get it this fast."

"I owe you, Jeremy." Favors were better than cash in the pocket, in their world, and the tally of who owed whom was scrupulously kept. "No matches, huh?" He wasn't surprised. Stalkers weren't your normal felons, who, starting in their teens or even earlier, served long apprenticeships in crime or violence or both and collided at regular, well-documented intervals with the law. Some stalkers suffered only one obsession in a lifetime. Others cruised from celebrity to celebrity. But unless and until they crossed the line from obsession to murderous possession, they didn't appear on the police officer's radar screen. "Well, thanks anyway."

"And as to the Dumpster diving down at the Moorings—the guys turned up zip. No glue tubes, no matchbooks or lighters, nothing. You've got a cute one there." Hearty male laughter sounded in the background, and Benton murmured, "Yeah, yeah, I'm coming," then asked hurriedly, "what about your end?"

"Lara told no one I ran out and got a bee sting kit. So that means anybody at that lunch day before yesterday who knows she never carries a purse would have had good reason to hope a bee would do the trick."

Benton grunted. "You warn her not to tell anybody from now on?"

"I did." Much better to leave the stalker thinking the bee trick might work next time than to have the person seeking a new method of attack.

"Good. You realize that if your Gillian babe isn't the freak, then whoever it is may not know for sure you spotted the bee. It could have torn its own leg off and flown away, or maybe it's still stuck in place and died of a heart attack, for all Sarah XXX knows."

"Or maybe she was watching and saw it all." The waterfront parking lot was open on three sides, with crowds of tourists strolling past. The stalker could have hidden there in plain sight. Trace rubbed his nape where his hair bristled. "And here's another thing. You asked me yesterday if a fan would know that Lara Corday is allergic to bees. The answer is probably not, *but*—hang on to your hat—Dr. Laura Daley, the character Corday plays in the soaps, is allergic to bees."

"What the hell, Sutton?"

"Yeah. Lara's husband had a habit of borrowing from real life to enrich his fictional characters, she tells me. So he borrowed his wife's allergy, tacked it onto her character and wrote an episode a few years back where Dr. Daley is stung by a bee during a hospital staff picnic. And guess who saves her life by doing an emergency tracheotomy with a pocketknife and a straw?"

"No. I don't wanna hear this."

"Oh, yeah. Dr. Daley's faithful surgical nurse and best friend, aka Woodwind's perpetual houseguest—Harriet Bristow."

Benton let out a sigh of disgust. "You got a butler over there by any chance?"

"Nope."

"Okay, so the butler didn't do it. He's the only one in the whole wide world we don't suspect. But it looks like it could be either of her stepkids, her personal assistant, her actress buddy. Or it could be a nutcase—one of ten—twenty?—million viewers who's confusing Corday with her TV role. We'll catch Sarah XXX someday and find out she's a fruitcake who hates all *doctors!* Meantime, I've got a hot date with a steak and pepper grinder across the street."

After cradling the phone, Trace sat scowling into space for a while, then dialed again.

"'Lo?" his sister snapped.

"How's it going, kiddo?"

"Ho—so glad *somebody* asked! Let's see. I'm stuck on a freeway—the wrong freeway, headed God knows where—someplace on the north side of Houston. Pre-rush-hour rush hour, apparently. I've been sitting here for forty minutes now, and the air conditioner croaked twenty minutes ago. And it's a hundred degrees in the shade, except there isn't any. Nothing but concrete and kudzu as far as the eye can see. Five minutes more of this and I leave the key in the ignition and walk."

"Stay calm, Em."

"I *am* calm. Five more minutes and I calmly walk!"

This was why you didn't hire relatives. "Fine. Before you go, tell me your latest, okay? What's Mahler's middle name?"

"Scott."

As bad as Sylvester. "Scott is a guy's name," he said with exaggerated patience. Unless it was a last name? Her maiden name? Meaning Mahler's her married name? His stomach did a nasty triple gainer off a high board. Gillian married. It made sense. Any man looking for a wife would—

"According to her next-door neighbor, Mahler's mother was married twice. She was a divorcée named Eleanor Scott, with a daughter named Gillian Scott in tow, when she arrived in Houston. Then she met a man named Ed Mahler, married him, and Ed adopted her daughter—"

"Who became Gillian Scott Mahler. Got it." He let out a long breath of relief. Not married. Even better, not Sarah. His eyes narrowed. So why had she lied?

"*Aaaand* the crowd applauds," Emily teased, "The sound is deafening. Wait, the're all getting to their feet! It's a standing o—"

"Good job, kiddo. Well done. Thank you very much."

"*Ohhh,* you're entirely welcome. You'll receive my invoice tomorrow. Now, can I *please* go?"

"Not quite yet." He ignored her yelp of anguish. "So Gillian Scott Mahler used to be Gillian Scott. What was her middle name back then?"

"I don't care! I want to go home."

"Emily, if you work for Brickhouse, it's a job, not a hobby. You stick till it's done or go find something softer. Research librarian maybe?" She'd quit that job last year after feuding with the head librarian about whether *The Hitchhiker's Guide to the Universe* was appropriate children's literature.

"Creep."

"The creep who's paying your bills this month. Mahler's original middle name, and I need it on the double. We had another attempt on my client yesterday."

"Why didn't you say so?"

"You were too busy whining." He told her about the bee, to a background of hooks and revving engines, till all trace of temper and tears had left her voice.

"Okay," she said humbly when he'd ended. "Mahler's original middle name coming up, ASAP."

"You could try to find the court in which Ed Mahler adopted her. Might be on record there. Or maybe you can think of some way to trick it out of her parents."

"'Fraid not. Her mother died two years ago—cancer. And Ed Mahler sold his house and went to sea. He's a merchant marine."

A family existed—a family blown away like dust. He and Emily were luckier than most. They were two of four children, with happily married parents thriving up in Vermont. He could go home anytime and find his high-school letter jacket hanging in his bedroom closet, his rock posters still tacked to his bedroom walls. But Gillian couldn't. She'd had not one but two families fall out from under her.

How much does it take, he wondered, to push a sensitive person over the edge? How much loneliness and dislocation does she suffer before something snaps—and she sets out in search of somebody to belong to who'll never let her down? Someone who can't really die because she never really existed? Someone like a TV mother searching for her daughter?

And when her TV mother rejects her?

"TWO MORE ALBUMS SHOULD do it," Lara decided, thumbing through the album they'd completed. "Or let's say three to be safe."

"We could run down to the photo shop in the Brick Market," Gillian suggested. "They should be open for another hour."

Lara glanced at her watch and let out a groan, just as a key turned in the door to the suite. Trace Sutton peeked in. "Twenty minutes till your rehab session."

"I just realized! Darn, I wanted these off the rug today." She looked down in dismay at their train of photographs.

"That's why you hired a personal assistant," Gillian reminded her. "If you could drop me on your way, I'll buy them."

"Terrific. Or better yet, why doesn't Trace drop *me* off, then he can drive you around to the shops?"

"No!" Gillian and Trace protested as one. Startled, Gillian swung to meet his scowl, then turned away. "No, thanks," she said briskly. "It's stopped raining and I'd like a walk."

Head cocked to one side, Lara stood very still. Then she smiled and shrugged. "Of course."

AFTER SHE'D PURCHASED Lara's albums, Gillian wandered back toward Woodwind, following Thames Street south along the harborfront. The storm clouds had cleared out, leaving the old town bathed in a rosy glow as the sun sank beyond the bay. Lovely light for painting. She'd been too long away from it. There just wasn't time, between Lara's assignments and her classes at the Y. But she was storing up images.

She stopped to peer down one of the ancient cobblestoned wharved toward the water. Old two-story shops leaned in from either side. At the far end where the wharf jutted into the harbor, the dark masts of sailboats striped a pink sky. She jumped as a car horn blared close behind her. She turned to see a black Range Rover, Joya smirking at her from the open passenger window, her brother, Toby, at the wheel. The sports ute cut off a gaggle of tourists venturing timidly out onto the crosswalk and sped on down the road. *I guess you could call that progress,* Gillian told herself. Usually, Lara's stepbrats either ignored her or patronized her when they crossed paths at all. A honked acknowledgment was a definite advance. Not that they'd bothered to stop and ask if she'd like a ride home.

Even if they had, she preferred her own company. Especially this afternoon, two days before her birthday.

For the past twenty years, Gillian had celebrated a ritual with her mother—her real mother Eleanor Scott—window-shopping together two days before her birthday. Eleanor would point out objects she thought Gillian might like for a present. Gillian smiled, remembering. *Isn't that beautiful? Oh, honey, what do you think of this bracelet?* Gillian would dutifully admire them or express tactful reservations, then they'd wander on to the next shop. At the same time, she'd keep a sharp eye out for a present for Eleanor—whose birthday was—had been—in October. Because her mother generally pointed out objects that pleased her own eye.

At the end of the excursion, they'd eat supper in some special restaurant—a carefully considered treat in itself. The following day, they'd sneak back separately to the shops to make their purchases. And the day after, Gillian's birthday on September 12, she'd receive the object she'd most admired, beautifully gift-wrapped and lovingly presented—and she'd express delighted astonishment. *Dear Mom.*

Last September, her first birthday without her mother, she hadn't been able to make herself shop. But this year, two days before her birthday, Gillian thought she could continue the tradition. Maybe she wouldn't buy, but at least she could admire, and listen for her mother's ghostly remarks at her shoulder. *Yes, Mom, it does match my eyes, but how often do I wear a scarf. Now, this hat...*

Still, she surprised herself by finding an irresistible pair of Victorian earrings in an antique shop that specialized in estate jewelry. Baroque pearls edged with garnets. She shouldn't—it would cost a week of the salary Lara was paying her. She bought them anyway. Who else would be gifting her this year?

Well, there was Chris; his birthday present arrived every September without fail. Which reminded her. She should stop by her old apartment, see if there was mail. She'd filed a forwarding address with the post office, but so far they didn't seem to be forwarding.

On her arrival she rang the bell for the upstairs apartment—it felt odd to no longer have a key—then heard footsteps clattering down to meet her. Michele, one of the two sophomores Debbie had added to their household to make ends meet. About Joya's age and rather like her, Gillian thought, looking up at her, poised uncertainly on the third stair.

"Oh, it's you." Michele decided to brazen it out. "I was just leaving."

"Not in my sweatshirt, you're not." Gillian made no move to step aside. Her favorite orange University of Miami sweatshirt, a Christmas gift from Chris when she was fourteen. She held out her hand. "Give."

"This is yours?" Michele caught a pinch of fabric and stared down at it, as if someone had slipped it over her head while she slept and she'd only just noticed. "I thought it was Debbie's."

"It's mine and I'll take it now, please."

Michele tossed her blond curls. "But I was just going out."

Was I ever this young? Gillian settled herself more comfortably against the doorjamb. "Oh? Well, you may want to find something warm to wear. It's getting chilly."

An hour later, arms now loaded with Lara's albums and a plastic bag stuffed full of her own missing clothes, Gillian cut uphill to Bellevue Avenue. Less than half a mile to Woodwind, she assured her feet. *And a treat when you get there,* she reminded herself. Apparently the package she'd expected from Chris had arrived this morning. Debbie, it seems, had delivered it to Woodwind on her bicycle, and had met Harriet just exiting the front gates.

"You know who she is, don't you?" Debbie demanded. "She plays that bitchy nurse on *Searching for Sarah,* and I guess she's typecast. I told her I needed to see you, but she claimed you were too busy working to entertain visitors. That she'd give you the package. She didn't?''

''She was still out when we left. Lara said she went up to Providence to talk to some theater director.'' But she ought to be back by now and Gillian smiled in anticipation. Chris gave wonderful, whimsical presents, often picked up on his wanderings around the world. Seashells, carved coconuts...a pareu from Bali one year— A horn honked and, still smiling, she turned.

''What perfect timing!'' Lara cried from the car window as Trace pulled over. ''Hop in.

''We're taking a short detour,'' she added as Gillian settled into the back seat and the car swung off the avenue. ''I remembered I needed something.'' Trace threaded through back streets with silent skill, while Lara admired the new photo albums and told Gillian about her rehab session. ''The therapist says I should be able to do anything I want to from now on. Just as long as I don't try to push through any pain.''

''Excellent. I've been meaning to suggest we start doing tai chi together, if you're interested.'' They settled on a time for their first lesson, then Gillian looked up as Trace parked the car in front of a small market that catered to the carriage trade. ''I think I'll just sit,'' Gillian said quickly, as Trace opened his door and walked around to Lara's.

Mr. Possessive, dogging Lara's every footstep. Having a man follow her everywhere like that would drive her wild. *How can Lara stand it?* Remembering his kiss yesterday, she supposed there were compensations. She ran a finger absently back and forth across her lips, then grimaced as she realized what she was doing.

A car pulled in off the street and edged into the one remaining space near the market's door. Red…its make came to her slowly, then Gillian sucked in her breath. A Mustang from the early seventies, clearly a collector's car. Not that vintage cars were unusual in Newport, where only last month they'd held a parade of antique Rolls-Royces that had stretched for more than two miles along Bellevue. This was a town where people came to strut their stuff.

A red Mustang. Like the car Lara had demanded before she'd sign the relinquishment papers. Hardly aware she was doing it, Gillian opened her door and stepped out, as if the Mustang were a magnet, hauling her home. She stopped when her outstretched fingertips touched the Mustang's shiny flank. *Lara traded me for one like this.*

She glanced aside as the door to the market opened and Trace and Lara walked out. Laughing softly, Trace stopped beside her. "I see you like sports cars."

"This one anyway," she murmured, her eyes fixed on Lara. "Such a lovely color."

Expressionless, Lara walked past her to the door to her own car. "Don't you think so?" Gillian added, coming to join her. "It's a beauty, isn't it?" she asked. *Am I turning the knife? I suppose I am.*

"Is it?" Lara said. "I wouldn't know. I've always hated Mustangs." Huddled into herself, she didn't speak again all the way home to Woodwind.

CHAPTER FOURTEEN

''I LEFT IT ON THE hall table,'' said Harriet.

Gillian frowned. Lara's reaction to the Mustang had driven all thoughts of Chris's package from her mind. She'd run upstairs to her apartment on their return, gulped down a bowl of yogurt and changed for the aerobics class she was scheduled to teach at 7:00. On the way down to her car, she'd remembered and dashed up to the mansion. ''Are you sure?'' she asked now. The table in the front hall was the logical place to look, since Trace left all the family's mail there excepting Lara's. ''I've checked and—''

Harriet bridled. ''Of course I'm sure.'' She glanced angrily around the terrace at Toby and Joya, who were lounging on the balustrade, sipping one of Toby's alcoholic concoctions—apparently they were dining at home this evening—then at Lara, who sat beside her, as if to summon their support.

Trace glanced up from his golf club in mild interest. ''Maybe you left it in your car, Harriet.'' He tapped the ball at his feet. It rolled twenty feet across the terrace and missed his crystal vase by an inch. ''Damn.''

''I didn't.'' Harriet stuck out her chin. ''Go back and check again. It's there.''

''Maybe Lucy moved it when she dusted,'' drawled

Toby. "What's the big deal anyway? Somebody sending you some special dope, Gillie?"

"It's just a package I was expecting from a friend," she said stiffly, absurdly near tears. Here she stood among uncaring strangers, blocked from contact, no matter how tenuous, with the only person left in the world who loved her. *I want my birthday present!*

"I'm sure it will turn up," Lara said quickly. "I didn't notice it when we walked through the hall. Did you, Trace?"

He shook his head. "Why don't we ask Lucy and Barbara? Somebody must have put it away for safekeeping."

"Never mind. I'm late for my class already," Gillian said, trying to be gracious. "I'll look for it afterward." The last thing she saw as she turned away was Joya's Cheshire-cat smirk.

HOURS LATER, SHE THOUGHT of the package again as she parked before the carriage house. She glanced over her shoulder, but this side of Woodwind was dark, excepting the window on the second floor that, she had learned, marked Trace's office. Should she go up and look?

It was nearly midnight. Three women in her class had practically shanghaied her off to a bar, for a drink and what had turned out to be an attempt to pair her with the brother of one of them. She'd been flattered but the image of Trace Sutton had intruded. When had he become her standard for comparison?

And what about my package? she reminded herself. The day after tomorrow was her birthday, so she wouldn't, by her own rule, open Chris's gift even if she found it. Still, not knowing its whereabouts made her uneasy. She'd be happier with it sitting safely on her table, giving her two days to shake it and anticipate its contents. Trace was right, she told herself. She'd find it tomorrow, on the floorboards in Harriet the Grump's car.

She opened the door to the staircase, then paused, looking over her shoulder. To the east a full moon was rising over the trees. A lovely night for a walk. She'd yet to do Cliff Walk by moonlight.

But she was tired. Tomorrow night the moon would be nearly as full. She flicked on the light, trudged upstairs—and stopped short. "Son of a gun!" A package leaned against the wall beside her door. "Were you there all along?" Had she overlooked it this evening, going upstairs with her arms full of the clothes she'd retrieved from Michele? Or did Trace find it for her and bring it up? The man might have all the sexual fidelity of a tomcat; still, she could see him doing that. He was such a puzzling mixture of aggressiveness and consideration.

Whatever. She swooped up her gift and carried it into the apartment, over to the coffee table—and frowned. A wide flap of brown wrapping paper dangled from the bottom. Upending the parcel, she found that one end had been neatly wrapped and sealed with duct tape. The other end had once been finished in the same fashion, but at some point in the package's travels, the folds had come loose and been torn. She grimaced. Post-office sorting machines, no doubt. Someone had patched the shreds together with clear tape, then sent the package on.

She turned it over and studied the return address: Christopher Scott, Yacht Malay, Tahiti. "Lucky dog!'' she murmured affectionately. He'd been in Hawaii last time she'd heard from him back in June. He'd called her to urge once again that she give up her quest, forget about learning anything about her birth parents.

Because her adoptive brother was the only person she'd told about that horrible letter of rejection, and from that moment, Chris had despised Lara on her behalf. *You don't need a reunion with a selfish bitch like that,* he'd pointed out. *She's the past, Gillian. You need to get on with your future. You need nothing from her.*

If you could meet her now, Chris, would you still think that, I wonder? That car today at the market... *I don't know what to make of her.* Chris had always been a shrewd judge of character. *I wish you were here.*

He almost was. Always a letter came with his present. She turned the package again and picked at the torn flap. *Hope you didn't send me something fragile.* Could the post-office brutes have broken it? She shook the package, yet nothing rattled.

Two days to her birthday, but there would be no celebration this year. The only other person who knew the significance of September 12 apparently didn't care. Had never cared.

She hugged the package to her breast. *Why am I so blue, all of a sudden?* Still embracing it, she drifted to the window overlooking the courtyard. Beyond the fluttering leaves of an elm, she could see the light was still on in Trace's office. He was working late.

On what? She hadn't a clue. She ought to ask him sometime.

She wouldn't. He was Lara's man. The less she

messed with him, let herself think about him, the better. The light blurred for a moment, and blinking, she let out a startled laugh. *Hey, what's the matter with me?*

Antidote time. Immediately. She sank onto the sofa, balanced the package on her knees and attacked it. Let Chris drive the demons out. This year she was celebrating early.

Inside the wrapping paper, she found a much-battered cardboard box, which was taped with clear tape. She frowned, a vague sense of…uneasiness pricking at the back of her mind. She rose to find a knife with which to attack the tape, then paused, glancing toward the courtyard windows. A feeling of intrusion, of being watched, was growing slowly within her. *Don't be absurd.* Even if someone stood down below on the gravel, looking up, he couldn't see her from that angle. But still…

She sliced the knife through the tape, then raised the box's lid. And looked down at a book, dark blue with an exuberant design of S-curves and curlicues in gold. With a tremulous laugh, she traced the familiar pattern. She hadn't seen this book in twenty years, but still she remembered it. Tears trickling down her cheeks, she opened the birthday card that lay on top of it.

"I found it at last," Chris had written. "It was up in Dad's attic, and he said of course you should have it, when I reminded him."

Hans Christian Andersen's fairy tales, an edition printed in the 1890s, with wonderful art nouveau illustrations. Her mother had read her a few pages of a tale every night before bed from the time she was three till she grew old enough to read for herself.

They'd reach the end of the book then start over again. Somehow it had been left behind when her parents split households, but she'd never forgotten. Had mentioned it wistfully to Chris only last year.

"I remember how much you loved the illustration of the dog with eyes the size of saucers," his note continued. "I can still see you, lying on your stomach by the fire, your feet waving in the air while you pondered that picture."

He then went on to tell her about the yacht he was delivering to New Zealand, a wonderful old tub, with every comfort in the world aboard, but he could have reached the islands faster by swimming. "Meantime I worry about you," he wrote. "Have you achieved any kind of reunion with your mother? And if so, was it worth it? Or at least, have you pried the real story out of her?

"I wish you'd leave well enough alone, but you were always a stubborn brat. And curious as the cat. Please keep in mind what they say about kitties who insist on answers."

"The only thing that might be hurt is my feelings," she assured him. She finished the card, folded it and sat smiling for a moment. The blues hadn't quite departed her door; still, Chris had driven them back to a respectful distance. She set the letter aside and opened the book. Paged slowly through it, pausing to admire the illustrations for the Ice Queen, Hansel and Gretel and the Dog with Eyes— Her gasp feathered out into the silence.

Between two pages of text only a ragged stub remained—one paw of the dog and a bit of delicate background. Whoever had ripped out this illustration had done so carelessly, with malice, intending to destroy, not steal, leaving the tattered page like a mocking signature. *I passed this way and I wrecked it!* With a shudder, Gillian glanced up at the courtyard window.

Darkness pressed its face against the panes.

"CLOUDY," SAID LARA distinctly.

Instantly awake, Trace blinked at the darkness overhead. *Damn, here we go again.* Her third nightmare in a week. *What's bothering you, lady?* All this anguish about the weather? And why now? Even in the hospital, the first days after her fall, she hadn't dreamed like this.

"It's all my...stupid, stupid, *stupid*...oh, Cloudy, I...she's gone and I..." A keening, tiny sound of unappeasable, unending grief.

Time to get up and wake her. Maybe he should let her sleep, let her work it through, but no one with a heart could allow such pain to continue uncomforted. He swung his covers aside and sat.

She swore, one sudden, crystal-clear word, coarse and brutal. He'd never heard her curse before. He padded toward the bed.

"He'll never drive that car again," Lara muttered. "Never! And *I'll* never..." Anger shaded into wordless, murmuring heartbreak.

Moonlight flooding in the French doors helped him find the decanter on her bedside table. He poured a glass of water, started to sit on the edge of her bed, but suddenly she rolled over. Hugged her pillow and let out a long, shuddering sigh.

He stood, waiting while her half-sobbing breaths deepened and slowed. *Good,* he told her silently. *Sleep, Lara, go to sleep. Sleep and don't dream.* She sighed again and burrowed her face in the pillow. He set the glass down and backed off from her bedside. *Good...*

He waited for almost five minutes, but the nightmare didn't resume. Good for Lara, but now *he* was wide-awake. He shrugged and padded into his dressing room, set into the opposite end of the suite from hers, then to his bathroom beyond.

When he came out a few minutes later, she was sleeping as peacefully as a child. He glanced at his watch. Three in the morning. No chance of sleep for him once his mind started spinning. And it had plenty to spin about.

Gillian Scott Mahler. *Why lie about your middle name, Gillian?* Could Lara have been right? *She took offense when I first questioned her. Were her lies ever since simply teasing?*

No, his instincts told him it was more than that. Lion eyes, with something moving in their depths. She stood always on the edge of things here at Woodwind, watching, waiting... *For what?* A chance to belong or a chance to strike?

The Mustang at the market this afternoon—what was that about? For that matter, what about Lara's reaction? He remembered once, back in his FBI days, someone had tried to shoot him at close range and he'd barely deflected the gun. For two days after, his left ear heard nothing but ringing. This was like that. As if urgent conversations filled the air around him at Woodwind, but he could see only moving lips.

Lara and Gillian, then Lara again—shopping for food at the market, baker's chocolate and walnuts. He'd lived with the woman since May and not once had she shown any interest in cooking. He'd tried to question her in the store and she'd brushed him off with a joke about craving chocolate. But baker's chocolate is unsweetened. No chocoholic would buy it for eating, not when the market also sold the finest Belgian varieties. So that was a lie. Gillian and Lara both lying...why?

He prowled to the French doors, moonlight diffusing through the diaphanous sheers that covered the floor-to-ceiling panes. Unlocking one door, he smiled as the sound of the sea rolled into the room. Better. He walked out onto the balcony. A full moon riding high. What a shame to stay inside on a night like this.

He leaned on the stone balustrade, breathing deep, looking out over the moonlit lawn bounded by the pitch-black slashes of the surrounding walls. Something flickered in the shadows and his eyes homed in on the movement. Something pale—the gate in the wall swinging open, then closing again. *Son of a bitch!* He straightened, waiting. *Come on, Sarah XXX. Here I am. It's high time we met.*

A minute pulsed by, two heartbeats to each second, but no one stepped forth from the shadows. Was the watcher standing perfectly still? Could the watcher see him? Or—it hit him. He'd just seen someone *leaving* Woodwind, not entering! His eyes swept beyond the walls, out onto Cliff Walk, and for a moment, he thought he detected movement where the path twisted—someone heading south. He raced into the suite, ticking off his needs as he went. His sweats, his shoulder rig to hold his gun, his running shoes. No way was he missing this chance to end the whole maddening masquerade. If Sarah XXX walked the cliffs tonight, she was his!

TWO HOURS OF TOSSING and turning had convinced her she wouldn't sleep tonight. She might as well get up, go out, see if moonlight and the ocean could drive this sickness from her heart. Dressed in a T-shirt and running shorts, a light cotton sweater slung by its sleeves around her neck, Gillian unlocked the gate in the wall, locked it behind her, then pushed carefully through the rosebushes onto Cliff Walk. Starlight tipped the dark waters with diamonds; the sea sighed against the rocks far below. She drew a deep breath—roses and kelp—and broke into a jog, heading out the peninsula toward the ocean. She had the whole night to herself.

Running through moonlight felt more like floating, her loosely curled fingers flickering dark, then milky before her as the bushes shrouded her in shadow or broke to show the glittering waters beyond. The growl of waves dragging down the shingle beach; the soft thud of her running shoes on damp stone—up a flight, across a stony flat, then down again. Then the gap in the bushes, the unnerving seaward tilt in the path—the spot where Lara came to grief. Gillian held her breath as she passed the drop, let it out in a grateful puff and ran on, fleeing from the knowledge, feeling it loping at her heels like a black dog. A dog with eyes the size of saucers...a dog that was no more.

Chris, did you look at that illustration before you sent me the book, or did you only recall it from our childhood? Maybe someone had torn it out years and years ago—past malice, not present hatred. Perhaps her adoptive father in a fit of rage, just after the divorce, twenty years ago.

No. Victor Scott had never bonded with her, but neither had he hated her.

She quickened her steps, but she couldn't run fast enough to escape the conclusion: Someone had torn open the package, not caring that she'd notice, then opened the box inside.

And read Chris's loving note. Shuddering as if bony, claw-nailed fingers stroked across her skin, she ran faster. The path sloped downward, speeding her flight; her feet jarred against the concrete, resisting gravity. Read Chris's message, so he or she knew what Gillian loved—the dog—then wrecked him. But why?

The towering chimneys of the Breakers reared against midnight-blue. Out to her left stretched a reef of black stones, the waves breaking white on them to give the mansion its name. *It could have been any sickie between Tahiti and Rhode Island. It doesn't have to be anyone I know...*

But she knew better. She would check with her ex-housemate tomorrow, ask Debbie if the package had been ripped when she'd delivered it, but already Gillian knew. *Someone here at Woodwind hates me....*

The same person who had removed the package from the front hall table. Or maybe Harriet lied and she never put it there at all. Ripped it open in the privacy of her car. Maybe she never meant to deliver it. Wouldn't have if Gillian hadn't asked for it. Harriet seemed to hate almost everyone. But why single me out? What have I done to her?

Come between her and Lara?

She'd reached the riprap. Not slowing her steps, she leaped from rock to rock. One misstep and her foot would slip into a gap; she'd break a leg for sure.

Didn't care. The malice behind her was what she feared tonight. *Joya...* Joya could have noticed her name on the package on the hall table. She could picture Joya reading Chris's note, see her searching the beloved book for the dog, laughing as she tore him out. But why?

Or perhaps the question with Joya was why not? Had it been a simple, malicious thrill, done merely because she *could* do it, the way a child torments a fly, pulls off a wing to see what happens next? *When she smiled at me on the terrace I thought she was enjoying my dismay about my missing package.* But maybe that had been a smirk of triumph. Of gloating. *I know something that you don't, Gillie.*

Up another flight of stone stairs as the cliffs rose again, Cliff Walk climbing with them to overlook a smaller cove, with the clatter of rolling shingle and an eerie phosphorescence where the waves raked the beach. Roses and the high walls of the mansions were on her right, empty moonlit space to her left, though not so scary here—the drop-off was only forty feet or so. More intimidating by far was the tunnel ahead, looming like a yawning mouth, surmounted by the Japanese teahouse… Copper dragons leering at her from its winged rooftop as she neared, her steps slowing to a faltering jog. Should she turn back?

Back to where somebody hated her? She couldn't, not yet. Catching her breath, she slowed to a fast walk and plunged into the tunnel, right hand grazing cold stone, not a ray of moonlight piercing the black. Twenty halting steps…thirty…forty. And now the faintest echo of waves, coming from up ahead, the palest moonlight promising the exit above. And then a velvety buttermilk sky, the moon a gigantic glowing pearl rolling westward.

Higher cliffs now and more riprap, more gaping

cracks between the stones. She took the boulders at a run, as if the mouth of the tunnel might suck her back inside. *Lara, Lara, Lara, could it be you?* Couldn't...could it? Chris had printed his name on the return address. She hadn't thought to warn him, had never dreamed that Lara might someday see a letter from her adoptive brother, with his telltale name of Scott.

Nine months before, when she sent Lara that shy letter of inquiry, she'd signed herself Sarah Scott.

So if Lara didn't know my adoptive parents' name when she relinquished me, she's known it ever since my letter. Could have spotted it on the package when she walked through the front hall this evening. Could have taken it up to her room to open it. *No, please, not Lara!*

But then who?

The face that was never very far from mind loomed in her thoughts, a face that called her, mocked her, disturbed her always. *Trace Sutton, who else?*

Because who else, the logical part of her mind demanded, was, despite his infidelities, fiercely protective and possessive of Lara? *If Trace knew that my name was Scott?* He'd only come to Woodwind in early May, she'd learned from Lucy. So he hadn't been living there when her letter arrived nine months ago. But if Lara had told him about it and then he'd noticed Chris's name on the package? Trace wouldn't be slow to put two and two together.

But to do this? She couldn't imagine it. The man might be her opponent, might see her as competition for Lara's affections and time, but the more she knew him, the less she could imagine him sneaking or conniving. *If he's my enemy, it wouldn't be behind my back. He'd tell me, show me, perhaps pick me up by the scruff of my neck and fling me through the gates of Woodwind, but he wouldn't mangle my book. No, whoever hates me, I can't believe it's Trace.*

Safely over the riprap, she'd come to the second tunnel. A less-fearsome one this, a corrugated steel pipe, burrowing under craggy rock for forty feet in a straight line. The light at its far end beckoned you as you entered it. Steps echoing, she flew through, then out the far side. From there to the end of Cliff Walk a mile south lay a wilderness of tumbled boulders, the path breaking down entirely in places where storms had washed it out. It ran only ten feet or so above sea level, straggling along the base of the crumbling cliffs. Because it was a wild and private stretch, very few tourists ever ventured this far, and none at night.

Gillian slowed to a walk, panting. No, whoever it was that hated her, surely it wasn't Trace. But then who?

She halted, looking down at a horseshoe of soft sand and powdered seashells encircled by massive boulders. She'd waded off this tiny beach once or twice this summer, though the big icy waves of Rhode Island daunted a Texan used to the bathtub-warm Gulf of Mexico waters. A few times at dawn she'd come here to do tai chi.

With that memory, she realized—she wasn't fleeing from but to. No trouble was so black that the ancient rituals of tai chi couldn't transcend it. She jumped from ledge to ragged ledge down to the sand. Stopped to unlace her shoes and set them aside. She walked to the water's edge. Stood facing the sea, the waves licking her toes, inviting serenity.

After a measureless time of slow breathing, she bowed to the moon and began.

CHAPTER FIFTEEN

WHOEVER SHE WAS, she was young and in superb condition. Trace had caught glimpses of her flying shadow from half a mile back, but he hadn't yet managed to overhaul her. Each time she vanished around a bend, he had to follow with caution. Every time he passed a side trail, he scouted up it a ways, assuring himself that she hadn't cut between two mansions up to the avenue. He had to scan every pathside boulder or clump of brush for fear that she might have spotted him following her, might now be crouching under cover, hoping that he'd pass her by, so she could double back on her trail. So Trace took his time. He didn't mean to lose her. Catch her tonight and this detail was done at long last. Once Lara was freed from danger, he could go home with a fat check and a clear conscience.

The thought didn't give him the satisfaction it would have even a month before. Home was nothing but a place, an apartment in San Francisco, comfortable surely, filled with his books and music. But home wasn't a person, as it was for his father or his brother Jon. He ran lightly, leaping from boulder to boulder as he hit the riprap, smiling grimly at the thought. *I need a woman.* Something about chasing this one through the moonlight had set all his instincts howling. *Finish this assignment and I could go find one.*

One came instantly to mind. Lion eyes, a soft vulnerable mouth, slender waist he could almost span with his hands, she'd bend like a willow. *Forget it. Pay attention.* Lose his quarry now and he was going nowhere but back to his lonely couch at Woodwind.

He slowed to a half jog when he came to the teahouse tunnel. The perfect place for an ambush. If his runner had looked over her shoulder and seen him, here was where she'd lie in wait. He considered drawing his gun, then dismissed the notion. Whoever Sarah XXX was, so far all her murderous tricks had been low-tech, another reason he was sure she was a woman.

Hugging the right wall, he stepped into the darkness with no show of fear. Ten feet in, he crouched and cut over to the left wall. Hands upraised to chop or protect his head, he padded on, left shoulder brushing stone, ears craning for any sound ahead, hearing nothing but the faint echo of waves off the tunnel walls.

When his outstretched fingers found the turn, he stopped. Listened. The logical place for an attacker to wait was just beyond, with a stone or a knife at the ready. *Come on, come on, make your move!*

Nothing but the faintest susurration of the waves. Slowly he stooped, brushed the damp earth with his palm, found a pebble. He cracked it hard against the far wall.

No reaction. *Nobody here but me and the boogeyman.* Or a cool and intelligent opponent who knew a feint when she heard it. He shuffled on, found the stone steps with his toe, rattled up them—he'd lost too much time in the tunnel, dammit!

Burst out into moonlight again, eyes scanning the

far end of the cove, the path curving above it. Nothing. *If I've lost her...* He broke into an all-out run, leaping from stone to stone along the riprap like a broken field runner. *Wait for me, Sarah, you bitch!*

He paused, panting, at the next tunnel, but no one was silhouetted against the milky oval of sky beyond, so he plunged on through, footfalls echoing off steel, to halt just inside its far end.

Nothing and no one moved out on the path. He cursed silently. *Lost her.* Perhaps she'd simply lurked on the far side of the teahouse tunnel and let him bumble past her, then doubled back the way she came.

Or maybe Sarah XXX crouched behind one of the thousands of boulders in the half mile ahead. If so, it would take an army to winkle her out of hiding. He should turn back; his place was by Lara. But, too stubborn to call it a night, he pushed on.

Passing a boulder the size of a house, he glanced down at the pocket beach beyond it—and saw her. Dancing with the ocean. One foot upraised, he froze.

Hands sweeping across the sky, limber body on tiptoe, a soft lunge onto one foot, then the dancer paused. His heart beat once, twice, three times and he realized. Not dancing exactly, but the flowing movements of tai chi.

And his quarry was Gillian. He should have known. After days of covert watching, her shape and way of moving were tattooed on his brain by now, but darkness and distance and his own hunting lust had confounded him. He padded off the trail and uphill to sit on a rock above the natural amphitheater. *You've lured me into the night, woman. Now dance for me.*

Silently, gracefully, seemingly mesmerized by the

night and the ocean, she danced, one flowing motion merging into the next, then a graceful stance held, while a wave washed in and the moon rolled across the sky. He could feel the ease of her muscles as if he moved with her. Feel his heart pumping steadily, the warm blood surging. His own discipline was karate, but these moves were similar, if softer. His body knew them all. He could have wrapped his body around hers, limb for limb, and moved as one with her, dancing…

Gillian, fey mystic woman, I need to know you. Mean to know you. There was no use denying it any longer.

And if you're the enemy? Lara's and therefore mine?

He couldn't believe it. Would not. A woman who danced with the moon and the waves? She was celebrating beauty out here tonight. Creating it. Whoever and whatever she was, she wasn't a person who could push another off a cliff, not and move like that, too.

Cobras are graceful, his inner cynic reminded him.

He wouldn't believe she was a stalker. Could not.

Because you can't believe it and have her, the coolly objective half of his brain pointed out.

Whatever secrets she was hiding, they couldn't be hurtful ones.

With a client's life in jeopardy, all secrets are dangerous. To be distrusted.

Then he'd make her secrets his own.

He sat and watched while the moon sank into the west. While the tide rose and his desire with it, dragged up by the moon and Gillian's flowing grace.

Higher than all those that had come before, a wave washed in, wetting her to her knees. She laughed, completed a final sequence—and turned. He saw her head snap up as she spotted him, then her hair fly out in a silken bell as she spun toward the rock. She froze. With him waiting at the top of the path, she was trapped and she knew it. Another wave washed in around her ankles. Deliberately she turned to face him, chin up, shoulders squared.

He stood, rising up out of the shadows thrown by the cliff. "It's Trace, Gillian."

"Oh..." She flattened a hand to her breastbone. "I thought..."

"I'm sorry. I didn't mean to scare you."

"Oh, *really?*"

He deserved her anger. He'd invaded a ritual as private as bath or prayer. But no man would have done otherwise. She turned around and bent over, hunting slowly along the rock. Another wave swept in. The sand would be entirely covered at high tide. "What are you looking for?"

"My..." She turned back, retracing her steps. "My shoes. I thought I left them over..." Another wave washed in and she whirled to the water. "Oh, *no!*"

He laughed in spite of himself. "Oh, yes. Tides do that."

One of her shoes was still visible, about thirty feet out, a jaunty boat heading off to sea. She took a step toward it.

"Don't even think about it," he advised, coming to the edge of the path, prepared to stop her if need be. "The currents are nasty, and sharks hunt at night."

"Oh, thanks," she said bitterly. She shrugged and started up the rock, her arms outstretched sideways for balance.

He climbed halfway down and caught her hand as she wobbled. "Easy!" His voice was husky with amusement and delight. Two miles of ragged rock back to Woodwind and not a cab in sight. He'd have thrown a kiss to the waves if she hadn't been frowning at him.

She stepped up wincingly onto the path, which wasn't paved this far out Cliff Walk. "Coming home now?" he asked rhetorically. There was no other place she could go. The last mile would have cut her feet to shreds, and it led farther out the peninsula, away from town.

"Yes, I..."

He could almost see the wheels spinning inside her head. Did she dare ask him to run two miles back to Woodwind to fetch her a pair of shoes? Theirs was a prickly relationship at best and whatever else Gillian was, she was both self-sufficient and proud. Joya would have blithely issued an order and expected him to hop to it. Gillian wouldn't ask.

And it was too early for him to point out the obvious. Instead Trace slowed his steps to match her halting progress. Ten wincing feet and his amusement started to fade. She stumbled and her hand flew up and he caught it. "Careful there!"

"You should go on," she muttered. "I plan to take my time."

"I'm in no hurry." He placed her hand on his forearm, covered it with his own, pressed insistently on her slender fingers when she would have withdrawn.

She let out an exasperated breath but stopped resisting. After a few more halting steps, she leaned some weight on him.

Her hand on his bare skin...he'd wanted this since

the first day when he'd frisked her, wanted it more after she'd lifted the bar off his chest, then massaged his cramped muscles. He'd thought of little else since he kissed her outside the bookstore. Her thigh brushed his and a flurry of goose bumps stampeded across his skin. *Oh, woman, what you do to me!*

They hobbled along for another twenty yards, Gillian in grim silence, Trace pondering, *Why this woman?* Take her feature by feature and she wasn't extraordinarily beautiful, but take her as a whole— Some inexplicable instinct simply cried, *This one.* Now. No compromise, no substitutes acceptable. *This one.*

Might as well tell the tide to back off.

No, the only way out was straight through. Once he'd possessed her, the desire would surely fade to manageable proportions. He'd be his own man again.

They reached the first tunnel. It was too narrow for a couple to go abreast, so reluctantly he let her precede him. The path was crushed rocks the size of a fist; she took it without a whimper.

How could a woman be so stubborn? His own pride was starting to kick in. Did she think he couldn't carry her? Wouldn't? Or was it something more fundamental—an essential, physical distaste? That would have stopped him cold, but somehow he didn't think that was the problem. As often as his eyes had sought her out these past few days, he'd found her watching him.

They exited the tunnel and Gillian drew a shaky breath. "I think I'll stop here awhile."

"Sure." He stopped beside her, his arm brushing hers.

She rounded on him. "Trace, will you just go *on?* I'm fine. Really."

"But I'd rather limp along with you." He brushed his knuckles down the side of her upturned face, along the corner of her mouth and felt his heart surge as he did so. "We've got all night." *Let's not waste it.*

"Dammit, I—" She sounded halfway to tears, half laughing. "What am I supposed to do, I can't—"

"You can." *I'm yours to command.* "Is there something I can do for you?"

She let out a little growl of frustration. "*Yes!* You could go get me a pair of shoes."

"There's a simpler solution." *Ask me.*

She shook her head fiercely.

Laughing under his breath, he touched her cheek and waited for it. *Come on, give up. Give in. Give yourself to me.*

"C-could I…" She drew a deep breath. "Could I have a ride?"

"Thought you'd never ask!" He swept her up, all long coltish legs and slender arms—she wasn't heavy, not with a bolt of pure male energy shooting through him, swelling his muscles, stiffening his spine. When he straightened, he felt half a foot taller. The night brightened around him, as if the moon had pulsed. Gillian in his arms, a perfect fit! Memory intruded gradually on stunned delight, reminding him that he'd offered to carry her, not simply hold her. He moved out, their bodies rocking warmly together with each stride.

"I…meant ride on your back," she murmured, sounding breathless.

"Oh? Call me old-fashioned, but I've always preferred face-to-face." Her eyes gleamed brighter. By God, she was blushing! He wanted to laugh aloud, whirl her around and around and kiss her senseless. Instead he strode soberly along, half his attention on the path ahead, the other half enthralled by the sunny scent of her hair and skin, the softness of her left breast pressing against his chest, the feel of her heart beating against his. *What a night!*

"Did you follow me?" she asked after a while.

The sane half of him couldn't help responding to the guilt in that question. "Why would I do that?"

"I—" She started to shrug, then froze as her breast moved against him. His arms tightened reflexively and she gasped. "I don't know, but—"

"I couldn't sleep," he said to let her off the hook. "So I came out for a walk. And you?"

"The same. I was sad, and this place...takes that away."

I could take that away. "Why sad, Gillian? He could have dipped his head and kissed her.

"I..." She shook her head, willing to share her feelings, but not her thoughts.

Her left arm was hooked around his neck, her right hand locked onto her left wrist. Gradually she'd relaxed as she realized he wasn't going to drop her. Her hand smoothed across the breadth of his shoulder, almost a caress, then stopped. "What's that?"

You ass! he cursed himself. He'd been so hot to hold her he hadn't thought once of his shoulder harness, the gun tucked under his left armpit. It wasn't pressing against her thigh, not quite, but still. "That? Just my suspenders. The waistband's gone on these sweats. Fiddle with that and they'll probably drop."

"Oh!" She snatched back her hand. It hovered uncertainly, then settled around his neck. Careful to hold her legs out from the gun, he hitched her a little higher. "You're getting tired," she said anxiously.

"Nope." Harder than a rock, but never tired. After another hundred yards, though, he had to admit he needed a break. Trace glanced around, looking for a likely place to sit. Nothing, but they were coming to the teahouse tunnel. Maybe beyond it?

"Kinda spooky, isn't it?" Gillian murmured at his ear.

"It's those dragons," he agreed. "Each time I pass I'd swear they've moved."

"Brr!" She laughed huskily. "I never noticed that. It's the darkness, and what might be hiding in it, I think about."

"Well, you're safe tonight." *Except from me.* He paused at the top of the stone stairs leading down.

"Really, I can walk," she assured him.

"No need." With deliberation he descended, feeling his muscles pump with the effort. Halfway down the stairs, the darkness closed around them entirely. Gillian in his arms in the dark—with no premeditation at all, he sat. "Just a breather," he assured her.

"You can put me down." Her voice had dropped to a whisper, barely louder than the distant echo of waves off stone.

"Can't," he lied. "I've stiffened up." Had he, indeed. "I think it's better if we stay this way." Better? No, the best, with her warm trim bottom resting on his thighs, her heart stampeding against his chest. *Keep talking, Sutton. Distract her.* Considering the way she was distracting him, it was only fair. "What scares you in the dark?"

"*Ohhh...*" She let out a slow breath. "The dog

with eyes as big as saucers…?'' Her statement lilted like a question.

''Yow! If you'd told me about *him*…'' He snuggled her closer against his chest, couldn't help doing it. ''Saucer eyes. Do they glow in the dark?'' He dipped his head, feeling the warmth of her face radiating against his own, her breath on his cheek. *Stop me if you're going to, Gillian. Surely you know what I want.* She had to feel his runaway pulse where her arm encircled his neck. *Say something, if you don't want what I want.*

''I…don't know. I never thought…'' She laughed shakily. ''Probably.''

''Yours do,'' he half whispered. *Lion eyes!*

''Do *not*.''

''They do. I can see them. Here's *one*…'' He dipped his head and kissed her eyebrow. She drew in a feathering breath as he brailled his lips slowly across her forehead, to find her other eyelid, closed now, a warm velvet curve. He brushed his lips through her quivering lashes. ''And here's the other. Like spotlights.'' Shining straight into his heart. She shuddered and his arms tightened. His lips traveled down the side of her smooth cheek, slowly, giving her time to protest, but her arm tightened around his neck, molding them closer.

Go slow, go slow, he warned himself, sensing the resistance in her body even as she sighed. His lips going slow, his heart in overdrive, his body starting to shake with desire. Oh, Gillian! His lips found her mouth—closed, but soft and trembling, not clamped. He traced the tender triangle with the tip of his tongue. *Open, for me, darling.* She moaned deep in her throat, a sound of protest, but it must have been her own actions she was protesting—she opened her mouth and stroked a hand up into his hair.

Groaning with delight, he plunged into her before the invitation could be withdrawn. Honey and sunshine and musk and twining, vibrant strength. He dipped his right shoulder to bring her down; he needed to be over her, in her; he dragged his mouth from hers, spoke her name against her lips, ''Gillian!'' Kissed her chin, her throat, a place beneath her ear till she squirmed and cried out, his tongue lapping greedily at her pulse, urging it higher.

Her hands tightened in his hair. ''Trace...'' There was a note of dazed, drugged pleading in her voice, a woman pulled two directions at once.

But he was of one mind only, and until and unless she told him otherwise... He lipped the side of her neck, lingering at that sensitive corner where the tendons run shallow beneath velvety skin. His teeth closed on her gently—she gasped and convulsed in his arms. He found her mouth again and she shuddered and took him deeper, tongue dancing with tongue in the honeyed darkness, an endless plunging celebration that might have lasted minutes or hours—he was losing all sense of time. Of himself entirely. There was only Gillian, like a golden moon at the center of his consciousness, drawing him down and in and down, a wandering astronaut caught in a field of gravity he was powerless to resist. Wandering no more, homing straight in...

She tore her mouth away and moaned as he traced the delicate rim of her ear with his tongue. ''S-stop...'' she gasped.

''Mmm?'' She could not possibly mean that. He rubbed his face through her fragrant hair.

"We've got to stop," she insisted, but without conviction.

"Who says?" He kissed the tip of her nose. *Don't do this, Gillian!*

She framed his face with both hands and held him off. "Stop!"

"You don't want to stop. I don't want to stop. So we're stopping?"

"Yes." She'd said the word softly but there was no compromise this time.

He sighed and lifted her upright, resettled her bottom against his thighs, stifled a groan. "Mind telling me why?"

She laughed incredulously. *"Trace!"* He could feel her shake her head. "Look..." She rested her hands on his shoulders. "In a word? Lara, that's why."

He swore silently, viciously, then tipped back his head to consult the invisible rocks above. *Let me explain!* Except that he couldn't. He couldn't break cover while there was one chance in a million Gillian was untrustworthy.

And he wouldn't have even if he *was* entirely sure of her. Being undercover meant you lived the part, night and day, till you were done. He'd learned that first as an FBI agent, then relearned it as a bodyguard. People died when you broke that rule.

Which meant he could come to Gillian only as Trace Sutton the faithless gigolo, not Trace Sutton the heart-free bodyguard. He blew out a frustrated breath. "Are you...sure?" And now *he* was torn. He wanted her to have character, but oh, God, couldn't she please have it later?

"Yes." She sighed and rubbed her palms along his shoulders, a frustrated caress. She brought them down his chest, then paused. "What's..." Her right hand settled over the butt of his gun just as he grabbed her wrist. "Ow!"

His move was sheer reflex to stop someone from drawing your own gun against you. He gentled his grip. "I'm sorry." Lifted her wrist to his mouth and kissed it. "Didn't meant to—"

"What the hell is that, Trace?" she insisted, struggling to sit up.

He stood, the best way to stop that. "Just my gun." Leaning slightly against the left wall, he carried her down the last steps to the tunnel floor.

"Your—put me down!"

"It's wet in here and there are probably snails." He kept walking and smiled to himself as her squirming stopped abruptly. Ah, snails. They'd worked to keep the girls in line when he was twelve and they worked still.

"Why are you wearing a gun?"

"The same reason I golf and play squash. Shooting's an ancient and honorable sport of gentlemen." Dammit, he didn't want her thinking of him as a feckless idiot, one of those gentlemen blowhards you met around Newport in their Breton-red yachting slacks. They thought they were at the top of the feeding chain, but take away their polo ponies and their platinum Visa cards and dump them in a jungle with nothing but a pocketknife and see if they walked out again... "I'm a crack shot," he couldn't resist adding quite truthfully.

She snorted. "If you shoot like you golf, Trace? I haven't seen you sink a putt yet."

Hey, I miss on purpose! He bit down on the words, reminding himself that more covers were blown over wounded pride than for any other reason. "I shoot better than I golf."

"Even if you do, what were you planning to shoot on Cliff Walk? Seagulls?"

"A gun's very handy for self-defense," he insisted. "You never know who you might meet out here. Gangs, druggies…"

"Ravening tourists," she said dryly, "or someone walking a vicious toy poodle? I've lived here just four months, Trace, but noise violations from the bars are the only crime I've heard about. This is tame country compared with Texas."

"Even so…" he said peaceably. The worst of his frustration was ebbing with movement, but with the scent of her hair in his nostrils, the supple weight of her in his arms, desire still rolled like a river through him. *Gillian, Gillian, what am I going to do with you?* If she thought she could end what they'd started back there with just a word…

But they'd ended for the night. The night was ending, for that matter. He paused and turned back to look at the moon, gone from silver to saffron as it drowned in the sea. She sighed against him and automatically he tightened his arms.

"Here's where it…happened," she murmured.

He refocused, and realized they were standing at the spot on the path where Lara had been ambushed. His mind stirred uneasily. "How do you know that?"

"Lara told me."

"Ah." He probed her face, homed in on her pupils, which were nicely expanded with darkness—and desire, he hoped. "About her…falling?" he asked, and watched. Then drew a breath of relief. They hadn't contracted as he pronounced the lie. Or maybe sexual arousal canceled out that response. Reading pupils was an art, not a science.

"Mmm," she agreed, sounding sleepy.

He wanted most urgently to kiss her. Walked on, instead. His arms were starting to ache along with the rest of him, but it wasn't far to the gate.

One last argument when they reached it. She wanted to be set down. He insisted, quite truthfully, that the ground had to be littered with rose branches. She managed to pull her key out of her running shorts and unlocked the gate while he held her.

He shoved it shut behind them with his hip, then leaned back against the wood, fresh out of excuses. He could think of no good reason Gillian shouldn't walk across Woodwind's velvety lawn on her own, though he'd rather have carried her to her door.

Rather have carried her on up the stairs, to the big bed in her bedroom.

Soon, he promised himself. Somehow.

"Thanks for the ride," Gillian said gravely.

"My pleasure." A painful pleasure, but then most of the best ones were, one way or another. He set her gently on her feet, then steadied her when she wobbled. His hands tightened on her arms and he swayed her against him. His hands slipped to her waist and yes, he nearly could span her.

"Trace—" she said on a note of alarm.

Yes, but he couldn't help himself. He kissed her on one cheek, then the other, then rested his brow against hers. "Good night, Gillian. Or I suppose it's good morning." He could imagine starting a lot of mornings like this one.

She shivered in his grasp and stepped backward. "Good night." She turned it into a mournful farewell.

No need, darling. It's not for long. Still, it took a conscious effort to straighten his fingers and release her. To stand there watching her go across the dewy grass without a backward glance. His heart skipped a beat as her stride broke for an instant—she was having second thoughts?—then gradually resumed its rhythm as Gillian squared her shoulders and walked on.

No matter. He had second thoughts enough for both of them. *Later,* he promised himself, promised her. She vanished beyond the corner of Woodwind, headed for the carriage house. He let out a sigh and turned his attention to the rest of the world.

Up on Lara's balcony, a curtain swayed. He'd shut and locked that door behind him—hadn't he?

CHAPTER SIXTEEN

GILLIAN SAT IN HER OFFICE, elbows braced on her desk, her aching head propped on her hands, her thumbs pressing the soft hollows below her brow bones till purple spots filled her inner vision. Lara had seen them this morning! She was all but certain.

Feeling Trace's eyes upon her like a physical caress, she'd focused her attention behind her when a movement ahead, up on Lara's balcony, had broken his spell. Her eyes had refocused on a form drawing back through the sheer curtains. Lara. No one else would be standing there.

And if she stood there, then she must have seen us. Seen Trace kissing me. Seen me, hardly resisting that kiss.

She grimaced and pressed harder against her brow bones, as if to gouge out that image. *We were standing very still, up against the wall. The sun hadn't yet risen.* Maybe Lara had overlooked them, had been looking, instead, far out to sea.

Dream on!

How *could* she have let Trace kiss her?

Could I have stopped him? she asked herself wryly.

But she couldn't weasel out of her guilt by blaming Trace, though his passion had carried her along like a surfer on the crest of a tidal wave. Still, in spite of his desire, he'd made it clear that she held the final word, that he'd stop if she insisted. He *had* stopped, once she'd found the will to stop him.

Lara, I never, never meant to hurt you. Yes, she'd come in anger to Woodwind, still aching from that letter of rejection, righteously intent on stealing her own history despite that repudiation. But stealing her own life story was one thing, stealing her mother's lover something else entirely.

So now it's over. Just as she and Lara were coming to know each other, to even like each other, just as she was laying her hands on the first few pieces of the jigsaw puzzle that was their shared history. Yet there was so much still to learn—why Lara hated Mustangs, when by all rights she should love them; if the young man in the uniform was Gillian's own father; why Lara had let her go… *You stupid, greedy little fool, trading Trace's kisses for all that!*

She ran the tip of her tongue over lips still swollen and bruised from those kisses. She could say goodbye to Trace, too, when Lara fired her. Tears stung at the back of her eyes. *It's all over.* No doubt Lara would be phoning her any minute now from her suite—she couldn't imagine Lara would fire her in person.

Or maybe she'd send Trace to tell her to pack her bags. Showing both of them at once who held the real power at Woodwind. She made a little sound of anguish deep in her throat. Better to quit this minute than wait for—

"Now that's what I call a righteous hangover." Two hands descended on her shoulders, began massaging her tension-taut muscles.

She glanced up to find Toby's face overhead, grinning down at her.

"And here Joya and I thought you were a straight

arrow, Gillie.'' His thumbs found her spine, dug into the muscles on either side, traced small circles up toward her nape. ''Where do you go when you party?''

She shrugged, but he didn't take the hint. Clever and insistent, too intimate, his hands rode the movement. Her body was craving a touch, but not this one. ''Cut it out, Toby. This isn't a hangover.'' Or maybe that's precisely what it was—a moral one. Whatever, he wasn't helping. She caught his wrists and tried to lift his hands from her shoulders, but he resisted with surprising strength.

At least his fingers stopped moving. ''If it isn't a hangover, then you're wasting the Newport experience. You should come out and let me show you the town. It doesn't start rocking till midnight.''

Gillian sighed, clamping down on her irritation. *What is this?* He and his sister had shown no inclination to seek out her friendship. So why now, just as she was leaving? She remembered for the first time in hours—her mutilated book. Could this invitation be connected to that? Toby's way of an apology? He and Joya were practically joined at the hip. If Joya had opened her present, Toby would have found out, sooner rather than later. And now this?

''What about it?'' His fingers rotated again. ''Say tonight?''

''Thanks, but I'm not much of a drinker. And I have a class to teach tonight,'' she added as she remembered it.

''Then tomorrow night,'' he said, turning the question into a statement.

''Maybe.'' By tomorrow she'd be gone. She twitched her shoulders, but again he ignored the hint.

"Gillian?"

She looked up to find Trace filling the doorway—as Toby's fingers moved seductively on her shoulders. "Yes?" Trace's eyes dropped from Toby's face to her own, and his dark eyebrows lifted. She felt her face pinken. Only hours ago, it had been Trace touching her. She wanted to smack Toby's hands aside, but if she humiliated him in front of the older man, she knew instinctively he'd never forgive her.

"Lara wants you in her suite, at your convenience."

Here it came. "Right away," she said evenly, then winced as Toby gave her back a hearty clap—his finishing benediction.

"When the boss says frog, we all jump," he said cheerfully. "Right, Trace?"

She'd never noticed how hard he could look when the mood hit him. As if he could have thrown Toby through her closed bay window and not bothered to watch him hit ground. She blinked and the expression was gone, or maybe she'd imagined it.

"Right you are," he said amiably, then turned and went.

SHE FOUND HIM WAITING for her outside Lara's door a few minutes later. They studied each other in silence. She couldn't read his mood at all, but it didn't seem much cheerier than hers. Perhaps he'd been enduring tears and tantrums all morning. Because somewhere within Lara was the woman who'd written that savage note to her own daughter nine months ago. Maybe Gillian was about to meet that side of her mother at last.

"She's still in bed," he said, unlocking the door

for her, then inclining his head when she hesitated. "Go on."

He didn't follow. The door closed softly behind her; the bolt turned. Locking her in with Lara. She wouldn't be able to retreat with dignity, if need be. Cautiously she moved into the room. "Lara?"

Lara lay in the center of the king-size bed, propped up on a heap of pillows, one arm hooked around something small and orange. Her stuffed tiger. She gave Gillian a wan smile. "Hi."

She looked about twelve, except for the purple shadows under her silvery eyes, the hollows that had deepened under her high cheekbones. Gillian's fear turned to dismay. She thought *she'd* looked bad, when she studied her face in the mirror this morning, after a night out on the cliffs. But Lara! *I did this to her. Trace and I...* "H-hi yourself."

"I know, I know," Lara said ruefully, answering her expression rather than her greeting. "I look like something the cat dragged in." She pulled Tigger onto the comforter over her stomach and clasped her hands on him. "It wasn't much of a night for sleeping." She patted the edge of the bed. "Sit down."

Reluctantly Gillian sat. Lara must have lain awake all night, wondering where Trace was and with whom. *And I didn't think of her once.* "I'm sorry." *So sorry.*

Lara shrugged slim shoulders. She was dressed in pajamas, with her silver locket dangling around her neck. "Happens. Sometimes I get...bummed. I guess today's going to be one of those days. Tigger and I just pull the pillows over our heads till it passes."

"Anything I can do?" If Lara had trusted Trace—however naively—and Gillian had shattered that trust,

it was irreparable. There'd be no way she could take
back the harm she'd done. She swallowed around a
lump in her throat. Unable to hold Lara's level gaze,
she glanced around, noticed the scrapbook near the
foot of the bed, reached for it with relief.

"Thanks, but no. I just have to wade through it. I
think I'll give a pass on my tai chi lesson, if you don't
mind. Maybe tomorrow?"

Gillian had forgotten—they'd scheduled the first
session for noon today. "Oh, of course, that's fine."
Her hands smoothed restlessly over the cover of the
scrapbook. This was the first one they'd filled, containing Lara's earliest pictures. "May I?" she murmured at last.

"Wouldn't exist but for you." Lara hooked a finger
under its cover and flipped it open.

Gillian sat, staring hungrily down at the photo of
the young soldier. *My father, perhaps?* And most
surely Lara's first love. *And now I've ruined her latest—maybe her first love since her husband died.
How could I?* A wave of self-loathing washed through
her and she shut the album abruptly. "I think I should
quit." Lara was too nice to fire her, she saw now.
But how could Lara ever feel at ease, ever hope to
repair whatever kind of relationship she had with
Trace, if she feared that her personal assistant and her
lover were meeting in dark corners? *She's been nothing but kind to me. I owe her this much.*

"What?" Lara cried. "But why?"

Gillian drew a nervous breath. *Don't make me say
it.* It was better for all of them if they pretended it
never had happened. If Lara simply accepted her resignation as the apology it was intended to be and let
her slink off. Her eyes filled with tears as she pictured

it. She'd lose everything she wanted if she left Wood-wind. But if she hurt Lara by staying...

"*Why?*" Lara demanded. "Have I been working you too hard or I'm not paying enough or—"

"No!" Gillian laughed shakily. "I just..." She'd spoken on impulse and she had no arguments at hand, aside from the truth she couldn't speak. "I just think maybe I...should go." It got harder each time she pictured it. She'd be throwing away her last chance at family if she turned her back on Lara. Chris, much as she loved him, was a brother in absentia. "Don't you think?" she added weakly. *Help me out here. I'm trying to be brave for you. Don't make it harder.*

"No!" Lara shook her head vigorously. "I don't!"

"Oh..." Gillian swiped at a tear rolling down her nose. "I thought maybe..."

"It's Trace, isn't it?" Lara demanded. "Is he...pressuring you?" She tugged a hand through her silvery hair, leaving it standing in soft spikes, which made her look like an exotic, indignant bird. "I would have sworn he was a gentleman, but..." She shook her head disgustedly. "Is that it?"

"*Ahhhh...*" Gillian found her mouth hanging open and shut it. "Um..."

"Because believe me, he'll back off if I tell him to—that or he's fired," Lara declared imperiously, sounding for the first time since Gillian had met her like the star of the soap opera. "I won't tolerate a molester!"

"He didn't molest me," Gillian said faintly, still scrabbling for some sort of reality under her feet. "Not at all."

"I didn't think so. I didn't mean to spy," Lara added hastily. "I was out on the balcony, since I couldn't sleep, and suddenly there you two were. You appeared to be enjoying yourself, I thought, but if I was mis—''

"Fired?" Gillian repeated. Trace seemed to be a man of no visible means—she'd assumed he was a gigolo. But was that considered employment by the parties involved?

Lara clapped a hand over her mouth. "Oops," she said from behind her fingers.

Gillian cocked a head at her, then an eyebrow. And waited.

"Look..." Lara said after a moment. She gazed at her stuffed toy, scooped him up, brought him nose to nose with herself. "Would it...change anything about your leaving if I told you Trace and I were just...friends?" she asked, apparently addressing the tiger.

Gillian's eyes dropped helplessly to the enormous bed. *Friends who sleep together?* No, that didn't make her feel better. Casual sex was fine for those who wanted it. As for her... Maybe she needed to leave Woodwind for her own sake, not Lara's.

"Platonic friends," Lara enunciated with precision. "Not even kissing cousins. Tigger and I get the bed— Trace sleeps on that couch." She gestured across the room.

"Oh," Gillian said blankly. A sun was rising somewhere inside her, along with an almost irresistible sense of the absurd. "D-d-do you mind my asking why?"

"Yes." They stared at each other, Gillian with utter mystification, Lara with embarrassed defiance, then all of a sudden it was too funny for words—they burst out laughing.

DEAREST LARA-MOMMY,
If they electrocute fifteen-year-old murderers
And you as good as murdered me
What do you think you deserve?
What do you think you'll GET?
A BIG shock!!!!!!!!!HAHAHA. Ha.
See you Soooooooooooooooooooooooon,
your (and you better not try to deny it) Sarah
XXX

Feet on his desk, Trace sat tipped back in his chair, holding a copy of Sarah XXX's latest filth in his lap. He'd discovered the original this morning when he collected the mail, and bad as the message was, its manner of delivery was worse. The letter had been hand-delivered rather than mailed. He'd found it taped to the estate's mailbox, for which only the postman and the occupants of Woodwind had keys. No Boston postmark on the envelope this time. No postmark at all. Sarah XXX had walked right up to the gates sometime between sundown last night, when he'd last driven through with Lara and Gillian, and this morning at eleven, when he'd gone for the mail.

Actually he could narrow that gap. The mailman delivered at roughly ten. He was, thanks to Trace's instructions, already on the lookout for questionable packages, as was the main post office. If he'd noticed an envelope taped to the outside of the box, no doubt he'd have called up to the house.

So she strolled up bold as brass between ten and eleven this morning and taped it in place. He could picture a faceless hag, all elf locks and frumpy clothes, fixing her hate-filled message in place, then standing for a moment, grasping the gate with nail-bitten hands and peering through the bars. Eyes bloodshot and wide-open, showing whites all around.

A chill skated down his spine and he shivered— the chair creaked ominously. He brought his feet down from the desk. *Sure, if Sarah XXX is your typical stalker, she'll look something like that.*

But if she's really a mask for an insider, as he'd begun to wonder after the bee attack? *Where was Toby at ten-thirty this morning? Or Joya? Or Harriet the Glum?* Or the maid or housekeeper, for that matter?

Or Gillian. He found himself shaking his head even as he thought it. No, absolutely not. Not Gillian. There wasn't a mean bone in her delectable body. He stared into space for a moment, lips crooked into the faintest of faraway smiles, then gave himself a mental kick in the pants.

If his FBI instructors could see him now, ruling out a female suspect because his gut told him she was innocent! Instincts might serve a man well when the quarry was male, but once you threw sex into the equation, then feelings were automatically suspect. *Give us the facts to clear her, and nothing but the facts,* they'd insist.

The fact was, Gillian had had the same opportunity every other one of his inside suspects had for delivering this message undetected. Because between ten and eleven this morning, he'd been napping here at his desk with a goofy smile on his face.

Yet another reason not to mix romance with duty. A man had only so much energy and he shouldn't divide it. Stifling a yawn, he realized he was bone-tired and glanced at his watch. Nine o'clock. A long

day, considering he'd barely slept the night before.
And not a happy one since dawn.

He'd returned to find Lara in a dismal mood. She'd
clearly not slept well, and had stayed in bed all day,
silent and withdrawn. Gillian had succeeded in cheer-
ing her around noon, but she'd relapsed to near tears
within the hour. He'd tried the direct approach—asking her why she was sad—and received sighs and
shrugs and damn-all else. Woman problems, he'd finally concluded, though she'd never showed this kind
of moodiness before.

Reminding himself that he was her bodyguard, not
her therapist, he'd left her to it and devoted his day
to Sarah XXX's letter. First he'd arranged for Jeremy
Benton to meet him down at the gates and pick up
the original, which was now being fingerprinted—
with the usual fruitless results, no doubt. Any doofus
who watched TV knew you had to wear gloves to
write a poison-pen letter.

He'd tried to discreetly check on the whereabouts
of all his insiders between ten and eleven this morning, and now knew any—or *every*—one of 'em had
the opportunity to post that message. Toby and Joya
had returned from brunch during that time period.
Gillian, Harriet and the household staff had all been
on the grounds. Any one of them could have strolled
down to the gates, then reached through to put the
message in place. All it would take was masking tape
and nerve.

Headlights swept across the wall above his desk.
He rose and went to the window. Gillian in her little
Toyota, returning from her weight-lifting class. Leaning out over the windowsill, he smiled, imagining her
in her gym shorts, her skimpy tank top, a stern and

serious expression in those big golden eyes as she lectured her women lifters. He'd like to be a fly on that wall, or watch her lead an aerobics class. She'd bounce in all the right places.

He heard her quick steps across the gravel, then the sound of the door opening and closing. Mentally he followed her up. *I could drop in, say hello. If she invited me in…?*

Down, boy. She had to be whipped after last night, then her class tonight. Besides, she'd told him to go chase himself. Or at least, Lara.

It would be a pleasure dissuading her of that notion one of these days. *First, all you have to do is catch Sarah XXX,* he reminded himself. Frowning, he picked up the letter again.

If they electrocute fifteen-year-old murderers…

Why fifteen years old? Just a random choice? Or maybe Sarah had read something in a newspaper or heard some news on radio or TV? Had there been anything about a fifteen-year-old, anyplace in the country, going to the electric chair? He'd ask Emily to do an Internet search, keying in the appropriate words. Maybe that would give him some clue.

Better yet, he'd skim yesterday's *Newport Daily News* for such a headline. Sarah XXX could have sat down at the Waves, sipping coffee and reading the paper, while she composed her letter.

And you as good as murdered me…

How did Lara nearly murder you, Sarah? Is it all in your poor twisted mind? Or is there the tiniest nugget of truth, no matter how distorted, that would point the way to you, if I could only pan it out of this dross?

He'd have to show Lara this message. Trace scowled and shifted in his chair. All his instincts told him to shelter his client from pain and fear, but if she could help him in any way... Dammit, showing her this note—now that would cure her blues!

For all their sakes, he had to crack this case soon.

Soooooooooooooooooooooooooon, Sarah kept promising. She was coming closer and closer, knocking at their gates now. He had to catch her soon. Before her next attempt.

She's clever. Too damned clever. A sick but first-rate mind, an odd combination.

Cleverer than me? He clenched his teeth. *No way!*

But then, she didn't have to be, when she held all the aces. The assassin got to choose the time, the place, the method. He had to defend against all possible variables, couldn't miss a trick. Ran himself ragged, trying to cover all conceivable possibilities, while Sarah XXX had only to focus on her one attempt.

He needed reinforcements. A backup. Another pair of eyes. Given two BGs, one could scout the town while the other guarded Lara.

But all four Brickhouse agents were out on assignment. And Lara had chosen Gillian over the subcontractor he'd had in mind. By now he wasn't unhappy with her choice—far from it—but still...

He was going around and around here. Time to give it a break. He glanced at his watch. Eleven, and Lara still hadn't sent him her good-night buzz from her locket, which was his normal all-clear to enter her suite.

She fell asleep, he told himself. Barring a trip or two to the bathroom, she hadn't left her bed all day. Not good. The client's morale was crucial. He needed her alert, ready to fight or flee if need be, with an unambiguous desire to survive. If she didn't perk up tomorrow, he'd drag the reason out of her. He didn't like secrets on the job.

Standing at the door to her suite, he glanced right toward the elevator, left toward the stairs and the corridor beyond that led to the other bedrooms. All quiet. Unlocking the door, he entered.

The bedside lamp showed him the tumbled bed-clothes, an open picture album lying on top of the comforter, her toy tiger glaring at him with glassy eyes.

"Lara?" He stood listening, dread curling in his stomach, all his instincts crying that there was no one here to answer.

CHAPTER SEVENTEEN

SOME TEN MINUTES LATER, he found her in the kitchen. Ten minutes that had probably sheared ten months off his life. Trace leaned panting in the doorway, too angry even to consider speaking, sick to his stomach with the aftereffects of his own adrenaline. Reaching inside the windbreaker he'd thrown on, he resettled his 9 mm in its holster under his armpit, then zipped the jacket. *What the hell, Lara?*

Oblivious to his presence at the end of the room, she leaned over the big kitchen table, her hand moving from a small box to whatever object was blocked from view by her body. She worked with the fierce concentration and painstaking movements of someone compensating for a drink or two. A bottle of wine sat half empty across the table. The kitchen smelled of chocolate. Baker's chocolate, he reminded himself. *We bought it at the market yesterday.*

She reached for another oblong box, fumbled, gave a soft exclamation of disgust, then came the *scritch* of a match lighting—a tiny flame underlit her face. The flame vanished beyond her body, but a warm glow pushed back the darkness, edging her in wavering gold. *She's lighting candles.* The smell stirred old memories of his own mother working in the kitchen. His younger brother, Jon, had always demanded a chocolate cake for his birthday.

Lara dropped the spent match on the table, then sat, contemplating her flickering shrine. "Happy birthday to you... Happy b-birthday to you..." She sang in a tiny, breathless, barely audible soprano. A tender secret song blurred by tears.

Trace swallowed around a lump in his throat. *Who do you sing for, Lara? Richard? Is today your dead husband's birthday?* That would explain today's inconsolable sorrow.

"Happy birthday, dear S-S-S-Sarah..."

God! It was what you didn't know that would get you in the end. Trace started grimly across the kitchen.

"Happy..." The song quavered away into the gulping beginnings of a sob. Her head dropped into her hands.

Pulling out a chair, Trace sat beside her. He rested a hand on her shuddering shoulder.

She jumped violently and turned to look at him. "Oh..."

Staring down at the birthday cake with its half-burned candles, he patted her absently. *Talk to me, Lara.*

She swallowed audibly and turned back to the cake. Silently they watched as the pink candles wept wax, drooped, then puddled. The flames flickered, then died, one by one. *Who should have been here to blow them out, Lara?* He counted the blackened wicks. Twenty-eight candles. "Tell me," he said finally, voice low and uninflected.

"I n-never have..." she said in a wondering monotone. "Nobody, except Richard..."

But now I need to know. "Sarah," he said uninsistently. "Who is she, Lara?" Or should he have said *was?*

She drew a breath that would have sucked the air out of the candles if they hadn't burned out already. "S-Sarah was...*is*...my baby. Sarah Cloud Bailey."

She's twenty-eight today. But Lara was only forty-three!

"Her father was my true love, William McCloud." She smiled, tears trickling. "His friends called him 'Cloudy.'" She knuckled her lashes, but more tears fell. "He came home on leave after basic training. We went to a New Year's party and then—" Her wistful smile glowed like a thousand candles. "I loved him so, and he was bound for Vietnam..."

Trace sat, aching for her as she built the story word by halting word. Two months later she'd learned she was pregnant. They'd been exchanging love letters all that time, but this was the test of their love. And McCloud hadn't flinched. He sent her one last letter, in which he pledged his devotion, promised her that he'd be home as soon as he could arrange leave with his commanding officer to marry her, that he couldn't be prouder or happier. Two weeks later his family received notice of his death in some futile, nameless skirmish in the jungle.

"What happened then?" She would have been maybe fourteen, living with foster parents by then, she'd told him once. No, she was fifteen! he realized, a chill raising the hair on his arms. *You're the fifteen-year-old murderer, Lara? But how does Sarah XXX know?*

"It...it took me years to piece it all together." Lara stood, picked up the cake plate and tipped her head toward the kitchen door. "Come with me?"

Trace followed, punching the code that disarmed the burglar alarm, then preceding her out the door. Bearing the cake before her, she headed for the seaside of the estate. Trace unzipped his windbreaker as he scanned the moonlit lawn. All clear.

"My foster father began to have money..." Lara said as they walked. Carter, a drunken, brutal layabout who lived off the child-support payments his downtrodden wife earned by keeping foster children. Suddenly Carter had enough money to buy an enormous color TV set. To drink in bars, rather than swill moonshine on their swaybacked front porch. Enough money even to take Lara to a doctor several times in her pregnancy. "He was always yelling at me not to lift things or run. I couldn't understand it—he called me 'little slut' every chance he got, yet he was so considerate." She laughed bitterly.

Twenty-eight years ago, Trace calculated coldly. The bastard was probably beyond his reach, gone on to his well-deserved reward, which was a pity.

"The last week, before my...baby came, he drove home in a red Mustang car. Claimed he'd won it gambling, but, oh, he smirked at me when he said that."

He sold your baby, Trace realized, and found his fingers caressing the butt of his gun. You heard the rumors from time to time of baby brokers, lawyers usually, who sought out young, presentable pregnant girls through ads in newspapers. Who arranged the sale of their babies to the highest bidder. Private placements were legal, and the adoptive parents could legally pay the girl's prenatal expenses. If those expenses were outrageously inflated and the lion's share of the money vanished into the pockets of the lawyer

and whoever delivered the girl to the lawyer, who was
to know or care?

They'd reached the gate onto Cliff Walk. Trace unlocked it, checked outside for any lurkers, then escorted Lara south along the path, his heart as sad-
dened tonight as it had been shouting with joy the
night before, though the moon was as brilliant as ever.

The birth hadn't been easy. Lara was tiny and the
contractions started too soon. The baby hadn't turned.
Carter had been in a drunken lather, frantically cursing her, ordering her to wait till they reached the hospital. She traveled the whole nightmarish way lying
down in the back of his car, then had been rushed
into Emergency and up to a private room. She'd been
delivered of her baby by cesarean, one minute before
midnight on the eleventh, as her stepmother told her
later.

"God, Lara." Fifteen, with nobody in the world on
her side. They reached the place where someone had
pushed her. Trace moved between her and the cliff
edge, though that put her on his right, in the way of
his gun hand. Once they were safely past, he reversed
positions.

She'd had two days to adore her baby. Two days
to nurse her, cuddle her, sing to her, tell her that her
name was Sarah Cloud. To tell her all about her brave
father. "She had blue-gray eyes just like Cloudy, and
she was the sweetest child. Not a cry or a whimper."
To tell Sarah of the wonderful life Lara was determined to make for her. Someway. Somehow.

But you were only a baby yourself.

On the third day her foster father had arrived along
with the breakfast tray. He'd made her take medicine
from a bottle, spooning it down her in spite of her

weak protests, insisting that the nurse had told him to give it to her. She'd begun to feel funny almost immediately, then had fallen asleep.

In her weakened, postoperative condition, any kind of codeine-based cough syrup would have done the trick, Trace figured.

"When I woke up—" her voice wavered "—there was a strange man in the room with my foster father. Very official-looking, white jacket, clipboard, stern and brisk." Carter stood with his back to the door—guarding it, she realized years later.

The stranger had presented her with a form on the clipboard and told her to sign it—so the health insurance would pay for her operation, he explained.

Lara had drifted to a halt, hugging the cake plate to her stomach. "I was so stupid, stupid, stupid, so *stupid!* I tried to read it, Trace, but he was leaning over me, breathing garlic on my face, telling me to hurry up—it was just a simple formality—talking and talking and talking at me. I couldn't concentrate, was sick to my stomach..."

Drugged...tranquilized. Trace clenched his hands to fists.

"So I signed it and he went away." Slowly she started walking again. "I...I slept most of the day." A doctor came to examine her in the afternoon and told her what a brave girl she was, what a good decision she'd made. She hadn't known what he was talking about, was too shy to ask.

Then a nurse arrived with a wheelchair and helped her into it, telling her she was going home. When Lara asked where her baby was, the nurse clucked, patted her shoulder and told her she'd have to ask

"Doctor." In the corridor, she'd handed the wheel-chair over to Carter.

Who assured Lara that his wife was collecting Sarah from the nursery. That she'd bring the baby to the car, meet them there. "We got to the car..." Lara said in a flat little voice. "I was hurting from my stitches, sitting up. He put me in the back seat, gave me some more medicine—for the pain, he said. I asked where Sarah was, and he told me to be patient, that it took a long time to check a baby out of a hospital. I f-f-fell asleep, Trace. So stupid, stupid, *worthless* and stupid! If I hadn't fallen asleep..."

"It would have ended the same, Lara." What chance did a kid have, when the adults who should be protecting her betrayed her, instead? Betrayed her profoundly, ruthlessly, with such single-minded greed?

"No!" She shook her head fiercely. "No, I could have done *something*. B-but when I woke up, we were speeding along, my foster mother driving, Carter sitting with me in the back seat. I asked where my baby was and he said she was in the front seat, to shut up, I'd wake her. I tried to sit up, and he kept shoving me down. I finally realized—somehow I knew—Sarah wasn't there. I started screaming, trying to sit up." She'd struggled till she fainted. When she awoke, she was home in her own bed.

She stopped. They'd come to a spot where the path dipped within twenty feet of sea level with a rough path leading down to the water below. She turned and started down it.

"Let me carry the cake, Lara."

"No. I do this every year."

Teeth clenched, he followed at her heels, prepared

to grab if her feet slipped from under her, but she made it safely to sea level.

Where a series of flat boulders led out into the sea—an eroded dike of slate, a giant's stepping stones to nowhere. Lara leaped lightly from the shore to the first boulder. He shouldn't let her do this, didn't dare to stop her. Trace leaped after her. Luckily the sea was glassy calm.

Balancing along the mossy ledges, leaping from stone to stone, they made it to the end of the dike. The ocean heaved and sighed at their feet. Lara put the plate down on the rock, stood staring out to sea. They'd kept her locked in her room for a week, she told him without emotion. During that time, Carter told her she'd signed papers that gave up her baby to the state. That the state knew she was too young to keep a baby, too wicked to deserve one, so they'd find Sarah a good home.

As soon as her stitches allowed it, she'd climbed down the tree outside her bedroom window, had hitched into town to the hospital. "But…" She shook her head helplessly. "It took me all day to hitch and walk there, some thirty miles, since we lived up in the mountains. B-but when I got to the hospital, it didn't look quite the way I remembered it. And when I demanded my baby, demanded to know where my baby was, they said they had no record of me or Sarah. That we hadn't been patients there. I insisted we *had*, they told me to get lost and I…" She drew a breath. "I started smashing windows. Smashing and smashing and *smashing* every piece of glass I could reach, till they called the security guards." Who'd turned her over to the police, who eventually remanded her to her foster father.

For a few more months she tried to find Sarah. But she never was able to locate the hospital where she'd delivered her baby—there were three towns within driving distance of Carter's house, each with its own hospital. Carter might have even driven her over the state line into Virginia or Pennsylvania, for all she knew. The more she wandered through emergency rooms, the more her original pain-blurred memories merged with the new places. The insides of hospitals looked much alike, and she'd been in no state to notice the architecture of the building, either coming or going. And she began to think that all the doctors and administrators were lying to her. "They could see I didn't deserve a baby. They weren't going to tell me where Sarah was, even if they knew."

At last she'd despaired. She'd been a little goody-goody before she became pregnant, trying to please her foster parents, working hard at school. Afterward, she ran with the wild crowd. She'd lost Cloudy's baby—stupidly signed the papers that let the state take her away. "Sarah was the last of Cloudy, his last chance to live on, have a daughter who'd speak his name, hang his picture on her wall, tell her own children someday about their brave grandfather..." Lara stood, tears streaming. "I let Cloudy down, so I deserved nothing. Was worth nothing. Which meant that any boy who wanted me could have me, I didn't care."

"Oh, Lara..."

"Yeah, I know." She wiped her nose. "But that was how I felt. Nothing mattered. I was numb." Until one night when she was seventeen. Carter, drunk as usual, had slapped his wife around—no novelty there—then had roared off in the Mustang, not so shiny or new now, to drink in town. Half-drunk herself, bitter and humiliated, Mrs. Carter told Lara the truth at last, while Lara washed the blood from her face. That her worthless husband had sold Lara's baby—the Mustang was his final payment.

"After she fell asleep I sat and thought for a while," Lara murmured. "I knew I'd never be able to make Carter tell me where my baby was. He was as stubborn as he was mean. And I knew if I stayed there I'd kill him, that if I did, then I'd go to prison and never find Sarah." Her hope of recovering her child hadn't quite died after all, she realized that night. So she'd packed her clothes in an old backpack. She'd stolen Mrs. Carter's pitiful stash of money, which she kept hidden from Carter in a can in the freezer—Lara hadn't forgotten that no matter how unwillingly, Mrs. Carter had conspired with her husband to sell Sarah.

She'd waited until Carter returned home and staggered into the house. Fell asleep on the couch in the living room. Then she'd slipped out the kitchen door, stopping only to fill the Mustang's gas tank with a five-pound bag of sugar. "I didn't want him to ever have another minute's pleasure in selling my baby." And then she had walked off into the night.

She stooped to the cake, rearranged it on the last ledge above the sea, where it was invisible from land. "The seagulls will eat it in the morning," she told him. "Maybe they'll fly off to Sarah, tell her I'm still searching."

She'd run off to New York City, she told him as they made their way back to shore. Some ridiculous notion she'd had that she might be a model. Instead she'd found a job waitressing, then working for a caterer—who catered for a soap opera production company, where she'd met Richard Corday, the lead writer. "If he didn't save my life, he saved my soul," she said as Trace helped her up the rocks to the main path.

"And he wrote *Searching for Sarah*," Trace prompted her.

"Yes." After their marriage, Richard helped her search. But twelve years had passed since Sarah's birth; the trail was obliterated. Carter had drunk himself to death, and his wife had moved away. Lara and Richard never succeeded in finding her. Two of the three nearby hospitals had merged, reorganized, then closed their doors forever. If they had ever possessed records of Lara's admission and Sarah's birth, they had lost or destroyed them. The state of West Virginia steadfastly maintained it had never taken custody of a child named Sarah Cloud Bailey. "We finally realized that most of what Carter had told me was a lie. That I'd never know how much of it, or what part of it, was lies, and what truth. In all likelihood, Sarah had been purchased on the black market, perhaps by someone who'd lost a child, who'd then given her that child's identity. That if she'd never been adopted legally through the courts, then there was no record anywhere that would allow us to trace her.

"I signed up with the matching registries anyway. You give them your baby's date of birth, the state where she was born and the town if you know it. If your child ever…wants to find you and enters the same information with the registry, then they contact you."

Wants to find you. The words echoed between them as they walked. "And the soap opera, *Searching for*

Sarah, was that just Corday using life to make art?''
As he'd done with Lara's bee sting allergy.

Lara shook her head. ''That was Richard's gift to
me. His idea of a way to reach Sarah. Like a nation-
wide Help Wanted ad, he always said. Wanted—one
daughter named Sarah, lost from birth, missed and
loved always by a mother named Lara. He changed
some of the facts—he didn't have complete artistic
control and the coproducer wanted my character to be
a doctor. But enough of the real story remained that
we hoped…thought maybe someday…''

That an adoptee name Sarah Cloud would come
knocking. A thousand-to-one shot, but if that was the
only hope you had… Except that the premise would
appeal just as strongly to any neurotic with delusions
of grandeur. If you can't be the reincarnation of Po-
cahontas, why not discover you're the long-lost
daughter of a prime-time celebrity?

They reached the spot again where Lara had fallen,
and automatically Trace glanced over his shoulder,
then scanned the bushes. Nobody. The one good thing
about this expedition was that it was a complete break
from their routine. It was hard to set up an inpromptu
killing, harder still to do it safely. ''So have you had
any applicants for the position over the years?'' Besides Sarah XXX.

''About one a year,'' Lara said, then laughed painfully when he swore. ''Come on, Trace, we discussed
that the first time I showed you Sarah XXX's letters.''

''Yes, but you didn't tell me… Was there any
chance that any of those applicants was the real one?''
Sarah Cloud, a pretty name. He pictured her with
Lara's platinum-blond hair, like a cumulous cloud,
and gray-blue eyes, five-two or -three like her mother.

"No." They'd reached the gate and he unlocked it for her, checked the far side, then ushered her through. "No, they were always too old, or too young, or born somewhere out west, or they had brown eyes or...no."

"And Sarah XXX?" He stopped, staring up at the unlit bulk of Woodwind. A long way from a loveless shack in the West Virginia mountains.

"I don't know, Trace. You've seen all her letters. She deals in emotions, not facts."

Red-hot emotions, resentment forging itself to a brighter and sharper point with each letter.

"She never gave me any address so that I could respond to her. Try to calm her down. Ask her questions that would help me to know."

"But you think there might be a chance." *God help you if that's so, Lara. You don't need a child like that.*

"I..." Lara shook her head, and kept on shaking it slowly. "The child I imagined all these years? Cloudy's daughter? He was the most sensitive, the kindest... To think that his daughter could cut the leg off a rabbit and mail me the bloody stump..." Her arms flew around herself and she shuddered. "But, Trace, I don't know what happened to my baby. Who got her, what they did to her...who she became..." Her head drooped till she stared at the ground. "What...she thinks of me. Maybe she *hates* me for giving her away. For not being there for her. I hate myself. Why shouldn't she? God knows why she thinks I did it..."

So this was the ambivalence he'd sensed at Lara's core, the resignation in the face of danger rather than vigorous indignation. *Half of her wants to meet Sarah*

XXX, however warped she may be...half of her thinks that if Sarah XXX is the damaged remains of her beautiful baby, then she deserves whatever punishment her child decides to mete out. God, we're in trouble here.

CHAPTER EIGHTEEN

YESTERDAY AFTERNOON, after she'd left Lara, Gillian had spent the day dancing on clouds. Trace wasn't Lara's lover! Never had been!

Which meant, at the very least, she needn't feel guilty for their wonderful night out on the cliffs. Better than that, it meant she was free to learn what that night had meant to him—just a passing impulse born of a warm, willing woman in his arms, the moon and the silver sea? Or a deeper, more personal attraction?

Dazed by Lara's admission—by its implications—she'd felt no hurry to seek Trace out. First, she needed to think.

She'd left Lara's suite with strict instructions to take the day off—Lara pointing out that if *she* intended to spend all of September 11 in bed, then her personal assistant should goof off, too.

She had. She'd gone back to her apartment and crashed till almost five, then had risen, pottered luxuriously around the place with a drowsy, dreaming smile, then driven off to her weight class at the Y. She'd returned home, contentedly exhausted, at nine and gone straight to bed.

She'd risen this morning, the twelfth—her birthday!—to clouds and rain. And dreadful doubts. So Trace was a free agent—so what? That didn't mean he was free for the taking. She'd been building castles in the air, on the most ephemeral of foundations—a few passionate kisses out on the cliffs? A week of meaningful glances? *Get real, woman!* Looked at like that, her hopes were pathetically feeble. *And aren't you forgetting that steamy little scene you witnessed in the basement, Joya and Trace entwined on the weight bench?*

She'd seen no interaction since that would lead her to think they were involved. Joya always fixed Trace with a smoldering stare when he entered her presence, but it seemed more akin to resentment than lust. Still, Gillian didn't pretend to understand Joya. For all she knew, they could be having a volcanically passionate affair.

Compounding her doubts was a niggling uncertainty born of ignorance. If Trace was just Lara's friend, why was he sleeping on her couch? *Maybe it's one of those unrequited relationships: she considers him just a friend; he loves her madly. Till she comes to her senses, Trace patiently waits on her couch?*

But if he's crazy in love with Lara, what was he doing night before last kissing me senseless in the teahouse tunnel?

Try another theory: maybe Trace was some sort of promotional gimmick, dreamed up by the public relations staff of *Searching for Sarah* to enhance Lara's image as a sexy celebrity. Wasn't it true that a generation ago the Hollywood studios had forced some of their gay male stars to marry to protect their box office image as superstuds? Maybe Trace had been hired to make Lara look sexily satisfied now that she was a widow?

It didn't *quite* wash, and why wouldn't Lara have explained, if that was the reason?

Or maybe he's just what she said and no more—a

friend. Come to sleep on her couch—why? *Because he's a friend in need, and Lara needs him right now?*

Or perhaps Trace needed *Lara's* protection.

She couldn't make it out, and not knowing made her uneasy. Wary. Uncertain how to proceed, or if she should proceed at all. Worse yet, she could see no way to learn the truth. Lara had made her promise she wouldn't tell Trace she now knew they weren't lovers. *What is this, a soap opera?* And wasn't Lara's concern that she not tell Trace weird in itself?

Once she'd shoved all her doubts into the back cupboard of her mind and locked its door for the moment, the blues had stepped forth. As she'd sloshed through the puddles up to Woodwind, she'd reminded herself, *Today's my birthday.* September 12. Barring last year, when she'd endured it alone, September 12 was always her favorite of days. Her mother had always made a fuss of her birthday. *All those years of cakes and parties, Mom, I was happy as could be, feeling loved and cherished. But what were you feeling, all alone with the knowledge that the one birthday we hadn't shared was my first one?*

Was it an uncomplicated day of joy for you, as it was for me—or something more poignant, tarnished by the lie you lived alone?

How could you have ever dreamed I would have loved you the less because we weren't of one blood? Didn't you trust me? Gillian stood before the kitchen door, transfixed by that terrible thought, wishing she could unthink it.

Gray clouds stormed up over the cliffs, to scrape the wet treetops. The wind moaned through the tossing branches. Leaves flew on the gale, some green, a few golden—autumn approaching on leaden feet, months before it would arrive in Texas. A chill hung in the air, which hadn't been present there yesterday. There was no way to unthink a thought. She shivered and pushed on into the house.

Harriet the Glum sat at the kitchen table, a spoonful of cereal halfway to her downturned mouth. "Did you ever find your package?" she demanded.

"I did." *Did you open it?* If Harriet had, she'd never admit it.

"I told you it was there," Harriet said smugly. "Hope it was worth all the fuss."

Are you hoping the book mattered to me? No way would Gillian give her that satisfaction. "Oh, it was just an old book someone sent me. Nothing important."

By the time she reached her office, the blues had settled in to stay. Kneeling on the window seat, Gillian pressed her nose to the glass and stared out at a gray, rumpled sea. Born twenty-eight years ago today, thanks to a woman who was still, in spite of her efforts, a stranger. She still didn't know why Lara had written that horrible letter.

If I didn't want you when you were born, why the hell do you think I would want you now?

Gillian could certainly understand a fifteen-year-old not wanting to keep a baby—how could Lara have hoped to raise her? But it was one thing to give up a child with tenderness and regret, for the good of them both. Quite another to relinquish a child with rage and resentment, as her letter seemed to suggest.

Which was it, Lara? I'd really like to know.

Maybe that was why she was so blue. Today was the acid test. There was no way that Lara could have forgotten the significance of September 12. No way in the world. *If she's grieving today, I could take that as a sign that she wishes she'd never given me away.*

Or at least that she remembers me with fond regrets. That she might someday be open to a reunion, in spite of last year's letter.

But if Lara was happy today, then that proved she felt nothing but relief. That casting her baby off had been the right thing to do. That she did not look back with regret.

In which case, maybe it was time to respect Lara's wishes?

Just when their friendship was blooming and Trace was suddenly an unanswered, tantalizing question? Gillian sighed and turned away from the glass. *I don't know, I don't know!*

To drive out the demons, she dug into the fan mail. Despite her reading headaches, she had made excellent progress this past week. Working backward from the present, she had only four boxes to go to reach the point where Joya had abandoned the job last spring. Once she'd caught up, it should be easy to keep up with the half dozen or so letters that arrived every day. *But will I be the personal assistant who benefits?* She had a feeling today that something was drawing to a close. The season turning outside her windows perhaps, or that she was—overnight—a year older? She jumped as the phone rang, then swooped it up. "Hello?"

"Hard at work," Lara observed with a warm chuckle. "Are you ready to take a break? Teach me some tai chi? It's noon, you know."

Gillian bit her lip. "I was w-wondering if you'd still want to. You seemed to be feeling so down yesterday..." The test, oh Lord, here came the test!

Lara said briskly, "Well, that was yesterday, kiddo, and yesterday's gone. I feel fine today. Why don't you throw on some sweats and come on down."

THE RAIN HAD STOPPED and a few streaks of blue showed beyond the clouds, out on a gunmetal gray horizon. Gillian gave her first lesson out on Lara's balcony.

Whatever mood had been troubling Lara, it had vanished today. Lara wasn't cheery so much as she was serene, looking determinedly forward instead of back, Gillian would have said. They discussed a training program to put Lara back in television shape by Christmas—weights, walking and tai chi.

So that's that, she told herself as she executed a series of movements while Lara watched. *Lara doesn't care about her lost child—about me—at all.* She meant what she said in that letter: *Go get a life! And stay the hell out of mine!*

Now it was up to Gillian to accept that. *If I could just learn the name of my father—if that photo is of my father. Maybe I should settle for that and go?*

"Wait, stop, do that again!" Lara cried, laughing.

After the lesson, Gillian suggested a walk outside. The sun should be breaking through any time now and the temperature had turned almost summery. Lara looked wistful. "Let me ask Trace if he has any plans, okay?"

Gillian stayed out on the balcony while Lara went in to call Trace on the house phone. *And why doesn't she simply unlock her door and cross the hall?* It wasn't twenty feet to his door. Gillian was coming to the rueful conclusion that Lara was bone lazy—not a trait she'd inherited, she hoped.

"I guess I'll pass," Lara told her, coming to the door, looking mildly ruffled. She sighed. "Trace has some errands to run and I...I guess I'll hang around here and finish a book I'm reading."

Your just a friend has errands to run, therefore you don't think you'll take a walk. I don't get it, Lara.

But Lara wasn't explaining. She suggested good-naturedly that Gillian take the afternoon off, as well. But Gillian thanked her and declined. The tai chi had cured her headache. She might as well earn her salary.

As LARA LOCKED THE SUITE door behind her, Gillian stood staring at the door to Trace's office. *What does he do in there?* On impulse, she crossed the corridor and knocked.

Within the room, she heard the creak of a chair, then footsteps. The door opened to reveal Trace's inquiring gaze, higher than she expected to see it—he was always a little taller than she remembered. His smile curled slowly. Her skin tingled wherever those beautiful, masculine lips had brushed her only two nights ago. "Um, hello." This was the problem with impulses, she'd nothing planned to say.

"Hello yourself." He stroked a skein of hair off her cheek with the backs of two fingers. "I've been thinking about you."

"Oh?" Her breath feathered out like silent, shaken laughter. Just like that, one touch and he'd chased her blues away! "I...was just being n-nosy. What do you do in there all day, anyway?"

His fingers returned to her hair. He captured another lock hanging on her shoulder and studied it gravely, rubbed it between his fingers. "I'm writing the great American novel."

"Why do I not believe you?" He was pulling on his prize now, a gentle teasing tug that sent ripples of awareness spreading across her scalp, shivering down her nape. At this moment, she would have followed him anywhere he cared to lead her.

Eyes dancing, he shook his head solemnly. "Beats me. Don't you trust me?"

About as far as she could have thrown the man, all 180 or so sexy, muscular pounds of him. "Nope. So why not show me?"

"Sure. When it's published." His forefinger rotated lazily, winding her hair around and around its tip, gradually reeling her in.

He was lying. *Teasing,* she amended. *What do you really do in there? Play computer games all day?* "That's too long to wait," she protested.

"I'll say!" The timbre of his voice had lowered and roughened.

She couldn't help smiling. "I'm talking about your so-called novel. What's the first sentence, then?"

His spooling forefinger had reached the level of her mouth. Now he stroked her bottom lip. "The first sentence?" he murmured absently. "'She had lion eyes. They glowed in the dark of his dreams.'"

"Sounds...racy."

"I sincerely hope so!" His fingertip found her lips again, traced the deepening curve between, coaxing entry.

Not here in the hall, where anyone could wander past! She smiled and turned her head aside, turned back again as he tugged on her hair. "I was thinking...would you feel like a walk later today? Out on the cliffs? You could tell me the plot to your novel."

"I'm afraid I can't." No excuse, no explanation.

One moment she felt utterly confident in his company, certain he felt what she was feeling. Then the next—like this—she was dangling, no sure ground beneath her feet. "Oh," she said flatly. *I thought...* She was making far too much of this. Just because a man enjoyed flirting with a woman, that didn't mean he wanted to come closer in any meaningful way. "Sure, well, some other time."

"Like tonight?" he said quickly. "I have to go into town, but I should be back about seven."

So he hadn't been brushing her off. "Come out for a drink, then?" she suggested—and remembered. *It's my birthday!* An evening with Trace would be a fine gift indeed.

"Can't go out, actually." He frowned abstractedly over her shoulder. "This business associate might call and I need to be near a phone."

Thoroughly frustrated, she gave up. He led her on—then slammed the door in her face each time she tried to enter. "Hey, well, never mind." She caught his wrist and began to unspool her hair from his finger. *One minute he's an author, the next he has business.* To heck with this man of mystery routine!

"I could…invite you to supper in," Trace proposed, his eyes not missing her hurt. "As I recall, you have an excellent kitchen. And I make a mean *steak au poivre.* I could pick up the fixings while I'm out."

"You cook?"

"All the men in my family do. Mom's a police officer. It was cook or starve, most days."

He was opening up to her the tiniest bit. *Tell me all!* Maybe he would tonight. "Sounds heavenly," she said in all truth, smiling again. "Okay. See you at seven?"

LARA'S LAWYER KEPT HIM waiting for almost half an hour after Trace's six o'clock appointment. And when he finally ushered Trace into his office, it was to face a briskly skeptical cross-examination. "Jeremy Benton vouches for you, of course," Dudley said, cleaning his wire-rimmed spectacles. "And I spoke with Margaret Feinstein, Mrs. Corday's business manager in New York, after you called. She tells me you come with the highest recommendations, that it was she who hired you for Mrs. Corday in the first place. But no one has explained why you want to see Mrs. Corday's will without her knowledge or permission. Although Feinstein has limited power of attorney and so may request this, ethically speaking this situation makes me...uneasy." He positioned his glasses precisely behind his ears. "Of course, Jeremy and I go back—all the way back—so..."

"My mandate for this assignment is twofold," Trace said easily. "First, I protect Mrs. Corday from direct harm." *Which means, you pompous pencil pusher, that I need to get back to Woodwind ASAP.* She'd promised him she'd stay safely in her suite, but still... He took a calming breath. "The second objective of a Brickhouse agent—always—is to solve the problem. Which in this case means find the stalker and see her convicted."

"Laudable. Laudable. But how would learning the terms of Mrs. Corday's will aid you in that?"

"Certain...facts that I've recently uncovered lead to the possibility that this isn't a conventional celebrity stalking. That there might be an underlying profit motive."

"I see," said the attorney. "Follow the money."

"Precisely." *So could I please have the damned will?* Trace clasped his hands loosely in his lap to keep from drumming them on Dudley's desktop.

"Seems a reasonable theory to explore," murmured Dudley. "But why withhold this from Mrs. Corday? I'd be a lot happier if she knew."

"Because that's all it is at this point—a theory," Trace said patiently. "And though reading her will may narrow my list of suspects, it may not eliminate some entirely innocent people. I'm not here to do harm but to cure harm. Raising suspicions in Mrs. Corday that some of her nearest and dearest might want to kill her..." He shrugged. "Trust is a fragile emotion. Hard to rebuild once the question has been raised. Better not to raise the issue with her at all unless and until I have some proof." He looked pointedly at the folder resting by the lawyer's right hand. "But if her will *leads* me to that proof and a cessation of the threats against Mrs. Corday's life..." *Will you get out of the way and let me get on with it?*

Dudley nodded. "Discretion is what I'd hoped for. Very well." He flipped open the folder. "Shall I summarize?"

"No, thanks." Trace held out his hand and kept it extended till the lawyer grimaced and surrendered the document.

TEN MINUTES TO SEVEN by his watch, Trace noted, standing third in line at the market's meat counter. Damn Dudley anyway for all his delays! He needed to check in with Lara, tell her he'd be across in the carriage house this evening. Extract a stern promise from her that she'd stay in her suite. And he'd wanted to take a shower before presenting himself at Gillian's door. *Call her,* he told himself, and pulled out his portable phone. He dialed her Woodwind extension as he stepped up to second place.

No answer. He snapped the phone shut. Out in the gardens, perhaps. Or showering, herself? His heart gave a funny little lurch at the image of beads of bathwater like diamonds on hot, velvety skin. Hang-

ing like crystal in her long lashes...Gillian... He
didn't know why she'd changed her mind about coming between him and Lara, and at the moment he
didn't care. *She feels it, too.* There was such a right-
ness between them, such an inevitability. He was
hardly a novice with women, but this feeling was all
new. Would have to be explored in-depth. Hopefully
tonight. Yes, most definitely a shower...

"Are you going to just stand there grinning, or
would you like something?" the blonde behind the
counter inquired, adjusting a curl behind her ear.

TRACE WAS FIFTEEN MINUTES early, Gillian thought,
as he rapped on her door. No matter. She was ready,
after spending the past hour showering, then dithering
over her clothes, changing outfits three times before
she settled on a burgundy silk shirtwaist blouse—it
matched the garnet-and-pearl earrings she'd purchased two days before—and a pair of olive green
tailored slacks. Keep it simple, for Pete's sake. They
were only eating in.

But her heart was cutting a complicated little fan-
dango as she hurried to the door. *Oh, Trace!* "You're
early," she laughed as she opened it—to find herself
gaping at Toby.

He looked her up and down and grinned. "It's
never too early to howl. You look wonderful."

But not for you! She'd forgotten he'd asked her out
for a drink, the day before. "Oh, Toby, I'm *so* sorry.
I h-had a change in plans. Trace is due any minute
now and..." *And would you please just go?* She
smiled at him apologetically.

He smacked his forehead. "You mean Joya didn't
tell you? That silly bitch! She said she'd stop by on
her way out. Must have forgotten."

"Forgotten what?"

"Trace called a little while ago. He asked Joya to tell you that something had come up and he was unaccountably delayed. Wouldn't be back till very, very late."

"Oh." She stood motionless, all her hopes for this evening popping like bright-colored birthday balloons. She'd gotten beeswax candles for her table, picked half an armful of the most fragrant roses, bought a special bottle of wine and salad makings in case Trace forgot, had chosen music to play—Brazilian guitar, light but not too romantic. For pity's sake, she'd even painted her toenails! *You silly, pathetic little fool.* The height of her anticipation was now the depth of her fall.

"Stood you up, did he?" Toby observed, staring over her shoulder at her table already set with crystal and china. "The rat."

She couldn't agree more. She'd sensed Trace's ambivalence this morning, when she kept proposing timid dates and he kept refusing. Well, apparently he'd had second thoughts about this evening. Fine. She wasn't going to sit home and cry about it. "Does that offer for a drink still stand?"

BY SEVEN TRACE WAS STUCK in traffic, waiting for the light to turn onto Bellevue. He should have taken a back route—had been so intent on his goal he'd taken the straight line approach to it without considering what lay between. He swore and whipped out his phone. Dialed and again got no answer. *Maybe she's up at the big house, looking for me.* Or maybe she was working late in her office. Well, ten minutes more and he could apologize in person.

Drumming his fingers on the steering wheel, he

forced his mind back to Dudley's office and what he'd learned there. It was just as he'd expected, only worse. Much worse, with the bombshell Dudley had dropped on him at the end.

Reading the will, Trace had been startled at the size of Lara's estate. Her own residuals from *Searching for Sarah* plus her recent inheritance from her late husband added up to roughly ten million dollars. Add to that a fifty percent share in Woodwind, with Toby and Joya owning the other half of the estate, plus an apartment on one of the classier streets of the East Side in New York, which Lara owned in its entirety— a gift from her husband while living. Value of her liquidated estate? Dutton estimated it at fourteen million. *That might be worth a murder or two...* He stepped on the gas as the light far ahead turned to green, hugged the bumper of the van in front—then swore as the light turned yellow and the van stopped short. "Come on!"

Roughly one-tenth of Lara's fortune went to charities—a foundation for aging, penniless actors and several funds for orphans here in the States and abroad. Then there were the minor bequests—a hundred thousand to Barbara Heath, the housekeeper who'd cared for the Cordays since they'd purchased Woodwind. A hundred thousand to Lara's friend and colleague Harriet Bristow. Smaller sums to the present maid, a former one now retired, a doorman down in New York, a teacher back in West Virginia, a makeup artist and a hairdresser from Lara's soap opera company. These sums were chickenfeed compared with the major bequests, but that didn't mean he should eliminate Harriet and the housekeeper from his list of suspects. A hundred thousand would tempt some people to murder.

And if a hundred thousand could inspire bloodshed, consider the remainder of Lara's estate, worth roughly twelve million. It was divided into three blocks, two quarter shares worth about three million apiece, plus one half share of roughly six million dollars. Serious money any way you reckoned. Seriously scary money, from the point of view of a bodyguard. *Why couldn't you leave it all to the SPCA, Lara?*

The light changed to green and he stepped on the gas, chasing the van around the corner and into the stop-and-go traffic of Bellevue.

Instead of the SPCA, Lara had willed the two quarter shares to her stepchildren, Toby and Joya. Who were already millionaires from their father's estate, Dudley pointed out. He'd estimated they'd inherited roughly three million each from Corday, with the rest of his estate going to his wife, Lara.

So if either Toby or Joya killed Lara—and escaped detection—they'd double their take. Some might call that greedy, but he couldn't swear Lara's stepbrats were among them.

It was the six-million-dollar bequest, though, that had raised his hair on end. If and when Lara died, six million would be put into a trust fund in the name of Sarah Cloud Bailey. The interest accruing from that fund would pay for detectives, hired by the fund's trustee, to search for her lost daughter and keep on searching. The fund would stay intact for sixty years; then, no daughter having been found, the money would be donated to a scholarship fund for orphans.

All Sarah Cloud Bailey has to do to earn six million dollars is kill her own mother. There were usually bonds of affection, all sorts of emotional taboos, that forbade matricide, no matter how much the offspring might be tempted. But in a case where the two women were essentially strangers? If shoving a stranger off a cliff earned you six million dollars? And how much easier would it be to shove a stranger you resented? Whom you felt had brutally rejected you as a child—and by doing so had somehow wrecked your life?

Arriving at the gates to Woodwind, he punched in the code to open them, sat watching their ponderous inward swing.

The will also made provision if any of the heirs died before Lara. If either Toby or Joya predeceased their stepmother, the surviving sibling would take the other's share, inheriting six million instead of three.

And if anyone could ever prove that Lara's lost child had died *before* her mother, then Sarah Cloud Bailey's six million would be divided equally between Toby and Joya, if and when Lara died.

So there he had it—three people with million-dollar reasons to kill Lara. Two more who'd earn a hundred thousand by doing so. And then Dudley had dropped his bombshell.

Trace wasn't the only one who'd been checking out the terms of Lara's will.

CHAPTER NINETEEN

BIG MISTAKE, GOING OUT with Toby. Gillian sat at a table out on the veranda of the Inn at Castle Hill, one of Newport's swankier watering holes, surrounded by half a dozen of Toby's tipsy friends. Newport's chosen, they clearly considered themselves, not townies but from the top of the hill. Their hooting, self-conscious laughter had risen to a level where patrons at the surrounding tables were giving them cool and cooler glances.

In spite of their gaiety, Gillian found them a mean-spirited bunch, whose conversation consisted mainly of back-biting gossip about members of their clique not present. Suki was pregnant for the second time this year, the slut, and of *course* she was getting an abortion, at that private clinic in Paris that everybody used. She'd come back with some decent clothes, at least. Buffy had bought—would you believe?—a Lexus. Turn thirty and you might as well be dead. Next thing you knew, he'd be going off to Manhattan to work at his father's brokerage! Had anyone else noticed that Pooh's nose was getting pinker and drippier by the day? The girl didn't have a hobby—she had a habit! (Hoots all around.)

Gillian smiled gently, rose and walked to the railing. At least the view was spectacular. The Inn was built on a high headland that overlooked the mouth of Narragansett Bay where it met the ocean. To her north arched the two-mile curve of lights that was the cross-bay bridge, connecting the eastern shore of the state with the western. Around the shoulder of the headland, Newport's lights bleached the sky. Some five miles away from where she stood.

She'd assumed Toby would take her for a drink downtown, on the harbor, an easy walk back to Woodwind. She could have had one drink for politeness, then bolted, taken herself out to a solitary birthday dinner at one of the waterfront restaurants. Instead, here she was, marooned out in the fashionable wilderness with a bunch of shallow, drunken brats.

The contrast with the company she'd hoped to keep tonight was brutal. And the beauty and romance of this place tore at her heart. If Trace had been there they could have strolled down the long sloping lawn to the cliffs that overlooked the water and watched the sailboats gliding downwind back to port, their wings spread to the moonlight like gigantic moths. Could have stood down there and drunk their fill of that beauty and kissed. Could have talked in half whispers of things that mattered. *What do you believe? What brings you joy? Where are you going? Who are you?* Instead—

"There you are, Gillie!" Toby loomed up beside her and smacked a tall glass on the railing. "Now, this you've got to try. Ever had a Pimm's Cup before?"

"No, but I think I've had enough, thanks. Why don't you drink it and I'll get an orange juice." And then she was out of here if she had to walk.

In high heels, she reminded herself, with no Trace to carry her home when she went lame. Her eyes suddenly blurred and she tossed her hair angrily. This was what came of building castles in the air! At her side, Toby was insisting that he'd bullied the bartender into making it especially for her, that she really must try it. She shrugged and took a sip, then kept the glass in her hands until one of the girls at the table shrieked and called for Toby's assistance, and she was able to pour the rest of it over the railing.

"Joy*uh!* Joy*uh!*" two of the boys at the table bellowed, turning the name into a jungle mating chant, which the rest of the pack took up. Gillian saw Toby's sister breezing along the terrace toward them, a haughty blond amazon flanked by two lesser blondes. Toby reached out and caught his sister's hand, and she leaned down so he could whisper in her ear. Then her wide blue eyes swung around to find Gillian— and she smiled.

As soon as he parked the car in the carriage house, Trace sprang up the stairs. He'd apologize, explain he had to run up to Woodwind for a few minutes, ask if she could hold out for half an hour more. Then a quick shower and change, and let the evening begin. He rapped on her door. *It's me, beautiful.*

Shifted impatiently from foot to foot, then rapped again. Cocked his head this time to listen, then frowned. No sounds of her light footsteps as she hurried to greet him. He knocked a third time, held his breath, then let it out slowly. So...

He'd dated more than one woman—usually very beautiful women—who refused to wait for a man, to cut him any slack. One had had a strict fifteen-minute rule, he recalled, after which she walked. He'd let her keep on walking. But Gillian—he wouldn't have thought she had that kind of brittle princess edge. *Maybe she's up at the house.* Yes, that was much more likely. He was only twenty minutes late. He rattled back down the stairs.

Half an hour later, after a tour of the mansion, a casual word with Lara—Trace wasn't about to explain why he was asking, but had she seen Gillian?—then a circuit of the grounds, he had to face it. She'd stood him up. Must have walked into town, since her car was still parked before the carriage house.

Biting down hard on his disappointment, he carried his steaks to the kitchen and threw them in the freezer, then slapped together a cold chicken sandwich and took it up to his office with a beer. So he'd struck out in love. All the better to focus him on business. He picked up his phone and dialed.

"'LO?" HIS SISTER ANSWERED absently.

"About damn time! I've been trying to reach you for two days now. What's wrong with your phone?"

"*I'm* fine, and how are *you?* Jeez, I never thought of it before, but Mom didn't perfect her socialization techniques till after the first kid or two, did she?"

"I suppose you, being the fourth, represent a culmination of all Mom's hard-earned child-rearing wisdom? To say nothing of Dad's."

"You suppose right, my little cabbage. Now, as to your question, day before yesterday I forgot to turn on my phone. Yesterday I was flying all day and not wishing to disrupt my pilot's navigation systems, antigravity systems, etc., etc., I—"

"You're back in Seattle?" He swung his legs onto the desktop and pulled the plate with his sandwich onto his stomach.

"I wish! I'm out in L.A., hot on your Gillian's trail. I found her father, Victor Scott. Well, almost." She'd struck out with learning Gillian's original middle name in Houston, Emily told him. But she'd found a helpful secretary at Gillian's elementary school, who'd dug up her record of enrollment there in fourth grade. An annotation on the card stated she'd last attended a school in Los Angeles. "So I called every Scott in L.A., Abelard to Vanya, and eventually I hit Victor Scott's second, well, latest wife."

"You always were a stubborn brat." Still, he felt his pulse ticking faster. "So what's Gillian's middle name?"

"Mrs. Scott didn't know and couldn't care. And I'm afraid I made a botch of explaining who I was or why I wanted to know. Halfway into it, she shut me down and said I'd have to ask her husband, who's due back tomorrow. I decided I'd make a better show in person—don't bother to correct that notion—so here I am."

"That's wonderful, Em, but I wish you'd checked with me first. Gillian Mahler's no longer our number-one priority. I'm now more interested in a woman named Sarah Cloud Bailey—that's Bailey with an *i* and an *e*."

"Oh, swell! That's just perfectly swell." This outburst was followed by an extended indignant silence. Time enough for Trace to down a couple of bites of sandwich. Then she said suspiciously, "Bailey. Isn't your client's maiden name Bailey?"

"This is her daughter, given up for adoption at birth."

Emily let out a long, appreciative whistle. "And she's only just told you?"

"That's right." He didn't elaborate and he didn't bother to remind her that anything he told her was to be held in strictest confidence. She was good that way.

"And you think this daughter might be Sarah XXX, come back with some very hurt feelings?"

"Looks like a possibility. She turned twenty-eight yesterday—September 11. Born somewhere in West Virginia. If she favors her mother, she'll be about five-two or -three, weight about 105, hair platinum."

"*If* she favors her mother," Emily pointed out.

"True. The one fact I have for sure is that her eyes are blue-gray."

"Terrific. So I'm supposed to track down every twenty-eight-year-old female in the country with blue-gray eyes?"

"I hoped you might think of something. A Lexus/Nexus search with all variations of that name, to start with, I'd say. Then the magazine subscription databases, with an emphasis on subscribers to soap opera fan mags and magazines for adoptees searching for their parents."

"Gotcha," Emily said quietly. "And if those come up blank?"

"Then we'll see how stubborn you are. Go to your phone databases and find the number for every hotel and bed-and-breakfast in Newport and start calling. She dropped a letter off here at our gates yesterday. My guess is she's staying somewhere in town. Describe her to every desk clerk you reach. She might be using the name of Sarah or she might not. Ask, also, for S. Cloud, and Sarah with any last name starting with *X* or *E-x.*"

"And dare I ask how many hotels, etcetera, there are in Newport?"

"A couple of hundred, at a guess," he said blandly over her groans. "If you find anything that sounds like a lead, call me. I'll keep my phone switched on."

She let out a long, put-upon sigh. "Okay." Comfortable with each other's silence, they said nothing for a minute, then Emily asked, ''What would Sarah Cloud inherit if her mother was to die? Have you thought about that, Trace?''

''Way ahead of you, kiddo. She'd clear about six million, and guess what, somebody obtained a copy of Lara's will back in May—three days before she was pushed off the cliff.'' He told her about Dudley's sheepish revelation. That on a night back in May, the building security guard had entered the lawyer's office by the front door—and heard the back door banging shut. A search of the suite of offices had shown the copying machine was on, when it should have been off. And in the copier was the last page of Lara Corday's will, though the rest of the original was safely in its folder in the proper file cabinet.

''I've done that one myself,'' Emily said thoughtfully, ''when I *wasn't* in a panic. I suppose whoever it was heard the guard coming, had just enough time to clean up, cover his tracks but forgot the last page.''

''That's how I see it,'' Trace stated. ''Dudley assumes somebody bribed one of his secretaries or paralegals to obtain a copy. Since he knows that they know he'd fire anyone he caught doing that, he didn't bother to question them. Besides, no one would ever admit it. And since he assumed the briber must be one of Lara's heirs being greedily curious, no more than that, he decided it was smartest to let sleeping dogs snore.''

Emily snorted. ''And three days later somebody pushes his client off a cliff! That didn't embarrass him the teeny-weeniest bit?''

''Since we've kept that under wraps, he didn't know.''

"Ah." She thought for a minute. "So this isn't really about stalking, is it? It's about money."

"If our premise is correct," he reminded her. "Or maybe it's about hatred plus money." An even deadlier combination.

"Or something even subtler," Emily murmured. "Hatred with money being the excuse your killer is giving herself."

"Possibly." If she hadn't been his kid sister, and therefore never to be risked, he'd have recommended Brickhouse hire her as a field agent. Her brains were first-rate, her instincts better. "Whatever, let's find her first, then we'll ask her. I need a full-court press on this one, Em."

"Mmm," she agreed, then added, "why are we ruling out Gillian?"

Because I think I might love her. He blinked, as if the phone had sent a jolt of electricity ear to ear. Where had that come from? "Um," he intoned, a sound to cover a temporary cerebral overload. *No way! No way at all.* He was happy single—had scheduled at least two more years of putting Brickhouse on a solvent footing, before he could consider a change in status.

"She's the right age," Emily was saying persuasively. "You sent me her job application, you know, and she's twenty-seven. If a woman were to lie, she'd reduce her age rather than add a year. So maybe she's really twenty-eight?"

"She has the wrong color eyes," he reminded her with a rush of relief. "Whiskey colored." Lion eyes.

"You never heard of tinted contact lenses?"

Gillian was sane; he'd bet his last dollar on her.

A person could be legally sane—*and* rapacious as a piranha, his inner cynic observed. He'd spent nine years in the FBI; he knew that too well. *But not Gillian.*

"What about contact lenses, Trace?" prodded his relentless sister.

"I don't think so." But every time he'd gazed deeply into Gillian's eyes, he'd looked as a lover, not Lara's bodyguard. "I'll check it out, however." Tonight. His pulse quickened with the resolution. He'd gaze into those big golden eyes tonight. See if he could make them glow in the dark.

"TOBY!" GILLIAN PROTESTED as he swung the Range Rover abruptly off Ocean Drive onto an unpaved side road leading down to the water. A sign posted in the shrubbery proclaimed this King's Point Park, closed from sunset to sunrise, except for those with fishing licenses. "Where are we going?" The wheels bumped over unpaved potholes, a ridge of rock. He stopped the car on a bare, sandy ledge overlooking a tiny crescent of beach, with flat boulders stair-stepping down into the sand.

"We're taking the scenic route home, Gillie. Ever been here?" Toby got out of the car and went around to lean against the hood.

"Dammit," Gillian muttered. She should have called herself a cab instead of accepting Toby's offer to take her home.

"Oh, *relax,* Gillie," Joya said cheerfully from the back seat. She got out, too, and joined her brother.

Gillian watched them through the windshield, talking quietly, their cheeks almost touching—then the two broke apart with a burst of almost hysterical laughter. Joya stepped away from the car, flung out her arms like a child and, head thrown back to stare up at the stars, whirled around and around. *"Whoo-eee-eee-eee!"*

Gillian groaned and climbed out to join them. The black of the night folded around her like a velvet shroud. The ocean sighed on the sand. Stars spangled the sky overhead. The moon that had smiled on Trace and her would rise much later tonight. She stared eastward along the ragged coast, over small craggy peninsulas of stone thrusting out one after another into the water. Walk two miles along the shore drive and she'd reach Cliff Walk. Another three miles along that and she'd come to Woodwind. *Trace, are you home yet?*

"Panoramic to die for, huh?" Toby murmured, dragging something from his hip pocket. He uncapped a silver flask and offered it to her.

"No, thanks, and you shouldn't, either." If she had brought her license tonight, she would have insisted on driving. She didn't know how many drinks he'd taken, but his mood was definitely affected. He seemed alternately reckless and morose.

"Shouldn't, shmoodn't. Who appointed *you* our big sister?" He tipped back his head and drank. Coughed. Staggered comically. "You!" Then handed the flask to Joya, who also took a hearty swig.

I practically am your big sister. Or stepsister, anyway, though she'd just as soon claim neither of them.

"This is our favorite beach in the whole wide world," Joya proclaimed with childish enthusiasm. "Didya ever swim here, Gillie?"

"No." It looked no better than a dozen coves she knew along the shore. And it was too close to the road for her taste, she thought, as a car's headlights swept around Brenton Point in the distance and prowled their way, zigging and zagging as the road followed the tortured coastline.

"Well, come on, then! It's the perfect night—calm, warm."

Lousy company. Now, if Trace had been proposing a skinny-dip... "I don't think so, thanks."

"Oh, don't be such a party pooper!" Toby hooked an arm around her waist and started toward the beach. "Come on, just a quickie. You'll love it."

"No!" She dug in her heels, tripped as he kept moving, then staggered on alongside him. "Toby, I'm not in the mood. Cut it out!"

"Hey!" said Joya tensely, in an entirely different sort of voice, as she spun toward the road.

Headlights turned the wild roses edging the road to black filigree, then burst into the clear to illuminate the Range Rover. A black-and-white police car glided past it like a two-tone shark.

"Shit!" Joya said, her knuckles at her mouth.

The black-and-white circled, then braked, its headlights playing full upon them. A car door opened, and a tall, backlit figure stepped out of the passenger seat and swaggered toward them. "Fishing tonight?" the officer inquired easily.

"Uh, no," Toby muttered sullenly. He stepped away from Gillian, and from the corner of her eye, she saw him struggling to stuff his flask into his back pocket.

"What have you got there, son?" The officer held out his hand. "Give."

"Damn, damn, damn, oh damn!" Joya swore in a vicious undertone. "Of all the filthy luck in the world..."

"Open liquor container in a public place," noted

the officer, recapping the flask. He hooked a thumb at the Range Rover. ''Who's driving?''

''She is!'' cried Toby and Joya together, pointing at Gillian.

Their timing was so comedically perfect she laughed. ''I am not! I don't have my license tonight, Officer, and it's not my car.''

''Then who's driving?'' he demanded.

She bit her lip. Much as she was starting to dislike the younger Cordays, she didn't care to tattle. ''I really couldn't say.''

He seemed to grow half a foot in the headlights. ''Who's got the keys? Who owns the car? Somebody tells me now or all three of you win a ride to the station.''

''My brother owns it, Officer,'' said Joya in a huskier voice. ''He's a bad, bad boy, and you're absolutely right, he ought to be punished.'' Hips swaying seductively, she approached him and reached into the bosom of her low-cut dress. ''If I paid his fine right now, plus something for your, um, trouble, could we forget all about this?''

The cop was shaking his head, more incredulous than disapproving.

Gillian clutched her head in her hands and clamped her teeth to keep from laughing again. *This is how they do it in Beverly Hills, Joya?* She'd just earned them a ride to the police station for sure.

CHAPTER TWENTY

NOW THIS WAS A BIRTHDAY to remember, Gillian told herself, half an hour later as she unlocked the door to her apartment. Or to forget. The cops had given her a ride as far as Woodwind's gates. Would have probably dropped Joya off there, too, with a well-deserved lecture, but she'd insisted on riding down to the station, where they meant to book an increasingly belligerent Toby on everything from drunk driving, to trespassing, to obstructing an officer in the course of his duty. Being a mouthy brat didn't go down well with the police.

Once inside she switched on a lamp, then headed straight for the shower. Something about the whole evening needed to be washed away. The last part of it especially—Toby's drunken insistence that she swim with them, his arm around her waist forcing her onward... A silly incident, with an inexplicably nasty edge to it. She shivered, stripped off her clothes and stepped into the tub. *Forget it.* Forget the whole sorry day.

She scrubbed herself under the hot spray, letting her muscles and her mind loosen, till the water ran cool. Then she stepped out, dried her hair, wrapped another bath sheet around her body and wandered into the living room. And heard the insistent knocking on her door.

''Who is it?'' she called through the paneling, but

already she knew. It wasn't an impudent knock like Toby's but a solid demand.

"Trace." His voice was as uncompromising as the two inches of oak it penetrated.

"So you came home at last." And now what, apologies? She wasn't in the mood.

"What? Open the door, Gillian."

She let out an exasperated breath and rested her forehead against the barrier. She didn't need this.

"Gillian?"

Swearing silently, more at herself than him, she unlocked the door and tipped her head around the edge. "What?"

After all that racket, suddenly he had nothing to say.

She opened the door an inch wider, the better to glare at him. "Well?"

His hand drifted up. His fingertips came to rest along her temple; his thumb stroked across her lashes, sending a shower of raindrops down on her cheeks. "You were in the bath?" he asked huskily.

She nodded, feeling heat climb from the towel she held clasped with one hand at her breast all the way to her cheeks. She shouldn't have opened the door.

His hand curled around under her wet hair to clasp her nape. A simple, compelling act of possession.

She wouldn't surrender that easily! But her hand, of its own accord, opened the door a foot wider. "So you finally came home," she said spitefully, then felt another wave of heat wash up her body. That sounded as if they shared a home!

"Me?" Trace took a step nearer, his shoulders wedging into the gap of door and doorjamb, then stopped, making his desire to enter clear, while still he waited for permission. For surrender, because that

was what it would be if she let him walk through her
door. "What are you talking about? I've been here
all night, waiting for you."

"Joya said—" And then she realized. Her own
lack of confidence was what had fooled her! That and
the fact that willful, blatant lying was something she
didn't expect from anyone. "Toby said that Joya took
a message from you, canceling our date. That you
wouldn't be back till late. So I went out." She shoved
the door wide.

"Son of a bitch," Trace said quietly. "I'm going
to have to do something about those twerps." He took
the last step to close the gap between them and stood
looking down at her. "I was twenty minutes late, and
I apologize for that, but wild horses couldn't have
made me break our date."

The wild horses had gotten into her blood somehow; her pulse thundered like racing hooves. "Oh,"
she said softly, beginning to smile. "That's...good."

"I'm starting to think so." His hand at her nape
threaded up into her hair, caught hold and tugged
gently.

In unquestioning obedience she lifted her face to
his. He groaned against her lips, then his tongue was
inside her; his other arm hooked around her waist,
pulling her up on tiptoe against him. She shuddered
violently and wrapped her arms around his hard waist,
then thought Oops!, as the towel began to slip.

But she didn't care—cared only that his tongue
danced with hers, that she could feel his heart ham-
mering against her breasts crushed to his chest, that
he was whispering her name again and again as he
laid a chain of kisses up the side of her face, across
her eyelids... That they were turning in a slow dance
of enchantment across the floor, her towel falling

around their feet and Trace kicking it aside. They kissed again, then another turn, and now they were at her couch and sinking onto it, Trace drawing her down on his lap without a break in their liquid, honeyed, heart-stirring kiss.

As if the weight of her kisses bore him down, Trace toppled sideways onto the couch, taking her with him. Arms braced on his broad chest, she broke apart to breathe and laugh. "You're really good!"

"With you, I am." His hands, warm, pleasantly hard, smoothed up her back, then down again. He'd recognized her sudden hesitation and he slowed the pace accordingly, his fingers soothing and cherishing, tacitly showing her that his control was hers to command. At least so far. His body trembled beneath hers.

Of course he was good, and practice had made him so. But she shoved the ghosts of all his women aside. *Tonight he's mine.* It was her birthday and he was the gift. She lowered her mouth to his and, asking, received a hundredfold, kiss after kiss after kiss— tender, playful, passionate, one mood unfurling into the next. His hands stroked down her damp shoulders; she moaned and pushed herself up from him so they could explore lower. He cupped her breasts and gave a hum of delight—answered a second later by hers two octaves higher as his thumbs rubbed back and forth across her nipples.

Yes, oh yes, Trace! She twisted around to stretch her legs out along the couch and he swung his up from the floor, so they lay finally entangled, pressed together from thigh to mouth.

Clasping her waist, he held her up at arm's length in the air above him. 'You are so beautiful!'' He brought her halfway down, his lips claiming her breasts, while she twined her hands helplessly through his thick hair in wordless, rapturous joy. He brought her down, then rolled with her, and she felt his whole weight upon her for the first time.

Glorying under his muscled length, she tugged impatiently at his shirt. "I want to feel you!" Skin to skin, not this damned shirt; she hated his shirt—wouldn't have it. She fumbled feverishly with the buttons, while he laughed and tried to help her. An easy job if he could have sat up and away from her, but neither of them could bear that parting.

Trace got it unbuttoned at last, and she rubbed her lips across him, hairy and hard, with a wonderful, indefinable smell that was his and his alone. "Oh, Trace..." She wanted more of him, wanted all. Now she tugged impatiently at his belt. He laughed breathlessly and undid it for her, and it sailed off into the dark. "The rest of you," she demanded imperiously.

"I'm yours."

She cherished him, inch by hard silky inch as he found the strength to stand, strip the rest of his clothes away, before falling into her arms. *Trace.* All of him for all of her. The best, the only gift she'd ever need. The gift she'd been born for.

DEEP IN THE NIGHT they awoke to find they'd been making love in their sleep. They coupled with the drowsy, dreaming tenderness of longtime lovers, something sweeter and stronger than passion, bodies and spirits merging without boundaries. Two hearts to make one whole. Afterward, Trace held her in place on his chest, cupping her face in the dark. Their lips met one last, liquid time and she sighed and fell toward sleep. He whispered words inside her.

"Mmm?" she murmured dreamily.

He kissed her eyelids and whispered them again. "I think I love you…"

"*Ohhh*," she said, a word like one note of a golden bell. And fell asleep smiling.

SHE WOKE UP TO SUNLIGHT, to find Trace propped on one elbow, smiling down at her. "Lion eyes," he said softly, and brushed a lock of hair off her cheek. Resting his forehead on hers, he stared deep into her eyes. "They really do glow in the dark. All of you glows."

That's just my heart shining out through my skin. She drew his fingers down to her mouth and kissed them. He dropped his head and took her lips in a lingering, coaxing kiss, and when they broke apart to breathe, he tipped an eyebrow. "Mmm?"

She laughed and shook her head. "Uh-uh. Not before breakfast. I skipped supper last night, you know." She'd yet to tell him about her night out with the brats, she realized.

"Deal. Let me cook, since I didn't make supper." He rose, stretched magnificently, grinned—a little embarrassed at her unabashed admiration, and retreated to the bathroom.

She lay, too happy to move. *I'm twenty-eight and a day.* If the rest of the year continued like this…! She hugged herself and stared up at the ceiling, a memory flowering in her mind—or had it been a dream? Could he have really said— She rolled off the bed to go ask, realizing as she sailed through the bathroom door that she couldn't possibly. But maybe she could read the answer in his eyes.

Trace stood peering into her medicine cabinet. She stopped short as his head swung around a little too fast. He blinked, changing from guilt to bland in the wink of an eye. Maybe she'd imagined it? "Did you need something?"

"The toothpaste." He shut the mirrored door.

"It's here, silly." In plain view, balanced on the toothbrush holder that stuck out from the wall.

"Why, so it is," he said a little too casually.

So he's nosy, she told herself as she adjusted the hot-water faucet and stepped into the shower. How could she blame him, when she wanted to know everything, from his shoe size to the name of the first girl ever to send him a valentine? Not that she didn't know the most important things about him already, she thought as he joined her. *Gentle. Kind. Intelligent. Sexy as the devil himself.* He took the soap from her fingers and turned her around, lathered her back with heavy, intimate strokes, as if molding a piece of wet marble. She purred her delight. Purred louder as he cupped her breast and kissed her nape. "We really have to eat first?" he growled in her ear.

"We do," she insisted, though she shuddered against him and backed up to rub against his hardness.

"Torture," he complained good-humoredly. "Save me some cold water, in that case."

They soaped and teased each other till they were long past squeaky clean, then Gillian slipped out and left him to it. Wandering into her bedroom, she noticed for the first time that it was chilly this morning. What to wear? Nothing restrictive or difficult to take off again, she decided. Skipping a bra, she slipped into her favorite orange sweatshirt, the one she'd rescued from Michele, then a pair of black silk bikini panties for contrast. The sweatshirt covered them and brushed the tops of her thighs. *Let him wonder if I'm wearing any at all.* She smiled, thinking of after breakfast and wandered into the kitchen.

She was breaking eggs into a bowl when she heard him come out of the bedroom. "How hungry are you, Trace? Three eggs or four?"

No answer. She looked over her shoulder to find him dressed in his jeans only, standing frozen in the bedroom doorway, staring. "Trace?"

He shook his head as though shaking off a fly and walked toward her silently. Something in his face made her think of a tiger, the way the muscles had clenched along his jaw. "Trace?" He reached her and gripped her shoulder—too hard. Turned her. "What is it?"

His eyes were fixed on her chest. "Where did you get this?" His finger traced one letter of the emblem across her breast, then he snatched his hand back as if the fabric had scorched him.

"My brother, Chris, gave it to me years ago. Why?" What was the matter with him?

He shook his head again, that same shaking-a-fly-off motion, shaking something unpleasant aside. "I...I used to know a woman who went to the University of Miami. That's all."

She swallowed. "Oh." *That's not all!* Whoever the woman had been, she'd meant something very special to him. Dammit! Should she go change? No, that would make too much of this. "So three eggs in your omelet or four?" she asked briskly.

"Uh...you know, I don't think I'm hungry yet."

"Oh." Something was seriously wrong. He was avoiding her eyes. "Coffee?"

He shook his head. "I don't think so. Not yet..."

"Then..." What? From easy intimacy and laughing tenderness to this. She stood stranded in her kitchen with a frowning stranger. Feeling suddenly naked with her bare legs exposed, which was absurd, considering what they'd shared.

He turned without a word and walked across to the couch. Found his shirt they'd abandoned the night before and slipped it on; returned, buttoning it. She read the answer in his face before he spoke, and braced herself for it.

"You know, Gillian, I think maybe I'll skip breakfast, if you don't mind. Hit the gym, instead. It's going to be a busy day and…"

And you won't be a part of it. He might as well have shouted those words.

"Of course," she said around the lump in her throat. "I understand." *Nothing.* How could he change this fast?

"Thanks."

Thanks? She could have slapped him. Thanks for nothing! He leaned down to kiss her cheek—her cheek, not her mouth—and she closed her eyes. "Bye," she whispered. It really was goodbye; there was no mistaking it. What the hell had she done? Or not done?

But she was damned if she'd ask, and he wasn't saying.

"Bye," he said. She opened her eyes to find him at the doorway, shifting from foot to foot.

"See you around," she said wryly. *But not if I see you first.* What a fool she'd been! Castles in the air, crashing down around her. *Little fool, giving yourself to a stranger!*

He shifted his weight one more time, then realized she'd dismissed him and he could go. She turned her back so she didn't have to watch him walk out her door. Stood, head high, listening to the door shut, the soft sound of his retreating feet.

When the bottom door closed, she dumped the eggs into the sink and took a step toward the bedroom. But her bed would smell now of him. Of them. She sank down at her table, dropped her head on her arms—and cried.

"WHUH?"

"Wake up," Trace said rudely. *I need your help.*

"Trace?" His sister yawned. "Whuh'suh matter?"

"Did you fly home to Seattle yet?"

"Do you have any clue what *time* it is out here?" Sleep was rapidly giving way to annoyance. "It's—jeez, you brute—it's five in the morning!"

"Out where, dammit? Seattle or L.A.?"

"L.A.," Emily said sullenly. "I didn't fly yet."

He breathed a sigh of relief. "Good." He wouldn't have to tell her to get herself back on a plane. "I've changed my mind. Forget the hunt for Sarah Cloud Bailey for the moment. I want you to talk to Victor Scott. Like yesterday."

"I was going to anyway," she growled around a yawn. "Why else would I still be here? I checked that job application you sent me. Did you notice what she put for a birth date? October 12. Almost a month to the day from September 12. That seems too much of a coincidence to me."

"Why not October 11?" he mused, momentarily diverted.

"Beats me. 'Cause she's crazy?"

Gillian, eyes of a lion. She was anything but crazy. But then, neither were lions when they dragged a gazelle down into the dust. He rubbed his aching eyes.

"When can you talk with Victor Scott?"

"Not till late this afternoon. His wife said he's coming in from Chicago around five."

"Then meet him at the airport, if you can figure out which flight. I have to know, Emily."

"What happened?" she asked quietly.

She tore a strip off my heart, that's what. Nothing he'd share with a sister—or anyone else, for that matter. Only with one woman, and her he couldn't ask, *I love you, but by any chance are you a murderer?*

"What about her eye color?" Emily continued when he didn't speak. "Did you check that?"

"She doesn't wear contact lenses." With the sunlight slanting in her bedroom window this morning, he'd made sure of that just before he kissed her. He touched his lips, then scowled. And he'd checked her medicine cabinet to be doubly certain. No lens solution, no lens case, but— "But I found the red sweatshirt. You remember that the runner Lara saw on the cliffs—the person I think pushed her—wore an orange University of Miami sweatshirt? Well, Gillian has one." Draping her long slender body, which he'd made his own again and again last night. To give her up now, when they'd only begun, was to tear out his own heart.

"Aha! I knew it! That's why I stayed here to see Scott. I got to thinking about her eye color."

"What about it?" He rubbed a forearm across his face. God, he was tired. *Let me sleep and wake to find that last night was real, this morning a nightmare.*

"What color are Risa's eyes?"

Their niece, Jon and Demi's baby. "Dark brown," he said absently. Like her spectacular mother's. Demi was a quarter Egyptian, a quarter French.

"So your client, Corday, told you her baby's eyes were blue-gray. But the last time she ever saw her baby was on the second or maybe its third day. What color were Risa's eyes when you held her at the hospital, Trace?''

"Blue-gray,'' he said faintly.

"Like lots of babies. They change color around the second month. Your client never knew that?''

A motherless fifteen-year-old when she gave birth? And since then, how many babies had Lara held? He could imagine her shying away from that experience. How could she bear to hold another woman's child when she'd lost her own? Or even to talk about babies. "I guess not. Quite likely not.''

"So there you go,'' his sister said triumphantly. "I think your Gillian heads the suspect list. I mean, she's there. She sought out that job.''

"So did some twenty-six other applicants.''

"But how many of them own a University of Miami sweatshirt, huh? Huh? Am I right?''

He felt his temper jolt upward and he took a breath. It wasn't her fault in any way; it was his, because he led with his heart, not his head. "You may be. Talk with Scott and find out, then call me immediately, Em. The minute you know, okay?'' *And meantime I'll pray.*

AFTER HE HUNG UP he glanced at his watch—8:15 a.m. Too early to stumble into Lara's suite and disturb her. God, he hated this job. No bed even to call his own—he'd never take another detail like this one. Bed...there was only one he wanted, one woman in it. He shook his head abruptly and rose as he heard a car's engine outside. He strode to the window—Gillian leaving?—but no. It was Toby's black Range Rover, coming up the driveway. The brats, straggling home from another night on the town. For some people life was nothing but party, party, party. *They have three million apiece from their father and no inclination to work at all. Wonder how long that will last them.* He glanced at his watch again—hours till Emily would contact Scott. Hours before he could know. Hours he wanted to murder. He sank down at his desk, put his head on his forearms and—saw eyes that glowed in the night. He drew a shuddering breath and followed them into darkness.

CHAPTER TWENTY-ONE

KNOCK, KNOCK, KNOCK. "Trace, are you in there? Trace?"

Gillian calling him—he bolted upright at his desk.

"Trace?"

Not Gillian, but Lara, calling half an octave above Gillian's range, but still, there was something about the voice quality. *And they both have that tiny stutter!* Why had he never noticed before? *Proves nothing, he told himself,* as he rubbed his face with both hands. *Wait for the proof from Emily.*

"Trace!"

"Sorry," he said, opening the door, "I was asleep." And it hit him. "Hey, I thought we had an agreement that you wouldn't—"

"Would stay in my box like a good puppy? Do you realize I've stayed cooped up in my suite since yesterday *afternoon?*" Lara glowered at him. "This is how you bodyguard me? Why don't I just rent myself a safe-deposit box and camp out there till this blows over?" She stamped her foot. "I'm sick of this!"

He could have pointed out that she should have let him hire a second bodyguard, that it was she who'd wanted a minimalist, low-profile detail. "I'm sorry." Trace glanced at his watch. It was past twelve. No wonder she was ripping! "I'm really sorry, Lara, I..."

She tipped up her head and appraised him, and the corners of her mouth twitched upward. "When you didn't come to bed last night, I worried about you. I thought maybe something...bad had happened."

It did. He nodded glumly. *I've been derelict in every way.* He'd had no intention of spending the night with Gillian, even though he'd known that Lara was safe in her impregnable suite, but once he'd touched Gillian, kissed her... *Was I sleeping with your enemy?*

He didn't know that yet. Didn't know it for sure.

"And where's Gillian?" Lara asked shrewdly—nothing wrong with her radar. "She's usually in her office by now."

"Um, she might be sleeping late."

"Might she indeed," Lara said with a wicked smile, which gradually faded when he didn't return it. "Trace, what's the matter? She's all right, isn't she?"

Remembering the stricken look in her eyes when he left her, he didn't know. Couldn't say. He shrugged.

"I'd better call her!" Lara spun and headed for her suite and he caught her arm.

"Lara, leave her alone. Please? We're all adults here."

"Some more than others, it seems!" she snapped. But she nodded, and he let her go. "Fine, you two settle it among yourselves. I'm warning you, though, Trace. I don't want her upset or unhappy with this job. She's a gem and I mean to keep her."

The first time Lara had met Gillian there'd been an affinity, he remembered. Gillian had reminded her of someone, though she hadn't known who. Some instinctive recognition? *You bonded twenty-eight years ago, and your subconscious knows her at the emotional level, even while your brain insists that her eye color won't do?* He nodded. "Understood." God, if Gillian was the one who'd pushed Lara off the cliff... *You don't deserve this!* He could guard Lara's body, but how to protect her heart once she learned that? *And I'll be the one who has to tell her. Your baby came back for your money, Lara, not for you. You shouldn't have searched for Sarah.*

"Just as long as you do," Lara said darkly, crossing her arms. "And now, in case you've forgotten, I'm due at the hospital for my rehab appointment in twenty minutes. Would you care to shave, or is it bodyguard au naturel this week?"

AFTER LARA'S APPOINTMENT, she wanted to go shopping. Trace had to drive her to a mall, then sit patiently while she tried on two dozen pairs of jogging shoes, before she found a pair that suited her. *Here I'm guarding Lara,* he thought grimly, as she solicited his opinion on the fit, *when the one person in the world who means her harm is probably still curled up in bed, sleeping off our night together.*

There's more than one way to keep a client safe, he told himself grimly, but the joke was sour. Hands in his pockets, he glowered at the passing shoppers and wished one would make a move. He'd like to punch somebody's lights out.

The closest he came was a couple of women, autograph seekers, who pounced on Lara once they moved on to a boutique. But Lara wasn't annoyed in the least. She accepted their giggling adulation with her usual self-deprecating grace, signed their shopping bags, assured them she'd be back on *Searching for Sarah* in the following TV season, then waved

them on their way. "I'd almost forgotten how nice
that can be," she murmured, taking his arm. She nodded at the men's side of the store. "And now, my
dear, what about you? We're stepping out on the town
tonight. Medium dressy. Do you have what you need
at home, or shall we get you something?"

A night out, and said with a determined glint in her
eye. She was paying him back in spades for his neglect. "A Brickhouse agent is always prepared," he
said equably. "Tuxedo to wet suit, with all stops in
between. Where are we going?"

"Providence—a play at Trinity Rep."

The famous repertory theater upstate, where Harriet
had offered her talents only two days before and been
politely rebuffed, according to Lara. The actress had
been in a foul mood ever since. "I see," he said neu-
trally. "What are you plotting?" He would have expected her to shun the place while her friend was
smarting. So if she wasn't…

Lara looked guilty, then defiant. "I phoned my
manager, Feinstein, in New York and found out she
has some connections to Trinity's director. She made
a call or two, and now Harriet and I have an invitation
to dine with him, just a light meal before the show,
and a bit of business discussion. Then he offered us
all seats for tonight's performance. That'll give me a
chance to look over his style—ooh and aah in all the
right places."

*You mean you're going to throw your weight
around on Harriet's behalf,* he realized. Maybe make
the director a deal he couldn't refuse—a reigning soap
opera queen, plus her supporting actress, for the price
of one? *You're very, very nice, Lara Corday.* She deserved nice things in her life, like a daughter who
loved her.

"I hope Gillian will come along," Lara added, as if reading his mind.

"Don't ask her," he said automatically. It was half personal dread, half professional. You don't walk your client into the lion's den and then plan to protect her there. A pro didn't take chances.

"Trace," Lara said with steel in her voice. "If you two can't get along…"

Then I'm a goner, he realized. Might as well stand between a mama bear and her cub. But then, that was his job, to take the bullet if need be. "Don't do it."

"Why don't *you* stay home tonight and I'll take Gillian," she suggested waspishly.

"If you invite her tonight, I'll have to resign." *And then tell you why.*

"Dammit!" She stamped her foot at him. "Why do I put up with this? Do you realize there's been no…no attempt on me since that bee, and I'm still wondering if it didn't just catch its leg in a crack. What am I paying you for? Reminds me of that old joke about snapping your fingers to keep the elephants away."

He smiled—couldn't help himself—and delivered the punch line. "Then if you don't see any, I guess I'm doing a pretty good job, aren't I?"

She laughed, but she didn't back down. "Are you?"

"Give me a few more days and I'll let you out of your box. I promise." By tonight even, with any luck.

Luck? Imagining Jeremy Benton taking Gillian away in handcuffs, he felt as though one of Lara's elephants had sat on his heart.

SOMETIME AFTER NOON, Gillian crawled off the couch. Her wet hair had dried all bizarre. She showered again, then blew it dry, dressed and threw some things in a shoulder bag. She ought to report in to Lara, but she couldn't face Woodwind, take the chance of encountering Trace. She hurried down the hill and out the gates, hunching her shoulders as she fled. Was he watching from his office window? Not that he'd care if he saw her go.

Too blue to settle, she wandered the town, staring in shop windows at tourist T-shirts, trudging the docks, passing million-dollar yachts without a glance. She bought a cookie and a coffee—breakfast or was it lunch?—and sat on a bench on Bowen's wharf. And fed the cookie to a seagull that strutted over the cobblestones to demand it. Somebody knew what he wanted, anyway. But what did she want?

Trace. She wanted Trace back—the Trace of last night and early this morning, with a smile in his eyes, a body that worshiped hers. What had she done? She closed her eyes to hold the tears in and listened to tourists wander past, to whining children, giggling newlyweds; it was still too early for the serious party animals, Toby's crowd.

She could go back and ask him, but the parting this morning had been so brutally final. *He used me, then when he'd had enough he was out of there. What's to ask about?* Men did that to women all the time.

No one had ever done it to her. She'd never let any man this close, before. Though "let" hadn't come into it—Trace had vaulted over her hesitations and simply claimed her, as though someone had given him the deed to her heart in a previous lifetime and that was that.

He had it still.

So…she opened her eyes to find the seagull standing before her. Sitting as she was, hunched over her knees, they were almost eye to eye. "I've made a botch of things," she told it. The gull blinked one merciless golden eye, then turned its head to study her with the other one. "So what do I do now?"

She'd come to Woodwind for Lara's sake and nothing had changed there. Maybe that was part of her blues, as well—nothing had really changed. She had glimpsed a photo of a man who might be her father, had befriended Lara, but she was no closer to knowing why Lara had written her that awful letter of rejection. She'd told herself that she was coming to Woodwind to steal her life history, but she'd found that was easier said than done. *What else can I learn without first confessing?*

And if she confessed, would Lara turn against her? Throw her out?

Once those gates closed behind her, she'd never see Trace again. Never have the chance of a family. Tears gathered slowly on her lashes. Not a family from her past, and not a family for her future. Last night when he'd said— "You dreamed that!" she cried aloud. Must have, or else how could he have changed so by morning?

The gull tipped up its beak, stretched out its neck and screamed, a savagely mocking *awk—awk—awk—AWK!*

"You think so too, huh?" She stood and it waddled hurriedly away, then flapped off, gliding low over the cobblestones, then out past the docked fishing boats to the harbor beyond.

Maybe I should fly away, too. The thought of staying, passing Trace in the halls of Woodwind, watching him avoid her eyes as he had this morning...*I couldn't bear that.* But the thought of going, never seeing him again, never seeing Lara...?

SHE SPENT THE DAY DREARILY pondering her dilemma. She could see that the logical solution was to
leave, but she hadn't the strength to embrace the decision. Maybe tomorrow... Trudging back to Woodwind, she heard the firemen's six o'clock horn blast
over the town—and remembered. Her last aerobics
class of the term was tonight at seven. *Skip it,* she
thought wistfully. But no, not with her students de-
pending on her. She groaned and broke into a trot.

THROWING HER GYM BAG into her car, she climbed in
and backed in a rasping circle over the gravel, started
forward, then heard a cry.

"Gillie!" Toby hurried across the courtyard, flung
himself at her open window and caught hold, panting.
"Where...are you going?"

"The Y. Got a class tonight, Toby, at seven." She
tapped his wristwatch, which read 6:40.

"I...I wanted to apologize for last night. Those
miserable pigs...a hell of an ending to a wonderful
evening. I...want to make it up to you."

"No need." *Besides, you lied to me,* she remembered. Why? Simply to cut Trace out?

"There certainly is! Come out tonight and let me
show you a proper time. The Black Pearl for a late
dinner, say?"

She shook her head. "I don't think so, Toby, but
thanks. Don't worry about it." Toby and Joya were
the least of her worries. Her eyes flicked to the carriage house and she realized for the first time that the
bay that usually held Lara's car was empty. She
couldn't resist adding, "Where is everybody, anyway?"

"Oh, they've all gone up to Prov to see some
dreary play. Won't be back till late. Sure you won't

come out for just a drink after your class? I feel wretched about last night.''

He didn't look so much wretched as impatient. And she couldn't understand his sudden yen for her company. She wasn't remotely his type. Maybe it was male competition—he'd noticed Trace's interest in her and reflexively set out to beat him. In which case, Toby's interest would soon die a natural death when he realized Trace was out of the running. ''Gotta go, Toby.'' She stepped on the gas.

THE PLAY MADE NO SENSE to him, possibly because he wasn't hearing one sentence in ten. Trace sat between Lara and Harriet—the director had given them the best seats in the house—and stared blankly at the posturing actors onstage. They were anxious about something, he'd noticed that much, or perhaps he was projecting. *Gillian, what are you doing right now?* Surreptitiously he turned his wrist and consulted his watch. Nearly eight. Did she have a class at the Y tonight? He couldn't remember, could remember only the magic of their lips moving together, the shape of her, trembling in his arms. Her smile when she woke in the morning. Her hurt when he walked out on her. He moved restlessly in his seat, earning himself a sour glance from Harriet.

Gillian as his perpetrator didn't feel right, didn't feel right at all, yet everything pointed her way. The orange sweatshirt—how many University of Miami sweatshirts could there be in Newport? The initial *S* for a middle name that she wouldn't reveal. Her fascination with Lara—she was as drawn to Lara as Lara was to her.

Still, it didn't feel right, a woman who danced with the moon, who'd laughed in his arms last night? She seemed vulnerable, not hard. Loving, not hating. *Don't think, don't feel, simply wait for the facts. Emily, where the hell are you?* It was five o'clock in L.A. and if Victor Scott had flown in late this afternoon—

He jumped violently as the phone vibrated in his pocket. Yes! He drew it out and flipped it open. "Hold on." Harriet had turned to glare her outrage. Lara was smiling and shaking her head at him—probably thought it was Gillian calling. The couple in front turned to stare as he stood. "Back in a minute," he muttered, and worked his way past a dozen outraged drama lovers. His seat *would* have to be the middle one of the row. He bolted up the aisle and into the lobby and clapped the phone to his ear. "Shoot."

Silence—they'd been cut off, or he'd pressed the wrong button in the dark. Crap! He nearly threw the phone across the room, paced savagely back and forth, till in a minute it vibrated again. "Emily!"

"I was right," she crowed without preamble. "Your Gillian's middle name is Sarah!"

So. He closed his eyes and nodded. So everything he'd felt had been a lie. Everything he wanted was dust. He swallowed and said hoarsely, "Go on."

"Scott says he and his wife, Eleanor, adopted her in Virginia—not West Virginia—twenty-eight years ago, when she was a week old. They were told her name at birth was Sarah Cloud Doe and that she was born on September *12*. They kept 'Sarah' to honor her birth mother's wish and gave her a first name of Gillian. Some of the facts are scrambled, I know, but they're so close to a match. If she was sold on the black market, maybe the broker altered some facts to prevent a later search?"

"So..." he said, but no words came after. It was

over. He sat down on a bench and stared at his re-flection in one of the lobby's plate-glass walls. A man alone, unsmiling. Not planning to smile for a long, long time.

"But there's also this, Trace," continued his sister. "Scott's a closemouthed, none-of-your-business type. I had to do some fancy talking to prime his pump. Had to tell him that a woman's life might be in dan-ger."

"You shouldn't have," he said sharply.

"Judgment call and I made it, Trace. I told him his daughter might be stalking our client, that we wanted to stop her before she did anything that could send her to jail. And you know what he did?"

"No."

"He almost fell over laughing. Said that was ab-solutely impossible."

"That's what any relative of a criminal says." It was what he felt, too.

"Scott said that she was a sweetheart and had been since day one. He remembered her at six, giving him hell because he set a mousetrap in the house they were renting. He had to go out and buy a live trap. Each morning he and she would walk down the street to a meadow and set the mice free."

He smiled, picturing it, Gillian earnest and big eyed, defender of mice, then hardened his heart. "Gil-lian moved to Houston at age eight, however. Did he see her after that? She could have changed."

"He didn't. He said he's always regretted losing touch with her. I got the feeling the divorce was pretty bitter, and he married shortly thereafter, a woman with two kids from a previous marriage, and he al-ready had an older son from an earlier marriage him-self, and anyway Gillian wasn't his or even his idea.

It was his wife, Eleanor, who was infertile, who wanted to adopt. So he gave her custody. But as to Gillian's changing, I tried that on him, and he wouldn't have it. Said you see a kid for the first eight years, you know what you've got. And that Gillian was quote—'sweetheart to the bone.'"

Like her mother, Lara Corday. He felt as though a hand were slowly unclenching around his heart, but still... "I don't know that I buy that. If something terrible happened to her over the next twenty years..."

"Scott said that although he hadn't stayed directly in touch, his real son, Christopher Scott, had maintained a relationship, and that Christopher said she'd turned out pretty wonderful. That's another quote. And Scott said he trusted his son's judgment completely. He said we're barking up the wrong tree, chasing Gillian. That it's completely absurd."

The doors to the theater burst open as the intermission crowd poured into the lobby. Trace almost had to shout as he said thanks and farewell. He tucked the phone into his sportcoat and sat staring at the carpet. Gillian—had he figured her all wrong?

His instincts had so violently approved of her he'd refused to trust them. But in his effort to be objective, had he swung too far the other way? Convicted her simply because he was so helplessly attracted?

Victor Scott hasn't seen her since she was eight years old, he reminded himself. A lot could change in twenty years.

But what does the Bible say? Give me a child for the first seven?

Still, if she was innocent, why had she lied from the start, hidden her true identity? He had a good ear

for false notes; it was no wonder he hadn't trusted
her in spite of their chemistry.

*Turn the problem around. Start with the given that
Scott is right, your instincts are right and Gillian is
a honey, whatever the hell she's up to. What does
that leave you?*

Two selfish brats who stood to gain three million
apiece if Lara died. But— His hair stood up along his
arms. My God, was this what came of guarding one
person day and night for months on end—you saw
everything in terms of the client? Tunnel vision. He'd
read the will thinking only of how it endangered Lara.
But there hadn't been an attempt on Lara since the
bee. What would happen if Toby and Joya learned
somehow who Gillian was?

If Lara's long-lost daughter died *before* Lara, then,
by the terms of her will, Sarah's six million went to
Lara's stepchildren, doubling their take. *They have to
kill Gillian first!* He bolted to his feet, stepped up onto
the bench and searched the intermission crowd, looking for Lara.

CHAPTER TWENTY-TWO

GILLIAN WAS ALMOST stumbling with fatigue by the time she came home from her aerobics class. Talk about a low-energy last class! Well, it had been the best she could do, she told herself as she shambled up her stairs. And somewhere in the midst of the cool-down, she'd had a revelation. She'd been trying to learn the truth of her life by lying. No wonder it had all come to grief.

No more lies. Not to Lara, not to Trace. No matter what the consequences. She'd decided that the decent thing to do was pack and move out tonight, take a hotel room somewhere. Tomorrow she would write Lara, try to explain what she'd done and why she'd done it. And at some point she'd try to see Trace. *There's one truth I owe you, whether you want it or not. I think I love you.*

She dumped her gym bag before the door, reached into her pocket for her key—and saw the note tacked at eye level. She pulled it down and read the neatly printed words:

> Gillian, I have reason to believe you might be my daughter. Could that really be true? I'm too excited to sleep, so I'm walking out to the end of Cliff Walk, then back again. Want to join me and talk about it? Lara

"Oh, my...*God!*" She stood, shaking her head. *How did you learn?* It didn't matter, only that Lara knew and didn't sound angry. Fatigue entirely forgotten, Gillian turned and rattled down the stairs. She didn't realize she still held the note till she reached the gate in the wall. Folding it, she tucked it into her pocket, then found the hidden keys and let herself out onto Cliff Walk. Breaking into a trot, she headed south toward the ocean.

"WOULD YOU KINDLY PLEASE tell me what's going on?" Lara cried as Trace hit the highway, swerved into the fast lane and stepped on the gas.

The car hummed up to seventy-five and he held it there, well over the legal speed limit, precisely at the unspoken limit the drivers and state troopers of Rhode Island apparently agreed upon. One mile over and he was courting a ticket. No time for that. He glanced at his watch. Thirty minutes to Newport, he figured, at this speed.

Lara punched his arm. "Trace? I'm the boss here, remember?"

No more. He'd told her only back at the theater that they had to go. Harriet had pulled a fit and decided to stay, would take a bus back after the performance, and that suited him fine. But he couldn't leave Lara.

"Trace!"

He reached into his jacket, pulled out his phone and handed it over. "Gillian might be in trouble, Lara." He was explaining no more than that if he could help it. In the end the secret was Gillian's to tell, and meanwhile the last thing he needed was a hysterical mother on his hands. "Would you dial her number for me?"

"No answer," she said tensely a minute later. "What kind of trouble?"

"Would the YMCA still be open?" She shrugged, so he said, "Then get their number from information and dial it."

By the time they got to the halfway-home mark, she'd tried the Y, which was closed, Gillian's phone number in her office—no answer there—and Jeremy Benton's cell-phone number, which responded with a recorded message that the customer had traveled beyond his service area. They'd also tried the chief of Newport police, Trace's only other contact with the cops, and been told he was up at some dinner in Boston and not reachable.

Trace would need at least fifteen minutes to bring any other officer up to speed, and he didn't trust just any cop with what might prove to be a hostage situation. He eased the car up to eighty and held it there, weaving in and out through the home-going traffic. *Gillian, hang on, sweetheart. I'm coming!*

SHE SAW NO SIGN OF LARA for the first mile, though she peered ahead eagerly each time she rounded a bend or reached a high point. Lara could have left that note hours ago. But no, Toby had said she and Trace had gone up to Providence. So she came back early, left the note and walked. She could easily be three miles ahead, at the end of the path, turning back now to retrace her steps.

At the first dike of riprap, Gillian slowed her pace. With the moon rising later and later each night, she had only starlight to see by; the deep gaps between the boulders were a net of shadows, laid to snare her hurrying feet. *Lara, Lara, wait for me, I'm coming!*

As she rounded the horseshoe of low cliffs that led

to the teahouse tunnel she looked ahead. Thought she saw a flicker of movement at the mouth of the tunnel—someone just entering the passage? Or perhaps she'd imagined it. Trace had said the dragons that decorated the teahouse eaves moved each time he looked. Maybe one had slunk to ground level and awaited her there. Her steps faltered, then she pushed herself on. *Don't be silly,* there was only Lara somewhere ahead.

She reached the mouth of the tunnel, drew a breath and entered at a walk. *Nothing to be afraid of,* she assured herself, trailing her right hand along the cold stones. The last time she'd passed through here she'd been in Trace's arms.

In his arms she'd been safe. But without him to keep the dragons at bay… Her steps slowed, as if the darkness were a cold membrane that resisted her passage.

Don't be a baby, she scolded herself. A child afraid of the dark. Around the corner ahead were the stone stairs where he'd sat down and kissed her. Her eyes squeezed shut against the tears. *God, I want that back!* More even than she wanted a reunion with Lara she wanted one with Trace. Tomorrow, she promised herself. She'd seek him out tomorrow and demand to know what was wrong, make him tell her. Anything was better than not knowing. Her fingertips found the corner and she swung wide around it.

A light flashed directly in her eyes—she cried out and threw an arm up to shield them. A hand gripped one of her wrists, then the other.

"Be still, Gillian," said a familiar voice.

"T-Toby?" He was using the light to blind her. Three hands held her, she realized, someone using two hands to hold her left wrist, while Toby held her right. "Joya!"

"Got it in one, Gillie," she chuckled out of the blackness, her laugh rich with contempt.

"Let go!" She tried to pull away, but their grips tightened bruisingly.

"See this?" Toby tucked the flashlight under one arm, then pulled something from his waistband and held it before her nose. "A gun, Gillie, and I know how to use it. So come along nicely. We just want to talk."

"I don't believe this!" she cried, as they guided her toward the bottom of the stairs. "What are you trying to prove?"

"Up," snapped Joya.

Toby pressed the bore of the gun into her ribs and held it there. "Go on. We just want to talk."

The second time he'd said that. *He's protesting too much,* she thought, her mind whirling like a merry-go-round in the dark. They were climbing past the spot where she and Trace had sat and kissed. She stumbled as she remembered, and they jerked her upright and hustled her on.

They meant to kill her; she could feel it in Joya's excited breathing, Toby's brittle gaiety that shielded him from shame. What she'd felt last night without understanding when they'd tried to force her to swim with them. "Why?" she asked as they reached the top of the tunnel and stepped out into starlight.

"Because you came nosing around," Joya said. "Couldn't take a warning and stay away, could you, Miss Greedy-guts?"

"What warning?" Then she realized. "You mean that letter last fall—*you* wrote it!" Of course they had. She'd never been able to reconcile its pure hatefulness with Lara. Should have known better, except that taking her original relinquishment as rejection, she'd half expected a second rebuff. "So you opened my letter to Lara." Although she'd written Personal and Confidential all over the envelope. That had probably drawn Joya to it, when she'd worked as Lara's personal assistant.

"You bet I did. No big surprise to find out she had a bastard somewhere out there named Sarah Scott. Little Lara was a shameless slut in her twenties when she stole our dad away. You just prove she was a slut from the word go."

"If you'd stayed away, everything would have been fine," Toby continued as they walked. "But we were damned if we'd share the money with you. Dad never should have willed it to Lara in the first place. He earned it through his writing. All of it should have come to us."

"She'd be nothing but a penniless waitress or a coked-up streetwalker by now if it hadn't been for Daddy," chimed in Joya. "With his connections, he made her a star. That should have been enough. She's got her salary. But giving her half of Woodwind and his New York apartment? Half his interest in all the shows he ever created? What are we supposed to live on?"

Gillian jolted to a halt. They weren't talking about waiting for Lara to die, then inheriting! They were talking about here and now. "You mean to kill my mother."

TRACE POUNDED THREE TIMES on Gillian's door, without hope. He'd seen no lights on from down below. Then he scooped up her gym bag and unzipped it. *Any note for me here?* He emptied its contents onto the landing and stirred through the pile as Lara came panting up the stairs.

"Trace, so help me God, if you don't tell me what's going on..."

"Someone may have kidnapped her, Lara." He'd keep the details for later. "I hope I'm wrong, but—" But there was no reason Gillian would leave her bag outside. Either they'd taken her here or something had distracted her, called her away. What? He patted Lara's shoulder as he clattered past her down the stairs. "I'll be up at the house." He glanced over his shoulder as he ran. Gillian's car was parked in its usual spot. Toby's Range Rover wasn't in its stall. They could have taken her anywhere!

By the time Lara caught up with him in her suite, he'd changed to running sweats and stood shrugging on his shoulder harness. "Shouldn't we call the police?" she demanded.

He snatched up a pad of paper from the bedside table and scribbled Jeremy's number on it. "This is a Newport detective, Jeremy Benton. Try his number again, would you?" While she dialed, he checked the loads in his gun, holstered it. The harness carried another twenty loads, much more than he'd need. *Pray I don't need a one!* Pray that Gillian was out on the grounds somewhere, picking roses. That she'd simply dropped her bag off and gone for a walk.

His instincts, though, said she hadn't.

"Same damned message!" Lara cried in frustration. "I can't reach him."

"So go check her office," he said, as he slipped into his running shoes. "Look for a note, or anything you can think of." That got Lara off his neck for a moment. He touched the knife in its sheath at his ankle, then straightened, closed his eyes and thought. *Gillian, where are you? Speak to me, baby.*

Silence... Still, he figured he'd know somehow if she was dead. Would feel a black hole of loss inside himself. He didn't feel that, only a rising anxiety that made him want to leap from his skin. *If I were Toby or Joya, where would I take you?* Every attempt they'd made so far had been low-tech. They were the bright kids of a brilliant father, keeping it simple. Each time so far they'd tried to make it look like an accident, but if they were now feeling pushed... *And frustrated.* The short-attention-span brats at the end of their patience? *I wouldn't kill her here if I wanted to avoid police attention.* And even with most of the household out for the evening, the maid and housekeeper lived on the third floor. Why risk an accidental witness?

"Trace!" Lara wailed from down the corridor. He spun and ran.

And found her seated before the computer in Gillian's office, her hands clamped to her temples, her face greenish white by the light of its screen. "Is it true?" she whimpered. "Gillian?"

Standing behind her, he clasped her shoulders and read the words on the screen:

Dearest Lara-Mommy,

I came here to kill you. You deserve to die, you slut, giving away your own flesh and blood, a helpless baby. What kind of a mother would DO that? But God tells me it's not for me to judge (though I do, I do, I DOOOOOOOO). He said the best way I can punish you is to give you what you WISHED for. (You gotta be careful with that wishing, you know. Somebody's always watching wishers.) So you wanted your baby gone? I'm gone for KEEPS. Bye-bye, Sarah, bye-bye!!! No more searching, she drowned, you can bury the bitch if you find me. So have a looooooooong, MISERABLE life, you selfish bitch,

Your late, loving Sarah XXX. aka Gillian Sarah Scott Mahler
(no joke).

"Trace?" Lara whimpered, biting her knuckle.

"Gillian didn't write this. Trust me."

"Then *who?* Somebody who knows I had a baby! Who is Sarah XXX?"

"Toby and Joya, I'm afraid." They'd been planning murder for months, setting up their alibi—a fictional suspect. An invisible stalker. They'd hoped to make Lara's death appear an accident, but if the police penetrated that veil, Sarah XXX was the backup plan. *Don't look at us, Judge. We didn't do it. That crazy, murderous bitch Sarah XXX is the one.*

"They're their father's children," he murmured, thinking out loud. "Spinning fiction from facts." Storytellers, liars. Corday had told his tales to entertain. They used theirs as a smoke screen behind which to operate. And as a road map to shape their future— wouldn't it be so much nicer to have nine million apiece instead of three? They had a fatal case of the storyteller's what-ifs. *What if Lara died?* It was only one short step from imagining a different reality to creating it.

What if Gillian conveniently drowned herself? Which meant they hadn't taken her away in their

car—that wouldn't fit the story of a lonely, emotion-
ally fragile woman killing herself to shame her
mother, which they'd concocted here. The Range
Rover was gone to serve their alibi. When nasty
things happened, the brats preferred to be elsewhere.

Gillian has to drown someplace within walking distance, since she didn't take her own car.

The roughest waters in the state were at Woodwind's back door.

So one of the brats drove the sports ute to the far
end of Cliff Walk, parked it, then walked east. And
the other is either walking Gillian west, or following
her. Once they've killed her, they'll return to their
car, celebrate out on the town all night, making sure
they're noticed, then come home all drunken inno-
cence at dawn. Simple as that.

"They're faking Gillian's suicide?" Lara spun in
her chair and gripped his arm. "Because that's what
this is, Trace, a suicide note!"

"I think so. Somewhere out on Cliff Walk. Now,
I want you to stay here, Lara, locked in your suite.
Keep ringing Benton's number. If you reach him, tell
him to drive to the far end of Cliff Walk and come
in from there. I'm heading west from this end." He
glanced at his watch. "I left at 9:25. Tell him that,
too. Can you do it?"

She shot to her feet. "I'm coming with you!"

He gripped her by the shoulders and stared into her
eyes, willing obedience. "No. You can't keep up, and
I need you here. Call in my reinforcements." He let
her go when she nodded and sank down in the chair.

"But why would they do this?" she cried as he
reached the door.

He couldn't leave her in utter confusion. "They told one truth, Lara. Gillian is your Sarah."

SHE WALKED DOCILELY between them for a dozen yards or so, too dazed to take it all in. Could this really be happening? Here in the midst of this beauty, with cricket sound and the hush of the waves for background and Venus hanging in the sky ahead like a crown jewel? She was meant to live in this world, share it with Trace, not be booted out of it by two ruthlessly selfish brats. *Trace, where are you right now?*

Up in Providence, if Toby hadn't lied about that. So if she wanted to see him again, tell Lara the truth, it was up to her. *Think. Where are we going?*

The cliffs ahead were only forty feet or so and descending, not high enough for a fatal fall. It hit her suddenly. "Did you push Lara off the cliff?"

"Of course," said Toby. "We'd have done that with you, but it's half tide already and rising."

"This time he checks it," Joya muttered derisively.

"Yeah, and you thought of it last time, too!"

Good. Fight. Please do. But they stopped, so after a moment Gillian said, "I don't understand. If Lara knows you pushed her...?"

"She didn't see me," Toby assured her. "And then she fractured her skull, you know. I don't think she remembers the fall."

"Oh." They kept walking, her wrists aching where they held her. *Think.* No high cliffs ahead, but once they passed the next tunnel a wilderness of jumbled boulders stretched before them till the end of the path. An utterly private place for a killing. So they'd wait till beyond the headland. Drown her or shoot her there. *Fight them here?* But there was no real cover. If Toby knew how to use that gun... Up ahead lay all the cover in the world, if somehow she could get away.

TRACE LOST PRECIOUS minutes crawling out to the edge of the cliff they'd pushed Lara over. He peered down, trying to see past the overhang. He could see no body below. The tide was already rolling over the beach. Since it didn't work last time, maybe they'd learned?

He rose and ran, pacing himself. Figure seven minutes a mile, with no more than two miles to cover, since they'd do her someplace in the middle of the walk. Not at the far end, where lovers sometimes parked. *The teahouse tunnel!* He shot ahead—to hell with pacing himself. Gillian, Gillian, why had he ever let her out of his arms? *If I get another chance,* he prayed. *Are You listening? If You give me another chance, I won't ever let her go again.*

The waning moon sulked somewhere below the horizon behind him; there was less light than he'd expected. He ran the riprap at half speed, leaping from boulder to boulder. Break a leg here and Gillian would die. *I won't permit that!* Guarding the wrong woman. *You fool! Idiot! Don't let me be too late.* He stopped, panting, inside the mouth of the tunnel, crouched and listened. Heard nothing but the echoes of her soft moans when he'd kissed her, how many nights ago? *If I'd held on to you there. Understood I held everything I needed in my arms, right then and there.*

He leaped to his feet and ran on. Rounded the corner and paused. They ambushed her here? Somehow he thought so. He took the steps up, two at a time. If they clubbed her with a stone as she came around the corner, then threw her unconscious off the cliffs up ahead, the fall wouldn't be enough to kill her, but she'd surely drown. Chest heaving, he walked out to the edge of the cliffs and stared down, scanning the shallow cove, searching for a darker shape floating in the dark water. Seeing nothing.

If not here, then beyond the next tunnel, somewhere out among the boulders, the most private part of the trail. Trace broke into a run, hit the next stretch of riprap, twisting and leaping—and leaped six inches too far. His leading foot shot off a smooth boulder and down into a crack and his momentum carried him onward.

CHAPTER TWENTY-THREE

"BUT WHY DO YOU HAVE TO kill me?" Gillian asked casually as they approached the second tunnel.

"Because—" Joya began.

"We just want to talk with you," Toby cut in. "That's all."

Joya snorted.

Yeah, right. Gillian rephrased the question as a hypothetical. "I can't see how killing me would do you any good."

"Lara willed half her money—Daddy's money—six million—to her beloved child, Sara Cloud Bailey. That's you, isn't it?" said Joya.

"Her *beloved child?*" Gillian stumbled. "It really says that?"

Joya burst out laughing, so she turned to Toby. "Does it? Please?"

He nodded rapidly without looking at her.

"She doesn't get it." Joya snickered. "The point of the story, Gillie, is the six million, not the window dressing."

She loved me all along! Gillian glanced triumphantly from one to the other, wanting to share the miracle, but Toby avoided her gaze and Joya's shining, shallow eyes held nothing but contempt. *Love? Joya doesn't know the meaning of the word.* Gillian tipped up her head and stared at the planet hanging in the black above, a blazing jewel. Such beauty, so much to live for, Lara's friendship waiting back there to be claimed. *And Trace...* most of all Trace. Glancing back over her shoulder, she saw the red rim of the moon rising over the jagged horizon. The same moon that had smiled on her and Trace only three nights ago. Toby and Joya pulled at her arms, forcing her onward, and she turned ahead, to see the mouth of the second tunnel gaping wide.

HE'D BROKEN HIS FALL with his right wrist and broken it doing so. Teeth clenched, Trace tried to rotate it and felt the bones grind. He knew the sensation well; he'd busted this same wrist years ago skiing. With exquisite care, breath hissing between his teeth, he shoved himself one-handed to his knees. Worked his left foot free from the gap between two boulders. His ankle was ballooning over his shoe already. Sprained, he thought, which could be more incapacitating than a break. *You moron, you fool!* he swore at himself as he struggled to his feet, then stood, listing to the right. Great.

So move it. Wincing, he shambled on, his teeth clamped in his lip. *Gillian, hang on, I'm coming.*

There were perhaps a hundred yards to the next tunnel, and one of them might be standing sentry there, guarding their back trail. He stopped to catch his breath—limping took more out of him than running—and pulled his gun. Awkwardly, since it was placed for a right-handed draw. Better to do it now at his leisure than later when he might not have a second to spare. He limped on, doubly careful of the cracks between the boulders now, after the harm was done. Clumsy fool!

Chest heaving, he stopped after another twenty yards to stare at the tunnel mouth—could see no movement there—then back over his shoulder. The moon was rising. No friend to him now. He could shoot left-handed but not with right-hand precision. He'd need to be much nearer to risk a shot. On two good feet, under cover of darkness, he could have padded up close enough to tap Toby on his shoulder or snap his neck. But now?

He needed all the help he could get. Darkness. Also a crutch, he decided, would help him move more quietly, though the time he'd lose finding one tore at his nerves. A clump of brushy trees grew uphill from the riprap; he headed that way. Stepped up onto the slope above the boulders—and slipped on a patch of gravel.

"Crap!" Twisting frantically to land on his good shoulder, he hit and rolled onto his back—and slithered downhill on a rattling cascade of pebbles, clawing frantically with elbows and his good hand at the hard slope.

He fetched up sideways against a boulder with a grunt and lay there, swearing breathlessly at the stars, assessing damage. Barring his wounded pride, there wasn't much more damage than before, he concluded after a minute. Some abrasions on his back, but— *The gun!* He flopped over onto his stomach and stared uphill—didn't see it. God, the gun! With him half disabled, he needed it. Toby outweighed him by ten pounds at least. Nothing to worry about normally, but tonight— *Where's my damn gun?*

He found it lying between the piled boulders and the side of the hill above it. Down a crack, five foot deep, six inches wide. As unreachable as if it had fallen down a well.

No time to waste cursing his criminal clumsiness. There was only Gillian. He limped up the slope again and vented his rage on a tree—tore it limb from limb till he held a piece some five feet long, with a fork at its upper end. Tucking that under his left armpit, he gimped on, faster now, the pain in his arm and foot only a spur. *Wait for me, lion eyes. I'm coming.*

THEY HAD TO WALK THROUGH the steel-pipe tunnel sideways, Toby in the lead, drawing her onward. She suppressed her own urge to fight them. She'd never break free in this enclosure, and she wanted them to think her cowed, dazed by her coming fate. She hoped they thought her state reflected her terror, not her growing resolution.

Beyond the tunnel, Joya glanced at Toby. "What time is it?"

He lifted his left hand along with Gillian's to look at his watch: "Nine-fifty."

"It's getting too late. I think we should shoot her."

Toby's fingers clamped down brutally as Gillian flinched. He shook his head and kept walking. "We've still plenty of time. The play finishes at nine-thirty, the box office said. They're standing around telling the director what a genius he is right now. If they start for Newport at ten o'clock, then they won't be home before ten-forty, an hour from now, at the earliest. And there's no reason anybody should go into her office and see the message before morning. We've all the time in the world."

But she hadn't. They were passing the beach where she'd practiced her tai chi with Trace watching. Gillian swallowed and stared at the boulder where he'd sat and waited, as if his ghost might be sitting there still, ready to rise and come to her rescue. But no Trace. *Think. Think!*

"You're just being squeamish," Joya complained.

"Look, we can't afford any more mistakes. Shoot her."

"Where would I have gotten a gun?" Gillian asked in a voice of desperate rationality. "The police will check that, you know."

"It's Daddy's," Joya said impatiently. "Toby stole it years ago and kept it hidden in the carriage house. We'd forgotten all about it. You must have found it poking around."

That was barely plausible. "They'll know it's murder anyhow," she insisted.

"Wish on," Joya sneered. "You walked out here and shot yourself in the head. They'll buy it."

"That's not in our script," Toby protested. "She said she'd drown herself."

"I didn't!"

Joya leaned around her to scowl at her brother. "So she changed her mind and decided to shoot herself, so what? She's crazy, remember? The cops won't think twice once they've read all her letters."

She'd never considered before, yet given the choice of water or bullets, she'd take her chances in the sea. But as they nudged her off the trail and out onto a smooth, house-size slab of granite rearing some ten feet over the water, Joya seemed to be winning the squabble. Or maybe her demise could be a compromise scenario; she'd shoot herself in the head, then topple into the water.

"The cops won't think twice," Joya insisted. "Do it."

Gillian found her tongue at last. "They'll think twice when I shoot myself with the wrong hand!"

There was a weighty pause while they stared at each other, then her. "You're right-handed," Toby said on a note of doubtful challenge.

"Am I?" She was trembling from head to toe, but still she smiled.

THEY WERE ARGUING, all three of them, it looked like, Gillian pinned between them on the end of a rock overlooking the sea. He'd have to cross a long, clear space with no cover, and Toby was holding a gun. Trace paused and leaned down painfully to pull his knife from his sheath. Left-handed he was a lousy thrower. He grabbed a stone for backup, jammed it into his pocket and straightened. *Keep talking, Gillian.* Whatever she was saying, she held their attention.

"SHE'S LEFT-HANDED," scoffed Joya. "She sat to your right, Toby, next to you out on the terrace and you bumped elbows three or four times, remember?"

Damn. What else, what else, what else to say?

"Hell, you're right," Toby agreed. "So guess what. That means *you* have to shoot her. She's got to be shot from the left." He laughed in relief.

"Trade places with me," demanded Joya.

"Huh! This is your idea and you can do it. Here."

Now, Gillian prayed as he passed the pistol behind her back. Joya let her go with one hand to reach for it—and Gillian spun, wrenching down on the wrist Toby held as she leaped for the sea, shoving a screaming Joya before her.

COLD! HOW COULD ANYTHING be this cold? She writhed underwater, entangled with Joya, frantically pushing her clawing limbs aside, and rose with a desperate gasp—to find Toby taking careful aim from above. "Don't!" she cried, and threw up a hand.

"Don't!" shouted a voice from the path.

Trace? Or was she dreaming? Treading water, Gillian swirled backward from the rock and saw him some thirty feet behind Toby, leaning on a stick.

"Don't," he said quietly, and limped forward as Toby spun to face him.

A few feet to Gillian's right, Joya also treaded water, while she cursed and wiped the hair from her eyes. "Shoot him," she said flatly.

"It's over." Trace limped on, closing the gap to twenty feet, fifteen…

"*Shoot* him, Toby!" screamed Joya. "Shoot, you *stupid—!*"

"That's too many bodies to explain, kid," said Trace, limping on. "Forget it. Put the gun down."

"Don't listen to *him*—listen to me, Toby, you *jerk!* Shoot him!"

Toby's arm straightened and—as Gillian screamed her heart out, he spun to jab the gun at Joya. "Shut up, shut up, shut *up!* And you, too!" The gun stopped, pointing at Gillian. "You come a step closer, Sutton, and I'll waste her—I really will, so help me God!"

"Well, do it!" cried Joya.

A rock sailed out of the darkness and thumped Toby in the thigh. He swore and wheeled in its direction.

"You put that gun down right…*now*, Toby Corday!" Finger pointing, Lara stalked down the path, sounding like nothing so much as an outraged mother.

His gun rose and centered on her small, unflinching form. "It really was you we wanted to kill…" he said in a wistful voice, his arm slowly extending—as Trace's crutch came scything out of the night at knee level to cut him off his feet.

TRACE SENT THE TWO WOMEN on ahead, while he limped along as the rear guard. Not that he was really worried. They'd left the brats to fend for themselves, Toby nursing a shattered knee, while Joya wept out her rage and frustration.

Trace would dearly have loved to haul them in, see their fresh-scrubbed faces behind bars, but Lara had insisted she wouldn't press charges.

He had no intention of marring her joy in Gillian with the hard truth tonight, but this wasn't a soap opera, where the heroine could forgive all at the end of the episode. Once Trace and Jeremy Benton laid the facts of the case before the district attorney, that official would prosecute—for assault, if not attempted murder.

Meanwhile, the bubbling talk of two blissfully happy women drifted back on the wind—laughter, exclamations. He thought he heard sobs once or twice. They walked with arms wrapped around each other's waists, occasionally stopping and smiling back at him. And each time he'd wave them on. They had twenty-eight years to fill in.

When he reached the teahouse tunnel, they stood waiting for him, each with her head cocked slightly to the same side. "I don't know why I didn't notice sooner," he said. "So many of your gestures are the same. I suppose it's the difference in coloring and height." And not knowing there was a missing daughter to be discovered.

"I figured out who she looks like," Lara said triumphantly as they closed in on each side of him. Gillian took his crutch away and slid under his left armpit, while Lara supported him as best she could on the right. They descended the stone stairs with care. "She looks like Cloudy's older sister. I only met her once or twice—she'd already left home. Gillian has her eyes and hair. And Cloudy's height.''

Gillian laughed happily and he felt his heart contract. *This is what she wanted. What she came looking for. A mother, a family, her place in the world. She doesn't need a lover right now. She needs Lara.*

Well, he'd told himself he didn't want a wife for another two years. Two years now seemed like two hundred. He turned his head to sniff the hair at her temple, but tonight she smelled more of saltwater than sunshine. Lion eyes. All that really mattered was that she lived. Anything else he could handle.

At the far end of the tunnel, Lara eased out from under him. ''I think I'll go on ahead now, Trace.''

''Don't do that,'' he said automatically.

But she just smiled and stood on tiptoe to kiss his cheek. ''It's over now, Trace, thanks to you. I'll be all right.''

''But—''

''No buts.'' She backed away from him laughing. ''I can't tell you how nice it is after five months to walk alone.'' She backed another step. ''See you two later.''

He stared after her small, erect departing figure with something like dismay. A feeling of loss. What a mother duck must feel watching her duckling paddle off over the horizon. Finally he smiled. ''Are you as stubborn as your mother?''

Gillian laughed. ''Oh, I hope so. She's something, isn't she?''

They stood there, unwilling to follow too closely, savoring the feel of their bodies molded together. She didn't try to draw away. He felt his heart accelerating.

Gillian reached across his body to touch his right forearm. ''You've hurt your hand.''

"It's nothing." He supposed he'd have to get it set tonight.

Slowly, leaning together, with her taking much of his weight, they started to walk. "I have to thank you," she said after a while. "Coming after me like that. You walked right into his gun." She shivered. "If he'd pulled the trigger…"

He laughed, embarrassed. "I'm a bodyguard, Gillian. That's what I do."

"But you're not mine."

He stopped and looked down at her. "Only if you say I'm not."

She stood for a dozen heartbeats, then sixty or more, head tipped, as if she could hear something he couldn't. There was just enough moonlight to see she didn't smile. "The other night…was it just last night? You said something."

"I said a lot of things," he said. *Yes, ask me that!*

"You said… If I didn't dream it, you s-said…I think I love you?"

"You didn't dream it, but I was wrong." He drew his hand over her damp shoulder, till he found her wet hair and laced his fingers into it. Tugged gently.

"Oh?" Her face tipped up to meet his; there was no question of resistance. Her eyes seemed to glow in the moonlight.

"There's no 'think' about it, lion eyes. I love you." As she started to smile, he kissed her.

Such beauty. Within—as their mouths joined and danced and Gillian's heart exulted. And without— waves whispering, the smell of wild roses. Past and the present knitting their ragged ends in the moonlight—Lara and Trace and herself, a father she'd never known. Family—stretching from the unknowable past into the unseeable future. The ties that bind and lead us onward into joy.

"And I love you!"

HARLEQUIN®
SUPERROMANCE®

Three childhood friends dreamed of becoming firefighters. Now they're members of the same team and every day they put their lives on the line.

They are

AMERICA'S BRAVEST

An exciting new trilogy by

Kathryn Shay

Available wherever Harlequin books are sold.

HARLEQUIN®
Makes any time special™

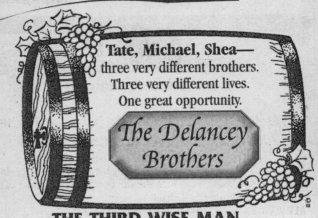

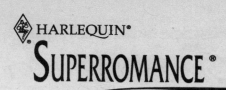